A LEGEND IS BORN

Had there been air, it would have been deafening —Zeke could feel the shock waves trembling the "ground" under his feet. The rest of the unit had readied the portable shield generators and thrown up a defensive screen. None too soon—the screens began sparking and shrieking almost immediately as the war machine directed intense fire on the group. They returned the fire, trying to take out as many lasers as they could.

They waited for Zeke to give them the command. Sylvie's holocams were focused tightly on him, expectant. But Zeke did nothing.

Zeke reached into the thigh pouch of the tight battle-armor and pulled out the seed. It glowed strongly against the steel-woven cloth of his glove, a pulsing orange flare.

"Back to the shuttle," Zeke ordered, still holding the glowing crystal in his palm. His companions stared at him strangely, as if he were some ghost, an apparition.

Books in the Dr. Bones™ series from Ace

THE SECRET OF THE LONA
THE COSMIC BOMBER *(coming in January 1989)*

DR. BONES™

BOOK 1: THE SECRET OF THE LONA
STEPHEN LEIGH

A Byron Preiss Visual Publications, Inc. Book

ACE BOOKS, NEW YORK

This book is an Ace original edition, and has never been
previously published.

DR. BONES
BOOK 1: THE SECRET OF THE LONA

An Ace Book/published by arrangement with
Byron Preiss Visual Publications, Inc.

PRINTING HISTORY
Ace edition/September 1988

Cover art by David Dorman.
Visual data by Joel Hagen.
Character design by Steranko.
Developed by Byron Preiss and Paul Preuss.
Edited by David M. Harris.
Consulting editor: Paul Preuss.
Book design by Alex Jay/Studio J.
Special thanks to Adele Leone, Jean Naggar, Susan Allison,
Beth Fleisher, and Gwendolyn Smith.

CHAPTER 1

The lioness slipped through the tall, dry grass surrounding the house, her muscular haunches down as she stalked. The rambling structure, set in the midst of the dusty Serengeti Plain, was quiet in the heat of the summer sun. The only disturbance was the slow, deliberate sounds of Mahsi, the old Bantu headman, as he cleaned the carcass of a gazelle in the side yard. The lioness hunkered down, sniffing the air; she could sense only the man and the sweet, compelling odor of gazelle meat. She rose and padded silently closer, staying downwind of the servant.

Now she was within striking distance, a scant few yards away, and she gathered her haunches together to rise, to cover the remaining distance in a tawny blur. Yet even as she streaked the first few feet, a horrible shrieking tore through the predator's concentration and slammed her back. The clamor rose to a painful, shrill crescendo inside her head, and the lioness stopped dead in her tracks. She howled in pain and confusion, shaking her head from side to side to rid it of the unseen screamer, but it would not go away. The mind-beast roared louder than the thunder of the spring rains, louder than the explosions of man's guns, louder than the mating roar of a male, as if the sound came from within her own skull. She broke off her attack to lope quickly away from the house and the loud resonance that still echoed inside her. Even when the noise had stopped she continued to flee.

Mahsi had lifted his head to watch, the bloody machete clenched in his fist just in case. Now he grinned and turned his attention back to the gazelle.

There had been another watcher. Zeke Bones had seen the confrontation from inside the house, sitting on his bed in his shadowed bedroom. The thirteen-year-old boy also smiled as the lioness fled from the unseen presence around the house—

1

the sonic generators had been Zeke's own invention to replace the old fencing. The acacia fences had been easy for predators to break through, and a chore to maintain. The sonics put out a high-pitched harmonic frequency beyond the range of human hearing, a banshee wail that kept out the prowlers in the surrounding grasslands more effectively than the fences: invisible, reliable protection.

He'd made the generators for two reasons: to see if he could do it, and to impress his father. But Leo Bones had watched the demonstrations with a tight-lipped frown—it had not occurred to him to praise the work of his young son. Leo Bones seemed to *expect* Zeke's brilliance as normal. "They work," he said flatly. "Good. We'll have some of the lab techs at the corporation duplicate these. Mahsi, take care of it. When you have enough of them, take down the fence."

Leo had turned to Zeke then, and Zeke had thought that his father would have at least complimented him on his ingenuity. But no; he'd only nodded to his son and gone inside the house. Zeke wanted to shout after him, to rage and yell. Instead, he could only gape, slack-jawed. Zeke could feel hot tears gathering at the corners of his eyes, and he used his anger to force them back, knowing that Leo Bones would consider them a sign of weakness. *I won't give you the satisfaction,* Zeke remembered thinking. Mahsi had sensed the turmoil inside Zeke. It had been Mahsi who'd acted the father, whose arms had gone around Zeke and hugged him close. "Damn good, boy," the Bantu had said in his gruff voice. "I'm proud of you. All of us are. Damn good."

"Dad didn't seem to think so."

"He did, boy. He just couldn't tell you, that's all."

"You shouldn't have to apologize for him, Mahsi. You know me better than he does. Sometimes I just hate him."

Mahsi's dark, lined face had gone stern with that, though he'd only clenched Zeke tighter. "Boy, you don't say that. Not to me, not even to yourself. Your father, well, life has beat him down for the moment. He'll come back, boy. He'll come back."

The memory dissolved the smile Zeke had given at the retreat of the lioness. He turned back into the house. In the heat of the afternoon, the Bones compound was utterly quiet except for the whisper of the air conditioners. Zeke's stepmother—the third since the death of Zeke's mother—was taking her nap. In the cool dark below the stairs the servants were using the lull in the day's schedule to polish silver and sharpen tools, to re-charge their weapons and start preparations for the evening din-ner. The Bones estate had originally been the site of an African hunting lodge, a sprawling bungalow used by "Ohio" Bones, the patriarch of the family and founder of the Bones Energy Corporation. After the upheaval in weather patterns at the end of the twenty-first century and the chaos that followed, the whole Bones family had moved in. In time, they'd started add-ing to the structure. That had been four hundred years ago. The Boneses had been energetic, and they had been at it a long time. The original hunting lodge was still the main facade, but it was surrounded now by newer outbuildings, each added onto the other so that the place was a warren, a maze, a boy's delight.

Zeke rolled off his bed and began to whistle what seemed like an aimless tune as he walked toward the back wall of his room. At the last note of the melody, however, the "wall" that had been there a moment before shimmered and dissolved, re-vealing a well-equipped, if tiny, lab. The workbench was strewn with biomicros and the chips of crystalline integrated circuits. A stereo microscope and miniature centrifuge stood in their cases to one side. Protein synthesizers and small vials of nucleic acid lined the back wall. It was better equipped than some college laboratories, and any normal adolescent would have been lost amid the technology. Not Zeke. He patted each piece of equipment familiarly, affectionately. His father had bought each instrument as Zeke had asked for it. He'd done so without marveling, without much comment at all: if Leo Bones was amazed by the precocity of his son, he had never said anything.

There wasn't much time—what Zeke wanted to do he had to do *now*, today, for this evening he would be leaving home and this world itself for years. In the fantasy in his mind, he thought that he might never come back here again; though he found that hard to imagine. From a shelf crowded with finished biomicros Zeke selected several of the tiny servos he'd constructed him-self, fastening them to the shoulders and jackets of his shirt. He went to the bedroom door and eased it open, peering around to see if any of the servants were about. The long hall was empty and quiet. Zeke stepped into the hall, stretching to get across the floorboard he'd deliberately loosened years ago so he'd know when someone was outside his door. He touched one of the biomicros, shaped like a large dragonfly. It fluttered gossamer wings and moved off down the hall. Zeke listened intently as it turned a corner. When he heard nothing from his small scout, he continued on.

The house creaked, expanding under the heat of the relentless sun; inside, the high-ceilinged rooms were dark and cool. Zeke moved carefully along the upstairs hall, wary of tripping on the loose rugs scattered on the hardwood floors, all those faded fabrics—woven in geometric patterns and smelling of camphor—that his grandparents, great-grandparents, and great-great-grandparents had brought back from distant places. The house was full of things like that: five centuries of the eclectic treasures of a family who liked to collect odd things.

Zeke paused at the head of the stairs, listening again.

He crept slowly down the wide, polished ironwood steps to the first-floor landing. In front of him were the house's massive carved front doors. This was the oldest part of the house. The doors had been the hunting lodge's, erected during the boom period before the weather had gone crazy, before the economy of the whole planet had been wrecked. Everything showed the ornate, neo-Victorian attention to detail of that time. The doors were a carved fantasy of the African jungle, teeming with wooden life. To Zeke's left was the formal sitting room with the table whose central pillar spread out into four great lion's paws, the chairs around it carved like African totems.

Zeke turned and went along the hall toward the back of the house. He passed a closed door, which gave access to the back stair leading down to the servants' quarters. There the hall turned, narrowed, and came to an abrupt halt. Against the wall stood a huge mirror of mottled volcanic glass. He could see himself in the mirror, blue eyes shadowed by gingery brows and unruly, sand-colored hair falling across a high forehead. After hours in the sun, Zeke's face was the color of old mahogany, deeply tanned with a sprinkle of darker freckles across his wide nose and cheekbones. He was bony-thin and short for his age, though in the past few months he'd been growing so quickly that he still had hopes of reaching his father's height before he slowed down again.

A servo in Zeke's pocket shrilled harshly, warning the boy that someone was coming. The door opened behind Zeke; before he could move, another reflection appeared in the smoky crystal of the mirror—a tall figure, darker than himself and wearing the uniform of BEC, the Bones Energy Corporation.

"Hi, Mahsi," Zeke managed, turning to face the man. "I thought you were dressing the gazelle."

"I decided to let some of the others finish," Mahsi answered. "It's too hot outside, and the flies. . . ." His voice was soft and round with the accents of his people. "Would your father know you're here?" Mahsi's chief job was to be Leo Bones's personal pilot. For generations his ancestors had been in the employ of the Bones family—Mahsi's great-grandfather had been born in a village on the plain not far from here. Mahsi, with the legacy of four generations of service to the Boneses, was more a citizen of BEC than of any tribe, country, or world.

Zeke evaded the question. He didn't like to lie to Mahsi, not when Mahsi was the only confidant he had here. Zeke smiled and rummaged in one of his shirt pockets. "I fixed your sniffer," he said. "I thought I'd put it in your lockers."

"So soon?" said Mahsi, obviously pleased. "Young man, you surprise me."

Zeke had done his best with the broken gadget, hoping to gain Mahsi's respect. He handed the servo to the older man. The little machine—looking like a silver insect—whirred inquisitively and lifted its delicate copper snout toward Mahsi. "Try it," urged Zeke.

"What should I have it analyze?"

"How about your hair?" Zeke suggested.

Mahsi gave a rich, deep laugh and took the tiny mechanism between his long fingers. He held it to one side of his head, where the tightly curled black and silver strands of his hair, gleaming with oil, lay close against his skull.

The sniffer whirred and chirped. Mahsi moved it close to his ear, and the servo emitted a stream of high-pitched squeaks. Again Mahsi laughed, his amusement shaking his broad chest.

"Well?" Zeke persisted.

"You've done well, Master Zeke. It told me exactly what's in the oils I rub on my hair. It even detected a series of complex lipids—a traditional ingredient known only to my family."

"Lion fat," said Zeke.

Mahsi's dark eyes flashed, and for a second Zeke thought that the man was angry. But a smile spread slowly across his face. "You've learned all my secrets, boy. You've a prying, curious mind; that's good. It's a Bones trait, eh?" He smiled again and perched the sniffer on his shoulder. He laid his long hand on Zeke's shoulder; it looked impossibly massive against the boy's thin frame. "Thank you for your good work. Did you see that your sonic generators worked again today?"

Zeke nodded and grinned. "I did. I was watching from my window while you cleaned the gazelle."

"I know. I saw you. A special night tonight, eh, young master?" Mahsi said it with a wink in his eye and a tone that hinted at unspoken words.

Zeke smiled up at the man. "I'm looking forward to dinner," he said flatly. Zeke tried to think of something else to say. Still, Mahsi looked down on him, his broad lips curving in a smile. Mahsi hadn't asked Zeke why he'd gone past the door to the servant's quarters, or why he was lurking in this dead-end hall. Zeke was hoping that Mahsi would remain silent—Zeke couldn't have answered. He knew that he couldn't have lied convincingly to Mahsi; he'd never been able to do so. With a faint shrug, Zeke disengaged himself from Mahsi and started back the way he'd come, as if his presence in this hallway had been a mistake, a wrong turning on his part. He could feel Mahsi's gaze on his back as he closed the door.

Halfway up the staircase, Zeke heard the servants' door open and close again. He paused, his heart pounding in his chest. Had Mahsi really gone below? Carefully, the boy retraced his steps. The detector servo in his pocket remained still, though he knew its range was very short.

Within a minute, Zeke stood before the mirror once more. Beside it, a tan Cycladic jar from the Aegean rested on a marble column. Zeke lifted the jar to reveal a keypad set into the top of the column.

He'd found the keypad by accident weeks ago. He'd just finished the dragonfly servo and had set it out on a programmed flight through the house. The device had a tiny imager built into the eyes. Among the twenty or so grainy pictures that Zeke had developed from the imager was one of Leo Bones standing before this mirror and pressing that keypad. In the next picture, taken a few seconds later, his father had been . . . gone: there were enough "secret" rooms in the Bones house for Zeke to know immediately that he had found another. It had taken him many cautious attempts to figure out how to get past the mirror. The trick was to make the keypad think that his touch was his father's; otherwise it would refuse to operate—if he persisted, he assumed it would set off alarms in Mahsi's quarters and in his parents' bedrooms.

Two weeks ago, he'd taken a wine glass with his father's

fingerprints from the dinner table. In his room he'd made a cast of the prints and programmed Mahsi's already repaired servo to analyze the components of the clinging oils. Afterward, he'd used the casting to make a membrane of thin latex to fit over his fingertips, smearing the rubber with a light coating of identical oils and amino acids. Zeke wasn't certain if all the precautions were necessary, but he would take no chances. Now he could freely handle the keypad; deducing its numerical combination had been easy—it had been his mother's birthdate.

Wearing the glovetips that allowed him to mimic his father's touch, Zeke rapidly tapped out the four-figure code. A mechanism behind the mirror whirred; the mirror slid smoothly sideways. Zeke stepped through the opening; the mirror door closed behind him.

Long rows of clear cases glittered in the subdued light. Against the walls stood sculptures and giant jars and broken bits of carved pediments from the ruined architecture of a dozen planets. His mother, who had been intensely interested in archeology and history, would have loved this room. Mary Carter-Bones had held two Master's degrees, in archeology and paleontology; Zeke knew that she had participated in several digs in the years before his birth. She would have been awed by the collection here, though Zeke felt certain that she had never seen it. It was almost as if this were Leo's shrine to Mary's memory and her interests—certainly Zeke's father had never much indicated that he shared the interests of his first wife.

Zeke had been in this room once before, ten days ago or so, and the impact staggered him as much this second time as the first, perhaps because now he knew. He knew what this strange collection was.

Contraband, all of it. Stolen.

There was an *Archaeopteryx* wing impressed in limestone—there were only five other fragments known in the world. Here were superb examples of Galian gyroform clay tablets, not mentioned in any of his mother's catalogues. Their hieroglyphs, like those of the original Minoans, had never been deciphered, and it was forbidden to remove them from the world of their origin. In the center of the room stood a group of strange, corroded zinc sculptures, found only on the homeworld of the !xaka!. By treaty between !xaka! and humanity, two mutually antagonistic races, no human was to own a !xaka!ian work of art. Yet Zeke knew these were not copies.

After his first visit, Zeke had used the estate terminals to find out all he could about this archeological treasure trove. He knew immediately that his father wasn't keeping this gallery hidden simply because it was worth a lot of money. The Galactic Council of United Worlds had strict rules governing the sale and transportation of objects of scientific, artistic, and cultural value. The items in Leo Bones's private collection had been smuggled past customs and sold on the black market. Although Zeke didn't want to believe that his father was directly involved in theft, even if he hadn't been directly involved, he must have realized that these acquisitions had been stolen. Leo Bones wasn't so naive as that.

Yet the most valuable object in the secret gallery had no history at all. It wasn't mentioned in any catalogue or encyclopedia. Zeke knew what it was as soon as his eyes caught it.

The gems called star seeds were among the rarest things in the universe. There were plenty of theories about where they came from, but nobody really knew. Only three of them were known to exist; they were all in the Galactic Museum, on Griynsh.

A fourth star seed was here, in Leo Bones's secret gallery.

Zeke peered into the case where the star seed lay on a pillow of purple velvet. It was small, the size of a large marble. A sphere of transparent stone, it appeared to be a geode turned inside out, a maze of tiny multicolored crystals radiating outward from a shadowy, murky core. "Do you know I'm here, seed?" Zeke whispered, bending close over the case. The cool seed began to glow.

That response was one of the strangest traits of the seeds; some natural mechanism within the crystal could receive and amplify electromagnetic energy. They didn't glow very often, and usually not very brightly, but at times the shadowy center of a seed would begin to turn a smoky orange. The surface would grow warm and it would pulse with light, turning almost pink and putting out a glow that could illuminate a whole room. When a star seed got that bright it was too hot to touch.

Zeke had the case open in seconds. It wasn't locked; why bother locking a display case in a secret gallery? He took the seed into his cupped hands. The lambent crystal vibrated against his palms. Somehow, Zeke knew that it was talking to him, trying to communicate with him; its warm glowing heart was reflected in his eyes.

His resources didn't say anything about star seeds talking. Yet Zeke was certain that the seed had tried to communicate with him on that first visit here. Then, he'd picked up the seed and it had glowed as it glowed now. A clear sensation had formed itself in his head in that moment. It wasn't a word, or even a voice, but more like someone else's emotions had somehow snuck into his mind in the same way that Zeke's sonic generator had set up sympathetic vibrations in the lioness's skull. There was relief and a certain amount of comfort, all mixed up with an insistent "openness": Zeke had translated that emotion as •Welcome/Hello•

Right now, the emotional broadcast was different: a tinge of fear and uncertainty: the seed throbbed gently, like the feel of two frequencies partially cancelling each other out.

•What are you going to do?•

Zeke wondered if perhaps the crystal wasn't simply sending back an image of his own mind. It was as if the seed had read his own emotional matrix and sent it back to him, amplified. Perhaps that's what the seeds were, he thought: emotional amplifiers, logic amplifiers, memory amplifiers. The seed's question nagged at him. Why *was* he here? Was it simply that he had to see this place again one last time?

This evening, after dinner, his father would fly Zeke to the launch complex, there to board the orbital shuttle. Zeke would transfer to the intersystem caravan in the morning; two months from now the airlocks of the Military Academy of Mars would close behind Zeke Bones. If he didn't flunk out or get himself expelled—and Zeke wasn't the kind of kid who would deliberately buck the system—he wouldn't see this house or his parents again for five years at the minimum. And afterward, who could tell? The shri, the race that had molded the United Worlds, were currently at war with another race—the lona. It seemed likely that aggression would spread to include mankind as well. Maybe Zeke would come from the Academy into war. Maybe he would never see this home again.

Once more he felt the throbbing questioning of the seed. •What are you going to do?• it asked.

He didn't think he'd just come to say goodbye.

He held the crystal in his hand. The seed grew warmer and brighter, and the answer to his questions came clearly to his mind.

Dinner took forever. There wasn't much talk around the table; mostly, Zeke heard the sound of his chewing and the rattle of silverware as the others ate.

Leo Bones sat at the head of the long table, bright in the candlelight, a huge, sunburned man with a gray-streaked blond beard, chomping heartily on the gazelle flank steak. "This is a special dinner, eh, Zeke?—the last time you'll have *this* kind of meal." Zeke knew that his father meant the question for a friendly overture. Still, it sounded more like an interrogation. "For a very special occasion," Leo Bones concluded.

Zeke nodded dutifully and kept chewing. Real meat—maybe that was a treat for Leo, who talked a lot about the needs of a good diet. A few years ago, Zeke had thought that the most fun in the world would be for him and his father to sit around a campfire well out on the plain, just eating synthmeat or something while jackals prowled in the dark. That was the way it had been, once. He knew it from the old image crystals of his father and mother, those taken before Zeke had been born. But after his mother had died, Zeke's father had changed. Leo Bones never had time to go camping after that. Leo Bones became some stranger who walked around in Zeke's father's body.

Zeke's thoughts were interrupted by his stepmother Laura, pushing back her chair and running into the kitchen again to check on some unimportant detail of the dinner. Zeke studied his plate, not wanting to look at Leo. After what he'd done this afternoon, Zeke was afraid that Leo would see something in his son's face. Zeke ignored the conversation, keeping quietly to himself. If anyone noticed how silent the young boy was, they blamed the impending trip. When his stepmother came back she was smiling bravely, though tears were trembling in the corners of her eyes. It was a good show meant for his benefit: Dutiful Mother, Brave Mother. She meant well; Zeke supposed that he liked her, though he still choked on calling Laura "Mom."

He knew his real mother mostly from the crystals; she'd died when he was three. He'd never really understood the exact circumstances of her death, and now, when it seemed important, he simply couldn't talk to his father. He asked Mahsi once, but Mahsi had only shook his grizzled head and said, "That's a thing for a boy to ask his father." He'd never asked.

After his own mother, there'd been Carol for a year, then, after a time, Alicia followed for four angry, argumentative years. And now Laura.

It was a relief when the half-eaten steak was cleared away. Zeke wasn't very hungry, not even for the chocolate ice cream. Mahsi appeared at the archway to the door as the dessert was being cleared away. The old man looked directly at Zeke as he strode into the room, and when he went over to Leo, Zeke was sure that he'd been found out. He waited for Mahsi to tell his father and for the anger to come. But Mahsi merely announced that the plane was ready. Zeke nearly jumped out of his chair.

He'd gotten away with it.

Mahsi handed up Zeke's strapped and belted luggage and climbed into the pilot's seat beside the boy. He pulled the bubble of the windscreen down over their heads and started the engines. Zeke was absorbed, studying the instrument panel and watching Mahsi's long, wrinkled fingers move surely over the controls.

"Zeke, you haven't waved goodbye to your mother," his father urged from the back seat. Zeke glanced out the bubble and saw Laura standing in a silvery dress at the edge of the rooftop pad. She was magnificently posed, a hand to her cheek, the picture of broken-heartedness. She'd probably been a decent actress before she'd married his father, but Zeke wished that she wouldn't continue to try to prove it.

Dutifully, he waved. Dutifully, she waved back. Leo Bones smiled at the picture.

The turbines screamed and the little jet wobbled into the air on a vertical column of exhaust. Zeke always loved the moment of takeoff. It was the only reason he could think of to look forward to the Academy—if he made it through the first three years, in the fourth year they'd teach him to fly, not just atmospheric craft but the ships that moved between the planets and stars. That was what Zeke wanted at that moment—to be able to fly, to be able to go wherever he wished and see whatever he wanted to see.

Complete freedom. Away from Leo Bones, away from the whole Bones Energy Corporation. Away.

Mahsi toggled the turbines down and shifted the flaps so the craft was ready for horizontal flight. The jet lifted quickly away and streaked across the starry African night.

His father said the gruff and manly things Zeke expected him to say at the spaceport's quarantine airlock. Leo shook Zeke's hand firmly, and Zeke resisted the impulse to pull his father close for a last hug, expecting that somehow Leo would not approve of that. Besides, he told himself, his perception of his father had changed since his discovery of the hidden gallery at the African estate. The old Leo Bones, his "real" father, would never have been a thief, Zeke told himself. With that thought, Zeke sniffed, blinking his eyes hard, and let go of his father's hand.

Mahsi had been following with Zeke's bags. Now he came forward to hand them to Zeke.

"Guess I have to carry these myself from now on," Zeke said, a bit too lightly.

Mahsi grinned back. "You'll learn to travel lighter now." Just before he stepped away, Mahsi patted the shoulder bag and said in a whisper too low for Leo Bones to here. "You take care of that thing, boy. You understand me?"

Zeke's face felt hot with a sudden flush. So Mahsi knew. Zeke should have realized that nothing Leo did could be a secret from the Bantu. The keypad was likely designed to accept Mahsi's fingerprints as well. "I . . . I didn't really steal it, Mahsi."

"I know. I'll let your father find the message for himself," Mahsi replied. Then he stepped quickly back. Zeke impulsively reached out for Mahsi, hugging him as he hadn't hugged his father.

For two days Zeke didn't dare take the star seed out of its wrappings. By then the transport ship was well along in its slow one-gee acceleration away from Earth orbit, and Zeke was safely alone in his tiny private cabin.

The cloth fell away and he felt the crystal seed tremble in his palm. The rocky heart began to glow and its message came to him.

•**Congratulations/Pride. You have done well. You have done well**•

CHAPTER 2

Mars was a month and a half away at *Johanson*'s acceleration, an ancient deuterium drive manufactured originally by Bones Energy Corporation. The liner traveled a long, looping parabola designed to intersect Mars in its own orbital path around the sun. After the newness had worn off, Zeke found the trip to be mainly tedious. It had taken humanity time to crawl back from the decline of the 22nd century, when the unstable weather and overpopulation pressures had ruined world economies and nearly destroyed civilization. Travel between planets was still something too costly to be undertaken lightly—in some ways, it was easier and even faster at times to travel between actual star systems than between the planets themselves. The *Johanson* carried mostly supplies destined for the Martian cities; the passengers were secondary. Most of them were business and government people, traveling at need. There were two families emigrating under the Settlement Program of the Mars Council. Both of those had younger children, but no one of Zeke's age. For company Zeke had only himself.

And Devon Charles.

Devon was the son of Bart Charles, one of the larger shareholders of the Bones Energy Corporation. Over the years, Zeke had had occasion to meet Bart Charles and Devon when the board had come to the Bones house for socializing and impromptu business meetings. Because they were the same age, Zeke and Devon had been forced together. None of those times were pleasant in Zeke's memory. Devon was, well, *ordinary,* and used to being indulged. He was strong, active, and big for his age; he was intelligent but mentally lazy. He was all the things Zeke was not. And yet...Zeke realized that labeling Devon "ordinary" was unfair. Devon reminded Zeke of the predators of the Serengeti: Devon had their sleekness, their instinctive cunning. Most people seemed to like him immediately, and when Devon *wanted* to charm, he could be seductively pleasant. Given their differences, it wouldn't have been surprising if they had come to be either fast friends or enemies. But Devon had sensed a rival in Zeke, and Devon's charm had turned acid. Zeke had come to loathe Devon.

"Bones! Dammit, Bones! Over here." The call had come from across the *Johanson*'s main deck, where Zeke was inspecting the listing of holovids available to passengers. He'd seen most of them already—one more indication that space-flight, to someone who was merely part of the cargo, would be boring. "Bones!"

Zeke looked up from the holotank. He immediately recognized the trim, athletic body, the dark hair and long face. It had been a year and a half since he'd last seen Devon Charles. A frown crossed his face, and then Zeke sighed. He waved back to Devon. "Hello, Devon," he said. A sinking suspicion came to him. "I didn't see you when we came on board. What are you doing here—a family vacation?" he asked hopefully as Devon approached, loping in the light, spin-induced gravity of the ship.

Devon scoffed. "No," he answered. "I'm bound for the Academy. I'm not going to waste my life working for the company, especially when somebody else owns it." He finished that with a belligerent, challenging glance.

"The shareholders own BEC jointly," Zeke answered, not wanting to defend the oblique attack on his father but feeling compelled to do so. "Even as Director, you still have restrictions. My father can't make any big policy decisions without consulting the board—and *your* father—first."

Devon laughed at that. "Yeah, that's easy for you to say. *You're* going to inherit the whole ball of wax—you're a shoo-in to be voted Director after your dad kicks off. It's all yours after your old man's gone."

The rude comment would ordinarily have irritated Zeke, but he wouldn't have said much; it was exactly the sort of unthinking remark Devon would make. But coupled with Zeke's guilty knowledge of the star seed hidden in his cabin, Zeke found that the words made him snap back. "You don't talk about my father like that, Devon," he said. "I won't have it."

The burly young man made a face and backed away in mock terror. "Hey, Bones, don't get all upset. I'm just telling you what we both already know, huh? With the shares your father controls, directorship of BEC can be kept in the family. Once my dad's gone, I get *his* shares—maybe—but that's it. There are no guarantees for me. I need to make my own life—and I can do that better outside of BEC." Then Devon shrugged. His eyes narrowed as he looked at Zeke. "Just what're *you* doing aboard, Bones?"

"Same as you, Devon. I'm Academy-bound."

"You?" Devon was incredulous. "Why? You've got everything you want at home, Bones. You're going to run BEC someday. You can stay at home and play with those electronic toys you make up all the time. Why should you bother to go to the Academy?"

"I have my reasons," Zeke answered, curtly. *Because I want to fly. Because I want freedom to go where I want to go. Because I want to see the other races of the United Worlds. Because I just wanted to get away.* He didn't want to explain it to anyone, and especially not to Devon Charles. Zeke wasn't sure exactly why himself; all he knew was that it felt right. "Dad and I thought it might be good for me to get away for awhile. Besides, I think there'll be war soon—with the lona attacking the shri, it can't be too long before we're all involved. If any race holds the United Worlds together, it's the shri: they'll drag us in, too."

Actually, the decision had been Zeke's, arrived at after long months of thought. *It's not the possibility of war: I have to get out from under and sort things out. I have to find out what it is that I'm good at. I don't just want to become the Bones heir if it's not what I want, and I'll never know unless I get away. There's too much to see. Besides, Dad's changed a lot since Mom died. He's not the same; being with him isn't the same.* Zeke remembered the secret gallery, and the shock of finding the stolen archeological collection stashed there.

Everything in his life had changed, but he couldn't explain that to Devon. Devon wasn't a friend. Devon would laugh, he'd think it amusing.

Devon reached out and slapped the smaller boy on the back, far harder than needed. Zeke grimaced at the sting of it, but he kept his footing and said nothing. "Hey, I'll take care of you, Bones," Devon said. "You stick with me; I'm going to be top dog at the Academy. You'll see."

We certainly will, Zeke thought. *This will be a long flight, indeed.*

• • •

Zeke spent as much time as he could in his room with the star seed. The gem fascinated him. Zeke could stare at the seed for hours, gazing at the warm glow that his touch evoked. After his first encounter with Devon Charles, the seed seemed to echo his feelings. It gave Zeke a definite impression of empathy and comfort. Without words but with a complex emotional feedback, it seemed to say •It's all right. I understand•

Zeke wondered if his father would understand when he finally read the note Zeke had left in the secret gallery: *Dear Dad, I have taken this because I think it needs my protection. I will keep it safe until I see you again. Love, your son, Ezekiel.* It was possible that the note still lay unread in the star seed's case. It had been obvious that the gallery was infrequently visited by Leo Bones, and Mahsi would have been the only other person to know of its existence. Zeke wondered how his father would react when he read the words Zeke had so hastily scribbled. Taking the star seed had been an impulse, an action that was unlike Zeke's usual caution. Zeke wondered again if the decision hadn't in some part been influenced by the seed itself. If so, the thing might actually be a sentient creature, one with unguessed abilities. If his father had known that, he'd be furious at the seed's loss. Leo Bones could be a hard-minded, stubborn man at need. Zeke wondered whether he might be angry enough at the "theft" to come after Zeke and the star seed.

The crystal radiated warmth in Zeke's hand at the thought. •Think• it seemed to say. •Consider/Reflect• It almost seemed an admonition. He tried to put himself in his father's position, tried to imagine how he might respond in the same situation. "Of course," he whispered. "Dad won't do anything. If he makes a fuss, he risks having others learn about the gallery. No matter how powerful he is, he can't hide from a Galactic Council subpoena. He can't do that, so he'll wait. He'll wait for me to make the first move."

•Yes/Satisfaction•

Zeke laughed; it was as if a burden had lifted from his mind.

During the long days of flight, Zeke also learned that the star seed was aware of things beyond Zeke's own senses. He was sitting at his desk, the seed sitting in his palm as usual, when he felt the stab of the seed's emotional matrix in his mind •Irritation• That was followed by the kind of dread that Zeke remembered from nightmares. Zeke had the feeling that he wanted nothing more than to pull the covers over his head and hide. He frowned, looking at the seed's glow. "What do you want?" he asked.

There was a knock at his door. "Bones," yelled an impatient voice from the corridor. "Bones, are you there?"

Zeke smiled. "Just a minute, Devon." Zeke put the star seed in its wrapping. He felt the seed radiate comfort at that. "So that's what you wanted," he whispered. "You knew, didn't you?" He quickly put the seed inside one of the drawers of the cabin and locked it. Also in the drawer was one of his sonic amplifiers like the ones that kept the animals away back home. This one was designed to drive away the human animal. Zeke was taking no chances with the star seed.

When he opened the door, Devon seemed puzzled by the grin on Zeke's face.

In time, the *Johanson* arrived in Mars orbit. The passengers, weary of the ship, gathered around the viewing screens to see their destination. Zeke was there with the rest of them. Even the presence of Devon Charles couldn't dampen the excitement Zeke felt.

Fantasy had become reality on Mars. Even from low orbit, one could see the changes man had wrought in the face of the red planet. Ironically, man had changed Mars into a vision that perhaps Burroughs or Bradbury would have recognized best. Humanity had taken this inhospitable world and made it a place where men and women could walk. The terraforming had taken a century and a half and was not finished yet, but great advances had been made. The Mars found by the early explorers had been harsh and violent. Its thin atmosphere was mostly carbon dioxide. Surface temperatures in the middle latitudes might reach 15° C at the heat of the day, but then the mercury would fall rapidly to $-80°$ C, rivalling the lowest temperatures ever recorded on Earth. It was only worse as one went closer to either pole. The poles were covered with frozen carbon dioxide —dry ice—in the winters, which further dropped the air pressure. There was little protection from ultraviolet radiation there, and that protection was what made life on Earth possible.

The worst feature of all were the ferocious Martian storms. Gigantic storms pushing huge clouds of choking dust would gust across the surface at speeds of 150 to 300 kilometers per hour. They could grow to be large enough to hide large portions of the surface from observation.

What had transformed Mars had been the work of generations. The polar caps had been melted by triggering "clean" thermonuclear devices there. The addition of water vapor and carbon dioxide to the air had stimulated the greenhouse effect, keeping the caps from totally reforming and again locking up the planet's water and CO_2; what there was of Mars' active volcanoes had been stimulated to produce more heat. With the addition of the CO_2 to the air, pressure had been raised to about a third of Earth's, roughly equivalent to Earth at 20,000 feet: higher than any human habitation on Earth, but liveable. That had three immediate effects—people could go outside without pressure suits (though of course they still needed oxygen masks), the horrible storms were tamed somewhat, and liquid water could exist. For underneath the frozen CO_2 of the caps was water ice. To move it and protect it, it had been decided to give Mars what the Mars of myth had once had: canals.

Genetic manipulation had been the answer to the lack of oxygen. Genetically tailored plants had been imported to Mars —most of them algae to flow in the roofed-over canals. They fed on the new atmosphere, taking in the carbon dioxide and releasing oxygen. As the atmosphere's content began to shift, other plants were brought in: low-lying trees to line the canal routes, and that favorite of man, the grasses that would hold the soil in place.

The Mars that Zeke looked down upon was still extraordinarily dry, still very cold, still prone to vicious storms larger than any Earth knew. Yet humans could walk there, could breathe that thin, cold air and survive. For people with heart conditions or muscular disorders, the low gravity was a benefit. Mars was also close to the asteroid belt and the mining stations there—much of the ore that fed the factories was processed here. Cities had sprung up along the canal routes; there were even a few small forests. Slowly, with great caution, an animal ecology was being brought into existence, again through genetic tailoring: Zeke had once seen one of the red "squirrels" in a display on Earth. The creature had been six-legged and squat, with large pads that enabled it to cling to the trees during the winds. He'd seen the creature spread its two front legs and show the sails of flesh that actually allowed it to fly in the low atmospheric pressure and gravity of Mars. Zeke hoped he'd be able to see one in the wild, moving along the low branches of the Martian trees.

The call came to strap in for docking with Marsport Up, the

orbital station. From there, they would ride shuttles to Marsport Down, on the surface.

Despite the reassurance the star seed had given him, Zeke half-expected to see Leo Bones there in the port lobby, or perhaps Mahsi, all quiet and solemn. His imagination made him fearful as he went through the customs inspection. The serious expressions of the guards convinced him that, yes, they knew. They'd been told. Zeke had hidden the star seed as best he could, hollowing out the heel of his shoe so that it fit there snugly. *Smuggler,* Zeke thought. *Now you're breaking the law, too.* Zeke's stomach was knotted and queasy as he left the shuttle and approached the queue. It didn't help that Devon Charles was behind him. "Hey, don't you know who this is," he said to the inspector as she checked Zeke's papers. "His dad runs BEC. He could buy and sell someone like you. Let us through."

"Shut up, Devon," Zeke had hissed through clenched teeth. He shook his head at the inspector, shrugging. He was grateful when the woman finally waved him through, and not at all surprised at the close inspection she gave Devon's belongings.

As they passed through the gates, a person in a military uniform detached herself from the crowds and came their way. "Ezekiel Bones and Devon Charles?" she asked, stopping in front of them.

"That's right," Zeke answered. He smiled, holding out his hand. Since she was obviously from the Academy, it seemed best to get on her good side. "And you're . . ."

She looked at Zeke's proffered hand as if it were covered with running sores. "I'm your superior, pups, and don't you forget it." She looked to be about seventeen, slender but powerfully built, her blondish hair tucked tightly under the cap. She frowned down at them. "You can call me *Mister* Huff."

Devon laughed. "Mister?" he said. "I thought you were female."

She smiled; it looked decidedly malicious. "That's right, pup. You call *all* the upperclassmen at the Academy 'Mister,' no matter who they are. I'd advise you to remember that, too. And I guarantee that I'll remember what *you* just said." She shook her head. "You two'll never make it, I can tell you that now. It's washout city for both of you. Pups. Groundlings. You should've never come here. You'd all run with your tails between your legs if the lona ever attacked us." A klaxon sounded down the corridor. "But it's too late now. That's the shuttle for

Marsport Down. Let's go, pups. And try not to get lost; I've got to collect a few more of you little ones. Nobody here's gonna go looking for you if you wander off. It's your first chance to wash out—the Academy'll even pay for the trip home. The two of you would be advised to take the offer, I think."

Huff gave the same basic pitch to all the new people she rounded up: two more from a liner inbound from Venus that happened to arrive within the hour, and five more who had been staying in a hotel in the port for the past week awaiting the opening of the Academy to the new freshman class. These five she made clean their rooms before they left, telling them that it would be good practice. By the time she herded all nine— seven boys, two girls—into the shuttle for Marsport Down, Zeke had realized that her bluster was mostly an act. He noticed that, despite her words, she watched them very carefully and made certain that the whole group stayed together.

Three hours later, they arrived at the Academy via an underground monorail. Huff escorted them up a maze of slideways and into a dormitory. There, she showed them their bunks and lockers. "Get your gear stowed and put on the uniforms you'll find in your lockers. I'll be back in ten minutes to see how you've done. It had better be perfect."

They would learn that nothing they could do would be perfect for Huff. That day, dissatisfied by the way they'd left their dorm, she took them out to the practice field between the low gray buildings of the Academy. There in the cold Martian wind, she ignored their panting as they tried to accustom their lungs to the thin atmosphere of the world. She took them through basic drills again and again. "Move it, move it, move it!" she screamed at them. "C'mon, pups, show me some of that energy you're supposed to have. Bones, what the heck do you think you're doing, taking a stroll? Move, I said!"

That day began the routine that would not end that year. After a while, the days began to blend into each other—the Martian day was only thirty-seven minutes longer than the Earth day, but it seemed far longer. Mars used a twenty-four-hour daily clock as did Earth; they simply adjusted theirs to run slightly slower to match the daily cycle. The cadets were roused at 5:00 A.M. They were expected to be showered, dressed, and on the field by 5:30. Drill practice took up the next hour and a half. At 7:00, into the mess hall for breakfast. Into the classrooms at 7:30 until 11:30, then another hour of drill until lunch at 12:30. At 1:00, classes again until 3:00. Then there was what was called Free Time until 5:00, but it was rarely free, not with the hounding of the upperclassmen and the demands of school. At 6:00, after dinner, there was more drill and Theory of Military History. From 8:00 to 9:00, the exhausted cadets studied or did other work. Nine o'clock was Lights Out, and woe betide the cadet who was found awake after that time.

Zeke found his adjustment to the demands of the Academy perhaps more difficult than the others. Zeke had been used to freedom; especially since his mother had died, Leo Bones had left Zeke on his own more often than not. Mahsi had never minded what Zeke did so long as he kept up with his studies— something that Zeke had never found difficult. He was used to setting his own schedule, to following his interests wherever they might lead him. This rigorous, unbendable, and unbreakable schedule of the Academy was a jolting change, and not a pleasant one. Zeke found the Academy to be a depressing place, while Devon Charles seemed to fit right in. More than once Zeke would have quit and gone home, except for the memory of the secret gallery he'd found. That sick feeling of disgust he'd felt then would come back, and Zeke would grit his teeth and vow not to go back. Not yet, not as a washout.

There were some things he liked at the Academy; for instance, Zeke found the science classes, in particular those dealing with archaeology, to be fascinating. He knew that was perhaps also in response to finding the gallery. Or perhaps he found ancient things fascinating because his mother had found them fascinating. Still, the subject tugged at him, and he spent what little spare time he had in the library, studying on his own. He enjoyed studying about the other races of the United Worlds: the floating, majestic cities of the air-dwelling shri, the rigid and warlike society of the armored !xaka! (who had given humanity its first interspecies war until the shri interceded), and the heavy gravity environment of the dwarfish hlidskji.

And he spent stolen time with the star seed as well, contemplating it when he dared, trying to understand its ways of communications. At nights, with the lights out, he would reach down under his bed and trigger the tiny heat/touch-activated switch that he'd rigged on the trip to Mars. A servo would whirr softly and open the compartment in the heel of his dress shoes. Then Zeke would take out the star seed and cup it in his hands as the others slept. Sometimes it would only be for a few minutes. At other times he would lie there for an hour or more, listening and trying to open his mind to the voice of the seed as the Martian winds howled outside. He couldn't help but feel that there was some significance to his finding the seed. He thought that if only he listened hard enough, the seed would speak and tell him about itself. It never happened, though. Still, more than once, when he'd been convinced that he would march into Commander Blaine's office and resign, his meditation with the seed had changed his mind. He woke with the will to endure another day.

Mahsi had always taught Zeke to ask questions, not to accept things as they were. Zeke soon found that to question the ways of the Academy was to invite trouble. He balked once when Huff was exhorting her "pups" to push themselves beyond the limits of their endurance. He'd learned quickly that Huff had a reputation as being one of the hardest officers of the senior class; Zeke was often sorry that she'd been assigned to his unit. She had them running around the track between the dormitories, again and again. Zeke was running with the rest of them in the middle of the pack. Suddenly he shook his head and slowed. He stood on the side of the track, watching Devon Charles lead the rest of them around. He heard Huff come up behind him. His classmates stared at the confrontation but continued to run around the track. "Whassa matter, Bones? Get up and run with your classmates, pup," Huff growled at his back.

"It's stupid," Zeke answered. His sullen anger made his voice break in an adolescent crack, and that made him set his jaw and harden his eyes.

"What?!" The tone in her voice should have warned him, but somehow he couldn't stop himself. Zeke turned around and faced her. "It's stupid," he repeated obstinately. "What's it matter if I can run around the track a hundred times? What difference will it make? It's not important."

"You don't question orders, pup." Her eyes were narrowed with irritation. "I'm not going to tell you that again. Now run —your classmates got five extra laps to make up because of you, and *you*, pup, get ten."

"It's *stupid,* Mister Huff," Zeke said again, angrily. He knew she felt the same way—she just wouldn't admit it. He'd seen the bored look on her face as she watched them. The running was just something to give the freshmen to do—all the upper classmen did the same thing.

"You're up to twenty extra laps, Bones, and ten for the others. You gonna run?" She said it loudly this time, so that the rest of them could hear it. "It's run or wash out, Bones. That's your choice—I don't give a damn what your name is or what kind of coddling you're used to. If you don't want to be here, just walk away and pack your bags. Now, boy. Make your decision."

Zeke stared at her, trying to find in her face the sympathy that he knew must be there. But her slender features were set in stone; the lips were tight with a grimace. Finally Zeke shook his head. Almost wanting to cry but not daring to do so, he broke into a ragged jog and back onto the track. The others ignored him as he ran, but he could see how infuriated they were. They were all inside before he finished his extra laps in the darkness and cold. No one would talk to him when he came back inside.

For the next three weeks, Huff made Zeke do extra laps every day. He hated her for it.

The incident that set his attitudes for the next three years came midway through that horrible freshman semester. By that time Zeke was already alienated from the others, who seemed to consider him a troublemaker. Zeke did well enough in his studies, especially in the sciences, where he was easily the top student. He performed acceptably if not outstandingly in the team sports, in the gymnastics, in the endless drills and training. Yet something seemed to keep him at a distance from the others. He didn't bother to hide his intelligence; perhaps that was part of it. It didn't help that Devon Charles, adopted quickly as one of the leaders of the freshman class, let everyone know just how he felt about Zeke—Devon speculated openly that Leo Bones would make certain that his son never washed out, no matter what happened.

Zeke kept to himself, did what he had to do, and contemplated the star seed at nights. He had no friends, no confidants, and plenty of people who seemed to be his enemies.

He'd thought that in the quiet darkness with the boys sleeping all around him, he'd have enough warning if someone approached. Huff sometimes made surprise visits to the freshman dormitory to make sure that all the lights were out and everyone sleeping, but she usually could be heard outside in the hall before she opened the door, and Zeke would slip the star seed back into its compartment and pull the covers over himself. When Huff passed his bed, he'd seem to be sleeping as peacefully as any of the others.

He didn't hear anyone that night. He held the star seed in his palm and watched it slowly brighten so that a pale glow played on Zeke's blond features. The star seed pulsed slowly, and Zeke tried to open his mind to the seed. •Welcome/Hello• it seemed to say. "Hello," he whispered back. Zeke could feel a prickling inside his head; the feeling that he'd come to know was the star seed sharing his emotions. •Worried/Troubled?• The seed radiated the question with an insistent force. Zeke nodded. He let all his anger and bitterness show in his mind and felt the seed recoil, backing away a little from its contact. Then there was a sharp jolt in his mind that startled Zeke. •Danger/Move• Zeke slipped the seed into the heel compartment and shoved the shoe under the bed just before he heard the scuffling of feet on the concrete floor and rough hands grabbed him. A light blinded him.

Someone slapped him across the face and Zeke gasped in pain. He hit out blindly, his eyes watering. His wrists were caught and held. "What were you doing, Bones?" Zeke recognized the voice: Devon's deep bellow. "We saw the light—you know the rules. We're not going to get punished because of you, are we, fellows?" Zeke heard others agreeing with him. Zeke blinked, trying to get loose, but two people held him on either side. "We're gonna make sure you wash out, Bones. We're gonna make sure you run home to Daddy."

Through the bright spots in his eyes, Zeke could see Devon's hand doubled into a fist. The fist smashed down on Zeke's mouth. Zeke cried out, feeling the blood from his torn lips, watching helplessly as Devon readied another blow.

"That's not going to make me give up," Zeke told him through the pain.

"We'll see, won't we," Devon said.

Zeke spat blood. "Then let me go. Give me a chance to defend myself."

"Too late for that, Bones."

Zeke tried to turn but the others held him. Devon brought his hand back again.

"Stop it!" Huff's roar made Devon halt in mid-blow. Zeke felt the hands holding him let go as Devon whirled around. Huff stood in the doorway with pure anger on her face. "Bones, Charles—outside," she said. "The rest of you hit the beds. NOW!" They scattered like the Martian sands in a windstorm.

It was frigid outside with only the light thermal nightclothes between them and the winds. Both of the boys were shivering after a few seconds, but Huff didn't seem to notice the cold.

Hands on hips, she glowered at them. "You two got a problem I need to know about?"

"No, ma'am," they chorused together.

"Charles, you think a cadet needs to have friends to help him settle a problem with someone else? You think that's the way a leader solves things?"

"No, ma'am," Devon answered.

"Good. I'm glad to hear it. And if I ever see you using friends to help you settle a fight, I'll make sure you bounce out of here so high they'll need a shuttle to retrieve you. *And* I expect to see you in the laundry for the next month. You'll solve the problem of washing your class's clothes—by yourself, pup. And I don't expect to see you neglecting any of the rest of your studies. You understand?"

Muscles bunched in Devon's jaw, but he lowered his eyes. "Yes, ma'am," he said to the frozen ground.

"Good. You can get inside and back in your bed." Then, as Devon moved toward the door, her hard gaze turned to Zeke. "Bones, you think you're different from everybody else? Is that why you think you can do whatever you want to do? You think daddy's gonna come rescue you?"

From the side of his vision, Zeke saw the look of satisfaction as Devon toggled open the door and went back inside. As the solid door hissed shut behind the cadet, Zeke answered. "No, ma'am," he said, knowing that was what she wanted to hear.

Huff only shook her head. Her short light hair rippled in the gusting wind. "Bones—" she began, then stopped. She sighed. What she did next surprised Zeke. She came close to him and pulled him into the circle of her arms, hugging him. For a moment, Zeke was too startled to move; then he returned the hug, marveling at how good it felt. "Bones, take a lesson from someone who feels like your older sister. You've got to stop banging your head against the wall, Zeke. You're only going to dent your skull. I know. I put a few dents in my own skull."

"You?" Zeke said incredulously.

"Yeah, me." With a final squeeze, Huff let Zeke go. When he looked at her, the harsh lines of her face were soft with sympathy. "I look at you and remember how hard it was for me, my first year. Maybe worse, 'cause I had to prove that I was as good as any of the damn *boys*. I stuck it out just to prove them wrong. Bones, what are you going to do if you wash out?"

"I'm not sure," Zeke answered. "The Legion of Ares, maybe . . ."

Huff snorted. "Yeah, that's what they all say. The Legion's a bunch of mercenaries and nothing else—hey, I've thought of joining 'em myself; I still might if I can't get a naval commission out of the Academy. But the Legion's not for you, Bones. You won't find whatever it is you're looking for there. I can tell you that."

"I'm not looking for anything," Zeke said. "I came here to learn, to be taught how to fly and fight and lead. The Iona war's going to come here eventually. . ."

"Is that really why you came?" Huff shook her head. "Uh-uh. I've watched you. I know better. But I'll take that explanation for now. If you want what you say you want, you need to learn to survive. You're clever, Bones, I'll grant you that. I've seen the bio-servos you've put together in Electronics, and they're incredible. The suckers look just like bugs, better than the ones in the textbooks. I wouldn't know them for mechanicals at first glance. But sometimes clever isn't enough. That one"—she nodded her head to the door through which Devon Charles had just gone—"They follow him because he's *smart*." As Zeke shook his head, she continued, not letting him interrupt. "He knows who to coddle, who to push, who to make friends with. He uses his brains and his muscle to get power and keep it. You, you're different. You seem to think he's dumb because he doesn't score as high as you in the school tests, but academic knowledge isn't the only thing an officer or *any* leader needs. You also have to know the tactics of people. Devon may be a creep in a lot of ways, but at least he understands that.

"You'll have to have that fight with him, Zeke. He won't let you get out of it. You're going to have to be careful of 'accidents.' You understand me?"

"I know."

Huff nodded. She frowned and then smiled sadly at Zeke. "He'll probably beat you—but I'm going to show you some tricks if I can. Things I learned. But even if he does, that doesn't matter—what matters is that you don't give in to him."

"I won't," Zeke said. The conviction in his voice caused Huff to smile even wider.

"Yeah, I figured that, or I wouldn't be wasting my time with you," she said. "You're gonna be good, Bones. I tell you that. I'm also not going to let you make me a liar, so when I start pushing you, you understand why, okay?"

Zeke nodded.

"You know how the Japanese make swords, Bones?"

"No," Zeke said, wondering where she was going with that. In the half-darkness between the buildings, her gray eyes glinted.

"They take the steel and heat it," she said. "Then they hammer the molten metal, folding it over itself again and again. More heat, more hammering. Time after time. When the blade's finished, it's made of layers and layers of that steel, and is incredibly strong and supple. Stressing the metal makes it strong, Bones: the heat, the hammering. You understand what I mean?"

"I think so," Zeke said. "You're telling me that all this trouble I'm having will make me stronger afterward."

"That's right," she told him. "And mean, nasty Huff is going to be your hammer, pup. I expect to see you out on the drill field fifteen minutes before the others for the next two weeks for calisthenics. And next time you're up at night, reading or doing whatever you were doing, don't be so stupid as to get caught. You get caught and the Legion might be your only option."

Zeke sighed. "Yes, ma'am," he said. "Anything else?"

She laughed. "Yeah. One more thing. I love my pups, but don't expect a repeat performance of tonight. I'm not your mother and I'm not your lover. Got it?"

"Got it."

Huff gave Zeke another quick hug and then let him go. "Let's get inside," she told Zeke. "It's cold out here."

CHAPTER 3

It was a leaner, taller, and perhaps wiser Zeke Bones that received the summons to Commander Blaine's office at the beginning of his senior year at the Academy. After that night with Huff, Zeke had been in several tense situations with the others of his class. With the memory of Huff's words in mind, with the strange calm the seed lent him, he'd been able to work through them. He still had no real friends among the cadets, he still considered most of them to be actually antagonistic toward him, but his pride kept him from letting his true feelings show. Even when Huff left the Academy that year (to join the Legion, the other senior cadets remarked scathingly) and another of the seniors was assigned to his unit, he was able to take the constant harassment in stride with a calm that sometimes puzzled the upperclassmen and the officers of the Academy.

Illness had further hampered him in the last few years. Zeke, who had always been active as a child, now found that physical exertion tired him more quickly. Though he'd grown inches over the course of the last four years, he had actually lost weight. He was stick-thin and often pale. Eating did little to add pounds to his lanky frame—if anything, too much food made him nauseous. The decline in his physical health made him concentrate all the more scholastically. He was far above the next highest cadet in that area.

Zeke entered the commander's office and saluted the gray-haired man behind the desk, noting that Devon Charles was seated in one of the two chairs drawn up before the commander's desk.

"Sit down, Bones, sit down," the commander growled as the two cadets exchanged glances. Zeke had met Blaine only a few times in the past years, exchanging polite and slightly fearful pleasantries. For the most part, the commander was only a figure seen on the podium at Academy events. "We have a bit of a problem," Blaine continued, "and the two of you are the ones that are going to have to solve it." Blaine grimaced. His hands, folded together on top of the desk, were white-knuckled with tension. The commander got up from his chair and paced over to his window. There he looked out at the grounds of the academy. He spoke to the two young men with his gaze on the landing fields and the ranks of cadets beginning their morning exercises.

"Three days ago, a robot probe detected an alien ship just outside the orbit of Mars, near the asteroid belt," he said without prelude. To Zeke, the commander seemed oddly troubled and ill at ease. "The ship was of an unknown design—neither lona, shri, or !xaka!: nothing we'd seen before at all. Following its programming, our probe beamed a set of welcome signals to the ship. The signals were in every frequency its transmitter was capable of putting out, the message was in all Earth languages along with the dialects of the other known alien races. In addition, several sets of signals were entirely visual in content, with a computer-generated human indicating peacefulness and welcome: open arms and the like."

The commander turned back into the room, looking at Zeke and Devon. What he'd said sounded so strange, so unlikely, that Zeke knew immediately what it had to be. *The exercise! Every senior class has their exercise. This has to be ours.* They'd all heard whispered rumors from the upperclassmen ahead of them. Every year there was a mock crisis which the cadets had to solve—always different, always unusual. The instructors always treated it as genuine; any cadet who did otherwise would have been shipped out immediately. There was always the possibility that it *was* real, since the Academy had been called out before in emergencies. The danger was real as well; cadets had been injured, even killed during the exercises. You never knew; you simply had to react as if it were real, knowing that your every action was being watched and judged. Zeke felt a thrill of excitement.

"There was no answer to any of the signals, though our probe kept broadcasting for several hours. Fifteen hours after the initial contact one brief visual contact with the intruder was made: visual only, no audio. Following that quick, enigmatic transmission, the probe was fired upon and destroyed by the intruder ship." The commander's face tightened at that, almost as if in pain. "Telemetry indicated that the intruder was on a course heading inward to Sol. As it passed a mining station at the inner regions of the Belt, one of our mining ships—which had no knowledge of the robot probe's fate—attempted to contact it. This time, there wasn't even the visual contact. The intruder fired upon the mining vessel within an hour of the initial contact and destroyed it. Of the crew of fifty, only twenty-three crewmembers survived. The intruder is continuing on its course inward. Toward *us*, gentlemen. More threateningly, it's on a direct intercept course for the Outward Food Stations—the farms. I don't think I need to tell you gentlemen what a disaster it would be to lose them."

The food stations, universally called the Farms, were huge complexes located between Mars and the Belt. In the hydroponic gardens crops were raised that fed the populations of Mars and the mining colonies within the belt. Millions depended on the Farms for food. If they were to be destroyed . . . Zeke's eyes widened at the thought of it. Food riots, panic, starvation—it could throw the outer colonies into chaos. If it were real . . .

"Then the navy should deal with it," Devon interjected. "They're obviously hostile."

Commander Blaine gave the cadet a long, appraising glance. Then he frowned. "The naval base here on Mars is currently involved in full-scale maneuvers near Triton. That means that all the medium and heavy cruisers are a week or more away even under heavy acceleration. They've nothing but a few intersystem patrol vessels in this area. The firepower the intruder has displayed so far would destroy the patrol ships as easily as it did the probe or mining vessel."

"What about other bases?" Zeke asked.

"None of them are close enough to get a cruiser here before this intruder arrives," the commander replied. "Given its current velocity and trajectory, it could arrive at the Farms within a day. No cruiser could get here earlier than a week. None. And while the Farms are protected from such things as terrorist attacks, they're not designed to hold off a ship with the firepower the intruder has demonstrated." Blaine seemed older than Zeke had ever thought. The lines of his face were carved deep with worry.

"Then what of the Legion of Ares?" Zeke said.

Disgust showed in Commander Blaine's scowl at the mention of the Legion. "The Legion is nothing but a bunch of mercenaries. They're showoffs and risk-takers, not a group you'd want involved in something as important as first contact with an alien race. And in any case, the Legion is out of the Sol system entirely at the moment, doing the dirty work they're best at. That's just as well."

"You think an organization that would have Huff is any good, Bones?" Devon interjected. Zeke ignored the comment.

"What about the Academy's two training ships?" he proposed. "They're older models, I know, Commander, but the shielding's the same and they have the heavier beam weapons. The navy could use them."

Commander Blaine nodded. "Good, Bones. That was thought of and rejected. Those ships require a crew familiar with them, a group trained to work with them. The navy has only a small force still in residence. Most of them aren't flight-trained, and they'll be needed to man planetary defenses here if it comes to that."

Zeke knew then that all alternatives had been covered. This wouldn't be a ground exercise. "Sir," he asked, "are you saying that the Academy will be involved in this?"

A quick smile fought with the commander's perpetual frown for just a moment. "That's exactly what I'm saying, Bones. Circumstances dictate the situation. In many ways, it's very unfortunate. I can tell you that heads will roll afterward, especially within the navy. The station should never have been left so desperately understaffed. But you've pointed out exactly the reasons that the planetary council has asked us to undertake this mission, and this is what you've been trained for. As you're both aware, the Galactic Council has strict rules governing contact with new races. We must not make a mistake here. If we act rashly a war could result, one that could have been avoided. That's why, Bones, even if the Legion were available, we wouldn't send them. We need trained people, bright people with good minds, to deal with the situation, and the Academy has them. This is a time of crisis, gentlemen, and you've been thrust into the spotlight. Charles, you're the highest ranking senior cadet, you'll command the Red Force and take the *Peregrine* up. Bones, you will command the Blue Force; you'll have command of the *Santiago*. I don't need to tell you how important this could be. You have three hours to get your people flight-ready, gentlemen. Three hours, and we go to meet this intruder. I'll be aboard *Peregrine* as an advisor."

Devon Charles shook his head. "Commander, I . . ." Then he stopped, seeing the commander's face.

Blaine's thick eyebrows lowered over his deepset eyes. The commander looked like a bear prodded from his cave before winter. "You want to know why I'm choosing Bones instead of Wojtowicz, who ranks second in the class. You want to know why I'm choosing a cadet who seems to you to be unqualified."

"With all due respect, sir, Bones is not the best pilot or tactician in the class. He spends inordinate amounts of time in the infirmary."

"He *is* the best scholastically. I'll agree with you that he's not the best cadet physically, nor does his attitude always seem quite standard. Yet he's in the top third of the class overall, and when he's healthy, he manages to hold his own; add them all together and you'd be surprised where he stands, Charles. Overall, Bones might be better qualified for command then you."

"He's also a Bones," Devon muttered.

The commander's craggy head swiveled toward Devon. "What was that, mister?"

To his credit, Devon didn't deny the accusation. "With all due respect, sir, I think a lot of the other cadets will wonder if Bones hasn't been given command of the second ship because of his father's influence. I know BEC donates heavily to the Academy. The inference—"

"The inference had better be kept to yourself, Charles. Do I make myself clear on that?"

"Yes, sir." Devon tightened his jaw. If he noted that Blaine had not bothered to deny the accusation, he said nothing. Zeke definitely noted the omission. He tried to tell himself that it was accidental.

"You think you can do it, Bones?" Blaine asked, turning to Zeke.

"Yes, sir." He should have been ecstatic. It should have been a milestone. Instead, Devon's accusation made Zeke answer almost listlessly.

"Then get going. Get your crews together and aboard the ships. You'll pick yourself the cadets you need—volunteers only, and seniors only: some of the juniors are under seventeen. All of you will have to sign consents."

Seventeen was the age of majority on Mars; Zeke understood the implications. Only those cadets who were adults in the eyes of the law would be allowed to go—Blaine was avoiding later legal problems. "When you have your crew, get them moving. You've got a lot of work to do and not much time to do it in. You're going up for real, gentlemen."

Later, Zeke would wonder at the strangeness of Blaine's orders. But for the moment, he was too excited to be struck at how odd it all was.

To crew the two ships fully required almost every senior cadet. Zeke wasn't surprised when most of the cadets he talked to waited to see if Devon would ask them first. Devon Charles was First Cadet—no one wanted to be on Zeke's ship if they could be on the *Peregrine* with Charles and the commander. Nor was Zeke surprised to find that the *Peregrine* crew was heavily stocked with the high-ranking cadets. He didn't care: he'd do what he'd been told to do. Huff's words came back to him: *Stressing the metal makes it strong, Bones: the heat, the hammering.* He could nearly feel the flames of the forge.

Three hours was very little time. It was barely enough to make sure that he had a person capable of running every technical position on the *Santiago:* engineering, navigation, internal systems, armament. Rushed, barking orders to his peers like old Huff at her worst, at the last minute Zeke made his way back to his dormitory. He took his dress shoes out of his locker and pressed the contact on the heel. When the star seed slid out, he palmed the crystal and put it in his pocket. "You're coming too," he said. "Our first command flight." There was the faintest flicker of a response from the seed. •Anticipation/Hope• Zeke rushed out of the dormitory and ran down the slideway to the linktubes that connected the Academy to its port. He couldn't help grinning as he did so, despite the situation.

Once his crew was aboard the *Santiago,* there was no more time for Zeke to relax or think at all. The ship's status had to be checked, a tedious hour-and-a-half process that would have taken days if not for the aid of the half-sentient ship. The ship's computerized brain was a complicated linkage of Artificial Intelligence circuitry, giving it personality and a limited ability to reason. Communication was always through the captain's nervelinks; Zeke had experienced one such linkage during training, aboard the *Peregrine.* That ship had seemed surly and bored—perhaps, under the constant hands of inexperienced and clumsy cadets, it was.

All support systems had to be verified and the backups tied

in: *Santiago* whispered into Zeke's ear with what seemed to be eagerness as they went through the checklist. Zeke though maybe the ship had caught some of the adrenaline rush tha pounded in his own temples. "Captain, I detect a loss of pressure in the rear hydrostatic valves on thruster four." Or: "Captain, please inform Navigation that the forward scanners are a half degree out of phase." Check and recheck—Zeke's green crew finished well behind schedule and twenty minutes after *Peregrine* had been cleared for takeoff. They all heard the throaty rumble of their sister ship's departure. Then it was nearly time for their own. Zeke, strapped into the command seat with the sticky pads of the nervelinks on his forehead, watched the digital readouts flicker away the seconds before the launch as *Santiago* droned in his ears. "Thirty seconds, Captain. Do you wish me to proceed on auto?"

"No, I'll take us up on manual, *Santiago*."

Zeke thought he could almost detect a hint of amusement in the ship's reply. "As you wish, Captain. Auto-sequence disabled. Take us up."

At zero seconds, Zeke flicked the toggle that fired the enormous rockets underneath them. *Santiago* roared like a wounded lioness, fierce and untamed, and then a gigantic hand shoved Zeke back into his padded seat as the ship climbed on its tower of fire.

Zeke couldn't hold back his excitement. The possible dangers of meeting the intruder were forgotten in the thrill of the launch. Zeke's unbridled shout was lost in *Santiago*'s thunder. He felt the echo of his excitement from the star seed in his pocket.

Through the ship's rearward screens, Zeke could see the column of smoke they left, rapidly scattered in the Martian jetstream. The rusty plains dwindled behind them, and he could see the curve of the world's shoulder and the spidery lines of the canals. The sky darkened to an utter pitch black and the stars gleamed beyond the glow of Mars. "Status," Zeke barked. "Green," the ship replied. Zeke touched one of the contacts on the command seat's arm. "Engineering?"

"Sir?"

"Full thrust until we reach orbit. We need to catch *Peregrine*."

"Aye."

"*Santiago*, take over auto. Com, send a message to *Peregrine* that we're aloft and right behind them."

"Aye, Captain."

That done, Zeke could relax slightly. He brought down the command seat's holovisor. "Okay, *Santiago*." he said, "let me see the pictures of the intruder."

The film relayed to the visor was grainy and two-dimensional, splattered and wavy with static. It didn't look like ship quality at all but something jury-rigged. Zeke squinted at the image, which showed an out-of-focus, smooth wall, and then the alien stepped before the camera lens.

Zeke wasn't sure what he expected to see; he certainly hadn't expected what appeared before him.

The being was humanoid—barely. The scale was impossible to determine, but it looked as if it were about five feet high. The head was small and covered with overlapping shiny scales that seemed to wriggle as it peered into the lens. A mound of ruddy flesh protruded at about the forehead, just above the one eye. The eye was set on a swelling of scales: the creature would have wide-angle but flat vision—Zeke wondered if it could determine depth at all visually. There were two narrow slits just below the eye; they vibrated rhythmically, so Zeke decided that they must be for breathing. Below the slits, where the mouth might have been on a human, there was only a ribbed disc that looked entirely rigid. Zeke wondered if that might be the "ear"; if so, stereophonic sound would be wasted on the creature. There was no sign of a mouth. Zeke found himself wondering how the creature talked, how it might eat.

It looked real. It didn't look like a fake at all. Zeke began to have doubts about his certainty that this was only an exercise. *You can't treat it that way in any case. Believe it's real.*

The film, relayed by the destroyed probe, was brief. The alien looked at the camera with its enigmatic face. It said nothing; it didn't seem to be making any attempt to communicate at all. Within twenty seconds, the transmission broke up in a flurry of static and was gone.

Zeke sat silently for a few moments, troubled by the scene but not knowing why. Even the star seed sensed his distress, for it sent out the rising emotional note he'd come to think of as •?•

"Nothing," he whispered. "Nothing, except that it's just not right." Zeke asked the ship to replay the sequence again, in slow motion this time, but saw nothing to explain his sense of uneasiness.

"Do you have a view of the intruder's ship, *Santiago*?"

"Onscreen now, Captain."

The holo before him shimmered. Now, dominating the center of a star-filled screen, Zeke could see the intruder ship. It hung there like a ball: a perfectly round, unbroken sphere. The surface looked utterly smooth, as if cast from plastic rather than welded from steel-alloy plates like the hull of *Santiago*. From the sphere trailed a thin line, a linktube leading back to an ungainly box, which evidently housed the drive systems for the ship. The ship looked fragile, yet it had ruthlessly destroyed the probe and the mining ship. As if sensing Zeke's thoughts, *Santiago* broke in. "Weapons are housed back with the engines, Captain. The sphere is the living quarters. I don't think much of it, sir. I could take it."

Zeke ignored the ship's comment. "Give me full magnification on the hull."

The image of the ship seemed to streak toward him. Zeke could see the surface, which looked like polished, opaque glass: unbroken, gleaming, and an off-white, cream color. There were no markings, nothing to mar the perfection of that surface. Zeke moved his gaze back along the sphere, and the image of the ship obediently tracked the motions of pupils until he was looking at the drive unit. He could see the tubing and nozzles of the drive unit. In class, they'd studied the ships of all the known races, even the scant information on the Iona; this was like nothing he'd ever seen before. The arms pack, mounted in a ring around the drive unit, looked conventional enough: a sand caster, the spiny turrets of beam weapons, even what was obviously the tube of a cutting laser. The rest . . . the very appearance of the intruder spoke of its strangeness, and there was a hollow throbbing in Zeke's mind, looking at the ship.

•**Sadness/Despair**•

"Because we'll probably destroy it," Zeke said, understanding the compassion of the star seed. "We'll destroy it without ever undersanding who they were, where they came from, or what they wanted."

The crystal sung a sad agreement. •**Affirmation**•

Zeke had forgotten that the ship could hear him. *Santiago* broke in. "Captain, I would remind you that this intruder fired on our probe unprovoked, that it killed the miners without warning. You should also remember that it may do the same to me." The ship's admonition drew Zeke out of his reverie.

"You're right, *Santiago*. I haven't forgotten that." Zeke sighed and pulled the holovisor up. He still felt that unvoiced fear. He felt that if he weren't there first, he'd have no say in whatever decision was made. *Santiago* was still behind *Peregrine;* from what Zeke knew of Devon Charles, he would have already made *his* decision. Something about the alien still nagged at Zeke. He wanted to see it on his own screens, wanted to be there before something was done that couldn't be undone. "Com," he said, triggering the nervelink again, "is *Peregrine* ready to break orbit for intercept?"

"They sent word that they are initiating, Captain," came the reply.

"Navigation, is our course plotted?"

"Aye, sir. We could initiate in about fifteen minutes."

Zeke opened the channels to the entire ship. "This is Bones," he said. "I know a lot of you are unhappy to be here instead of on the *Peregrine*. Just remember this—they didn't think you were good enough to crew with them. Over on that other ship they're thinking that we're the backup group while they're the elite. They're probably wondering if we'll make rendezvous at all. And they'll be right if we don't show them differently. Navigation, what's the safety factor in your equations?"

"Standard ten percent, sir," was the startled reply.

"Take it down to five," Zeke ordered.

"Sir—" the head cadet in Navigations began—Stewart Nickelhoff, who ranked in the lower third of the senior cadets. Zeke cut in on his protest.

"Are you telling me that Charles was right about you, Stewart?"

A pause. Then: "No, sir. I'll cut the new equations."

"Good. Engineering, what's the margin on the overdrive for the deuterium systems?"

After a moment's hesitation, the reply came back. "I'm not sure, Captain. Maybe twenty percent—they don't want to risk a meltdown of the components."

"Twenty-five percent, Captain," the ship interjected.

"Thank you, *Santiago*. Did you hear that, Engineering?"

"Yes sir," came the uncertain voice.

"Then I want the drives red-lined and more on the initial thrust. We can risk it; watch your readouts. *Santiago*, can you take the extra hull stress?"

A row of LEDs flashed green across the left arm of Zeke's chair. "Yes, Captain."

"Okay, then. I'll take responsibility for the decision—log that, *Santiago*."

"Logged."

"Then start initiation. Com, let me talk to Captain Charles." Deliberately, Zeke left all the channels open so that his crew could see and hear Devon as a frequency opened to *Peregrine*.

"Hello, Bones. I only have a moment—*we're* ready to leave orbit." There was no mistaking the gloating sound of Devon's voice.

"We'll be a few minutes behind you," Zeke said. "I'm requesting that you wait so that we can arrive at the intercept point together. A few minutes isn't going to make any difference in the encounter. We can back each other up."

"I think *Peregrine*'s quite capable of dealing with this herself, Bones," Devon replied.

"There may be things to consider when we get there."

"The only thing to consider is that twenty-seven miners are dead because of that thing, and it's heading for the Farms. That says enough. It'll be in pieces when you arrive."

"Is that Commander Blaine's order?" Devon might have come to that conclusion already; at seventeen, he was headstrong and impetuous, convinced that his decision was always the right one. But Zeke couldn't believe that the commander would have made such a decision without actually seeing the alien vessel. If nothing else, it was counter to Galactic Council regulations, which stated that "reasonable" attempts for peaceful communication had to be made in any unknown contact.

"It's *my* decision, Bones. Blaine says he's here to act as advisor, not commander. Unless he says otherwise, I've already given my orders. You"—Devon scoffed—"you people can clean up afterward. They'll want the pieces to analyze."

•Displeasure/Disgust•

Zeke closed his mind to the emotions of the star seed. "I'm asking you again to wait. Two ships might be needed."

A klaxon sounded aboard the *Peregrine*. Devon shook his head at Zeke. "No way, Bones. I have to get this ship out of orbit. See you and your group of incompetents there." Abruptly, the other cadet cut the transmission.

Zeke took a deep breath and then spoke to his own crew again. "Navigation, is our new course plotted?"

This time the reply was firm and decisive. "Aye, Captain. Feeding it into *Santiago* now."

"Engineering?"

"No problem, Captain. New red-line limits are set."

Despite the tension he felt, Zeke smiled. "Let's get going, then," he said.

• • •

The journey was four hours under heavy acceleration. Zeke was quite happy to order the engines cut as they arrived at the coordinates where the alien ship should be. Freefall lifted him out of the seat slightly as the restraining web held him back. Around the bridge, he could hear the sighs of relief as the drone of the engines and the uncomfortable pull of the acceleration eased. Zeke immediately checked the readout from the forward screens. Yes, there it was: a blip in the screens. Zeke switched to visual and saw the gleam of the ship moving against the backdrop of stars. "Give me full magnification, *Santiago*."

The stars raced inward, centering on the dot of brightness, which expanded into the sphere-and-box shape of the intruder. "It's an ugly craft," *Santiago* commented. "Human cruisers are far more aesthetic."

"Prejudice, *Santiago*?" Zeke asked, amused.

The ship sounded slightly irritated by the mild rebuke. "I don't think so, Captain. Aesthetics are universal."

"Tell it to the !xaka!—there aren't uglier ships than theirs. Navigation, match courses with the intruder. Let's stay parallel for the moment; no closer until *Peregrine* arrives. Com, keep the visual channel open for any communications from the intruder. Engineering and Weapons, be ready for immediate action. Stay alert, everyone. And crew—to all of you, not a bad job for incompetents."

Zeke could hear the appreciative laughter echo through the ship. The bridge crew grinned back to him.

Peregrine arrived five minutes later. "Santiago calling *Peregrine*," Zeke called over the open hailing frequency.

"*Peregrine* here." Devon Charles' face was flushed with anger, but he said nothing about *Santiago*'s quick appearance at the intercept point.

"Captain, please tell Commander Blaine that we've matched course with the intruder. We've been alongside her at a distance of forty kilometers for several minutes now with no response."

Commander Blaine's face suddenly appeared on the screen next to Devon Charles. "Have you attempted to make contact with the ship, Captain?" the commander asked.

"No sir," Zeke answered. "It didn't seem a good idea after the response of the last two. Commander, I had a few questions about the intruder. I don't see any antennae on the ship at all for external communications. What did they use to broadcast that video signal?"

Blaine pursed his lips at that. He touched his finger to his ear and Zeke knew that he was consulting the ship's brain via a nervelink tap. "The probe analysis indicates that they used part of the weapons system, rigging the beam generators to send out a damped, low-level signal. Why, Bones?"

Zeke shook his head. "I'm not sure, Commander. This whole thing doesn't ring true. I feel that we're missing something. For one, the creature didn't seem to have a mouth—how do they talk?"

"What's it matter, Bones?" Charles broke in. "The thing's heading for the food support stations. They don't have any defenses at all. If that ship destroys them the way it did the probe and mining ship, thousands could die of starvation on Mars. We're wasting time. We don't have days to sit here and puzzle it out. I say we destroy it now."

It was obvious Devon considered it only an exercise, something to be taken care of as quickly as possible. *Always the brutal, quick path.* "All I'm saying," Zeke declared earnestly, "is that we may not have communicated with them at all. Maybe we never used a frequency they could understand."

"They understood enough to rig the video signal," Charles said.

"It's still not right," Zeke said doggedly.

"Too bad, Bones. We've done all we need to do by the Galactic Council regulations. Isn't that right, Commander Blaine?"

Blaine nodded, though his gray, wizened face was noncommital. "The intruder has demonstrated hostile intent and ignored all attempts at communication. By the regulations, we've done all we *have* to do." There was a strange emphasis on the statement, but Charles didn't seem to notice it.

"Then I'll give the orders for *Peregrine* to commence firing. *Santiago,* you may fire the second salvo."

"No," Zeke said.

"Bones," Charles told him, *"Peregrine* is the command ship on the mission. Therefore my orders take precedence."

"Commander, I appeal to you." Zeke refused to give up.

Blaine seemed to shrug. "Captain Charles is correct," he informed Zeke. *"Peregrine* is the command ship. You are technically under the captain's command."

Zeke looked from one to another, from Blaine's blank stare to Charles' sneer. "Aye, sir," he said, and quickly cut the connection. Their faces shattered into static. "It's still wrong," he muttered. A hand slid into the pocket where the star seed nestled. "How do they talk?"

•**Welcome/Hello?**•

The star seed's voice rose in his mind with the familiar greeting, but followed now by the rising interrogative. Zeke's young face creased into a frown. "What do you mean?" he whispered.

•**? Fear/Despair? Welcome/Hello? Pride? ????Think!!!!**•
The crystal wailed in his mind, like someone screaming in his ear. Zeke put his hands to his head in pain. "Stop it," he said. "Stop—" He cut off the plea in mid-word.

"That's it," he gasped. He lowered his hands. *How do* we *talk? How do* we *communicate?*, the star seed was asking him. "I understand. It all fits. Com, get me *Peregrine!* Now!"

"What is it, Bones?" Charles asked wearily when contact was finally made. "We're about to begin the first attack."

"You can't do it," Zeke said excitedly. "Is Commander Blaine on the bridge?"

Another screen flickered into life. "Here," Blaine said.

"Commander, Captain, I know what the problem is. Our problem hasn't been that we've been unable to communicate with the aliens; it's that we've communicated far too well. As far as the alien ship is concerned, we've *already* attacked them."

"What do you mean, Captain?" Blaine asked.

"Look at the alien. No mouth, no ear, just that hard ring-membrane on its face. It can't talk—it doesn't make sounds the way we do. It doesn't move air to make sounds."

"We don't know that, Bones," Charles interjected. "It could have a mouth lower down on the body."

Zeke shook his head at that objection. "No," he insisted. "Look how we're viewing each other now. We wouldn't show each other pictures of our chest or stomachs without the head—no, we focus on the parts of us that do the communication. They'd do the same. What they showed us included their method of communicating with themselves. They didn't show us an organ to make sounds; therefore they don't use audible sound."

"Are you talking *telepathy*, Bones?" Charles seemed near laughter.

"Maybe," Zeke shot back. "I don't know. Telepathy, maybe radio frequencies, some type of electric discharge—I don't know. But look at it. The knob on the head; maybe that's holding a lobe of the brain that they use to communicate. The 'mouth'; that's the receiver. No antennae on the ship—so they don't use any type of radio link in frequencies we use. Their ship's round—a curved surface like that will scatter a lot of electrical energy beamed at it. Inside, the parabolic surface will reflect and amplify any transmission they make among themselves. They used the video link to show us that they heard, but *we* couldn't hear *them*. Maybe they used too low a wattage. Maybe their transmission was entirely telepathic so the robot probe missed it entirely."

"So they destroyed the probe and killed the people on the mining ship."

"You still don't understand," Zeke continued. "Let me finish. The probe and the mining ship both beamed powerful transmissions toward them on all kinds of wavelengths. These creatures are communicating electrically, telepathically. What we did was jam them. What we did was like turning on the largest amplifier in the world right in their ears, screaming with white noise. I think their one contact was a plea to turn off our transmission. When we didn't answer, they did what they thought they had to do—they were under sonic attack. When the mining ship did the same thing, they responded." Zeke paused and looked directly at Devon Charles. "The same way you're thinking of responding."

"It doesn't make any difference," Charles insisted. "None at all. Your theory's all fine by itself, but it still doesn't tell us how to communicate with them."

"I've thought of that. Try one frequency at a time," Zeke suggested. "That way we shouldn't overload them too much. Keep the power low on the transmitters—just enough wattage to penetrate that hull. And start with a video signal since they can obviously understand them."

Charles was shaking his head; Blaine simply looked neutral. "No," the young man said. "And what if they decide to respond the same way this time? If the intruder has enough firepower to destroy our two ships, then there's nothing between it, the Farms, and Mars. We can't take the chance."

Commander Blaine cleared his throat, gaining the attention of both cadets. "Captain Charles, are you then saying that you'll give the command to fire on the intruder?"

Devon set his mouth. "Yes, sir."

Blaine nodded gravely. He turned to Zeke. "Captain Bones?"

"Sir?"

"What will you do if that order is given?"

Zeke didn't hesitate. "I've just now keyed *Santiago* to move into position between *Peregrine* and the intruder. I will also be beaming a video signal to that ship. I'm sorry, Commander, but I feel that Captain Charles is making a mistake that may eventually cost more lives than have already been lost. All I'm asking is that we give the intruder a last chance."

"One more chance," Charles scoffed. "And if you're wrong, it may destroy both of us. Those are heavy armaments on that weapons ring. If we fire first we have the advantage. Bones, you'll never be able to block us before our first attack. All you've done is disobeyed a superior and ruined any career you might have had after the Academy."

"That will do, gentlemen." The harshness of Blaine's voice surprised both of the cadets. "We'll take up this discussion in my office. For now. . ." Blaine pitched his voice higher. *"Peregrine, Santiago*, this is Commander Blaine. The exercise is now terminated. Commence auto-return sequences."

"Yes, Commander," both ships echoed.

"Exercise," Zeke breathed.

"Yes, exercise," Blaine told them. "I think you both realized it from the beginning. Did you really think the navy would leave the Farms entirely unprotected, even during maneuvers? Did you think that the Council would leave such a momentous encounter in the hands of *children?*" The scorn in his voice raked at them. "The Academy trains good people, but even *I* might be slow to do that." He smiled, but there didn't seem to be any friendliness in it. "The intruder was a drone rigged up by your teachers. The photos are fakes. No probe was destroyed; no lives lost. Take your ships back to the Academy. Bones, Charles, I'll see the two of you in my offices immediately afterward."

CHAPTER 4

Back in his office, Commander Blaine growled at the two cadets like one of the Serengeti lions. He reached into his desk and pulled out a small servo. It scuttled across his desk toward the two nervous cadets. Going to the edge, the machine made a small hop and landed on Devon's arm. The servo plunked itself down there and whirred. A tiny LED glowed. "Report," it chirped. "Now recording."

"Sir?" Charles asked the Commander, looking at him quizzically. Blaine looked at the cadet unsympathetically.

"All exercises involving the ships have to be documented, Charles. Reports go to the Martian Council, the navy, and in your personal file. I want you to pretend to be an unbiased observer who saw this exercise. Give me a report on your performance."

Devon flushed. He glanced at Zeke. "Report," the servo said again.

"Okay," Devon said. "I, uhh, thought that overall I handled it fairly well."

"Error," the servo cheeped. As the two boys stared at the device, Commander Blaine explained. "This servo has the ability to monitor pulse and nervous system variances. In other words, Charles, it's a sophisticated lie detector. It seems to feel that your opinion isn't quite so high. I'd suggest you reevaluate yourself."

Devon's neck turned bright crimson above his tight uniform collar. "Yes, sir. I think that considering that we all thought this a genuine emergency my crew and I responded well—insofar as handling the ship," he added hastily. "We did a complete systems check and were in orbit well before the *Santiago*, as you know. Technically, I think our performance was better than average."

"And as to the tactical side?" Commander Blaine prompted.

"Sir, all my advisors and I felt that considering the potential threat of the alien ship, we had little option but to destroy it."

"Do you still feel that way?"

Devon took a deep breath. He looked at Zeke and there was a deep anger in his gaze. "No, sir," he said. "I suppose not. We hadn't noticed the anomalies in the picture. There was still a possibility that by"—he paused and swallowed hard—"by using the suggestions of Cadet Bones, we might have success-fully made peaceful contact with them."

"Good. That's all I need from you, Charles." The servo lifted up, emitted a brief squawk, and leaped from Devon's arm to Zeke's. Zeke felt the slightest prick as its sensors went through his sleeve to his skin. "New report," it said. "Record-ing."

"Bones," the Commander said, "Your turn."

Zeke nodded. He inhaled deeply to calm himself, feeling a sudden nervousness. "Technically, sir, considering the caliber of my crew, I thought we did a competent job handling the ship. It could have been better, I suppose, but under the circumstances I was pleased with them."

The servo whirred. An amber light flashed on its body. "Evasion," it chirped. "Subject holding back pertinent details."

"I am not," Zeke insisted. "I hadn't finished." He looked up at Commander Blaine, who waved at him to proceed. "As you know from my log, sir, I took chances that I probably should not have taken. I'll accept responsibility for those—my crew isn't to blame. I thought them necessary because I knew that if *Santiago* wasn't on the scene, *Peregrine* would immediately deal with the situation. I wasn't certain why at the time, but I was troubled by some of the anomalies and wanted to be there."

"You disobeyed regulations deliberately. You also disobeyed direct orders from Cadet Charles, who was your superior in the field."

"I did," Zeke acknowledged. "But, Commander, under the same circumstances, I would do it again. As captain, I saw a reason to bend the regulations and narrow the safety factors for *Santiago*. I had confidence the ship and my crew could handle any problems resulting from that. As to my reasoning—which of us was right in your scenario, Commander? If I'd obeyed the orders from Cadet Charles and this had been a genuine emer-gency, we might have made a critical mistake."

Zeke glanced over at Devon and saw that the flush had crept into his cheeks. *I'll have to stay out of his way for awhile,* Zeke thought. *And Blaine doesn't look any happier.*

Blaine leaned back in his seat and crossed his hands on the desk. He shook his head at the two cadets. "End report," he said. The servo retracted its microphone and turned on Zeke's arm. It jumped to the desk and waddled across the polished surface until it stood in front of Commander Blaine, where it sat and waited. "You're both aware that senior cadets are granted a leave from the Academy near the beginning of the senior year. This is to allow you time to consider your future. What you didn't know was that each senior class is posed its own unique problem to solve before that leave. This was yours. Usually, the problem is posed so that the senior class must break into groups to solve it—those that do so successfully are given a longer break as a reward. We watch the leadership of the captains; for the rest, we evaluate how well each performed their job, and part of *their* task is the choice of captain that they made. After all, a soldier lives or dies by his commander. We want to see, given the choice of commander, who each cadet would choose."

Commander Blaine turned to Devon, and his stare was harsh. "Cadet Charles, your task now is to return to your Red Force and inform them that they have failed the examination. I expected better than mere technical expertise from a group that was largely the cream of the crop."

Then he turned to Zeke, and his stare was just as unsympathetic. "Cadet Bones, I don't want you to think that I condone *anyone* who would be quite so independent in the field. Your actions smack more of the Legion of Ares than the Academy, and I will so note that opinion in your personal record. I think the navy might think twice before accepting you into officer school, if you decide to apply there after graduation. You may find that there would be conditions attached to such acceptance."

Zeke's optimism fell. The commander's words stung him. *But I only did what I had to do,* he wanted to say. *If I hadn't, Devon would have fired on the ship.* But his protest died as he heard the Commander's next words. "On the other hand, you *did* best solve the puzzle presented to you, and your crew performed far better than we had expected, given your roster. That's one of the marks of a good captain. With some reluctance, I'm granting Blue Force early leave, effective immediately. You may tell your crewmembers to book passage home as soon as possible."

"Sir!" Devon protested. "That's hardly fair. You're rewarding him for disobeying strict orders. It's his father again, isn't it? He's using BEC's donations to pressure you."

"Charles, I told you that you were to keep such opinions to yourself."

"Tell me one thing, sir," Charles persisted, his eyes full of hatred as he stared at Zeke. "If Bones *had* obeyed me, what would have happened?"

"Get out of here, Charles," Blaine shouted at that. "And consider yourself grounded—you'll be the last damn cadet to take senior leave because of that outburst. Now, both of you, get out of here."

Home. At first Zeke was elated, bubbling over with happiness and pride. His Blue Force cheered him when he gave them the news. For a time, he was as happy as they were, laughing and whooping through the corridors of the senior dorm and making plans for their extended vacation. The full impact didn't begin to hit him until he'd already sent a radio message home and made his own plans for passage aboard one of the liners. When he finally sat down and thought about it, he wasn't so sure that he wanted to go home at all. By then it was too late— he was already on the liner, Earthbound.

For the entire month of the voyage, he brooded about it. Home meant seeing his father. The star seed sat in his pocket like an accusation. He'd heard from his father in the four-plus years he'd been away, but none of the letters or radio contacts had mentioned the star seed or the secret gallery. It was as if his father was afraid to mention it in public where anyone could hear, and that bothered Zeke most of all. It made him feel guilty, made him ashamed for his father if he couldn't be ashamed for himself. Zeke knew that a confrontation had to be coming. He didn't look forward to it at all.

He brooded most of the time in his cabin. When the liner docked at the orbital station, he sent a terse message to the Bones estate that he'd arrived and would be taking the next shuttle down to Cairo spaceport. As the shuttle shook in its turbulent passage into the atmosphere, Zeke grimaced and shut his eyes. •Sympathy/Pain• "I know," Zeke replied to the star seed's empathy. "I should be happy, coming home. But all I've got is a big knot inside my stomach. It's not right, it's not fair. I used to love him. Why don't I feel that way anymore?"

The star seed had no reply for that. Zeke could feel it at the edge of his mind, trying to soothe him. •Sympathy/Pain• It didn't do any good.

Zeke moved with the crowds through quarantine and customs and out into the lobby. Cairo spaceport seemed smaller to him than it had when he'd last been here. Always before, the spaceport had seemed huge and bustling. Now, having seen the orbital stations and the huge Martian ports, Cairo seemed provincial, inconsequential. Zeke took his bags and moved into the lobby, peering over the shoulders of the people ahead of him.

"Zeke!"

"Mahsi!" Zeke spotted the tall man in the BEC uniform. The flashing smile on Mahsi's old, dark face made Zeke forget all his worries. "Mahsi," he said again, dropping his bags and letting himself be gathered up in the Bantu's strong embrace.

"You have grown up so much," Mahsi said at last, holding Zeke out at arm's length. "You're not a boy anymore." Then Mahsi hugged him again. "It's good to see you again," he said softly. "Look—" Mahsi let Zeke go and pulled a tiny servo from his shoulder. "The sniffer you fixed; it still works. It will tell you how much lion fat I have on my hair, eh?"

Zeke laughed at that and the memory it evoked, and then he remembered what had happened afterward. The smile dissolved. "How's my father?" he asked.

"He's well," Mahsi replied, but his eyes narrowed as he looked at Zeke. "He's waiting for you back at the house."

"And his current wife? Laura?"

"Your *mother* is fine as well." Mahsi's inflection scolded Zeke for his choice of words, and he immediately felt sorry. "She's in London at the moment, rehearsing for a play," Mahsi continued.

"Then things aren't good between her and dad," Zeke commented. "I thought as much, from some of the hints in the letters."

"She doesn't stay very much at the house," Mahsi said shortly. "But let's not stand here and talk. We can do that in the plane. Here, I'll take that bag—you get the rest. The jet's waiting at the last gate. It's truly good to have you home again, young master. Your father . . . well, I won't say more. But I think he has missed you most of all, even if he will not admit it."

• • •

The house looked the same. Herds of wildebeest scattered at the noise of their jet as they swooped over the house on their approach. When the hatch opened, Zeke could hear the acacia trees whispering, louder than the dying whine of the turbines in the breeze off the plain. The wind brought the smell of zebra. Locusts buzzed in the swaying grasses. Engrossed in the sights, sounds, and smells of his boyhood home, Zeke didn't see the man watching from the doorway until he turned to look back at the house.

If Zeke had changed in the intervening years, his father had changed more. The alteration was dramatic. Zeke remembered him as being big, with a wide barrel chest and muscular arms. But the man who greeted him from the doorway of the Bones house was obese, out of shape. The muscles had gone flabby, the hair and beard that had once only been touched with gray were now thoroughly peppered with it. In the heat of the plain, Leo Bones sweated and panted as he moved across the pad toward them. He was *old*. Zeke felt the impulse to run to him and throw his arms around him as he used to do, but something held him back. The awkwardness touched his father as well, for he stopped a pace away from Zeke and simply extended his arm. Zeke felt that he shook the hand of a stranger.

"Welcome home, son," Leo said.

"Thanks, Dad. I'm glad to be back." Zeke almost expected a servo to chirp "Error" with his words. For several seconds they stood there, just looking at each other with meaningless, empty smiles on their faces. Then Mahsi came around them with Zeke's bags and Zeke quickly grabbed the opportunity to break away. "Here, let me help you with those," Zeke said, and took a case in either hand.

When he looked back his father was still standing there on the pad, his back to them as he stared out at the plain from the roof.

Zeke went inside.

After he was settled into his room again, Zeke went prowling through the house, as he'd done as a boy. The place seemed more empty and huge than before. There were fewer servants around; with his latest stepmother gone and no guests in the many bedrooms, the house echoed with ghosts.

He'd put the star seed in his pocket. Even the crystal was oddly quiet here. Zeke found his steps taking him down the stairs and into the hall where the secret gallery had been. The volcanic mirror was still there, and he watched his dark reflection grow in the smoky glass. He was far different now than the Zeke Bones who had last looked in this mirror. He was taller than his father by a few inches, thinner, and with an intense look in the blue eyes nestled in their deep sockets—far older than the skinny blond boy who'd last walked here. Zeke shook his head. He lifted the Cycladic jar from its pedestal next to the mirror. The keypad was gone; where it had been was only a single button. Zeke frowned, then pushed the button. The mirror swung aside, revealing the gallery.

Empty.

"I moved it all." Engrossed in his memories, Zeke hadn't heard his father approach. Now he turned to see Leo Bones. The man was staring past Zeke into the empty recesses of the gallery. "What a thirteen-year-old boy could break into—no matter how bright he might have been—someone else could find as well. It wasn't safe. So I moved all of it." Leo's voice sounded angry, but when his father's gaze swung around, Zeke was surprised to see more pain than rage there.

"It wasn't yours in the first place," Zeke said. "History belongs to everyone. You stole it."

His father scoffed. "What about the star seed? Are you going to tell me that you didn't steal that?"

"I don't know why I took it," Zeke answered truthfully. "Somehow I just thought it was better in my hands than yours."

"Is that what they teach you in the Academy—that you're better than everyone else? I pulled some strings to make Blaine give me the records of the little exercise that let you out early. I'd hoped that letting you go to the Academy would teach you something, but you're still the same as when you left. Because you're smart, you think that you can do whatever you want."

The unexpected attack made Zeke fist his hands at his side. "I was *right*. That's what I told Blaine; that's why I got the extra leave. And I still think I was right to take the seed. You'd have just hidden it away forever." Zeke looked into the older man's eyes; he couldn't tell if he saw anger or vulnerability there. "You've changed, Dad. I don't know why, but you have. You've become greedy since Mom died. It's like you want to possess everything and everyone. Like you thought that if it wasn't locked up it'd all go away. Maybe that's why all your other wives left you; maybe that's why Laura's in London instead of here." As quickly as it had come, the anger left him and Zeke shook his head. "Dad, I didn't want to come home to fight. Please."

His apology was too late. Zeke could see that in the deep lines that creased his father's face. He knew his accusation had wounded his father; if he could, he would have taken back the words. Leo's mouth was fixed in a sour grimace. Leo Bones glared at his son for a moment, then stiffly turned and walked away.

Leo wasn't at dinner that night. Zeke ate alone at the big table in the dining room. The dinner, featuring an excellently prepared pheasant, tasted like ashes in his mouth. He shoved the tender pieces of meat around his plate and finally pushed it away after a few bites. One of the servants cleared away the setting.

Mahsi came in then, settling his huge frame in the seat nearest Zeke and putting a leather-bound case on the table in front of him. "Your father asked me to send his regrets for not being here at dinner," he said. "He's not feeling well this evening."

"I could see that," Zeke answered. Then, thinking that perhaps he sounded too abrupt and not wishing to offend his friend, he stirred and sat up. "I'm sorry, Mahsi. But I wish I'd just stayed at the Academy. We did nothing but argue today."

"I know," Mahsi said. "He told me. You didn't see him after you'd left. He won't tell you, but he was afraid of what you'd think of him after you found the gallery."

"I never thought Dad was afraid of anything. It always seemed like he bulled his way through life."

"He began to get scared after your mother died. He was away when it happened; I think he blamed himself, thinking that if he'd been here he could have done something. That was about the same time your father found the star seed." Mahsi patted the case. "This is his journal from that time. I thought you would like to hear it."

Zeke reached out to touch the case, then drew his hand back. "Did he tell you to give this to me?"

"No," Mahsi said simply. His deep brown eyes looked at Zeke without apology. "He spoke of giving it to you more than once, but he always changed his mind. He was afraid that you'd hate him. I took this from where he had it hidden, and I will take it back when you are done with it. Will you listen to it?"

"I . . . I don't know."

"I think you should," Mahsi said. "Your father was much

like you when he was younger. In many ways, you are both the same type of person. You won't like much of what you hear in this journal. I think you will be angry and ashamed. But you might understand him better, and it may mean that you can avoid the same mistakes. Take it, young master. I will return it in the morning."

Mahsi slid the case toward Zeke. After a moment, Zeke reached out and took it.

Mahsi gave Zeke a quick smile and left the table.

Outside, a lioness gave her coughing hunting cry; a jackal howled from under an acacia. In his room, Zeke locked the door and drew the shutters closed after a glance out to the moon-washed plain. He sat the case on the bed and touched the clasp. "Hello, Leo," the box said at his touch, and then laughed brightly. Zeke started—he didn't remember much of his mother, but her voice was still fresh in his memory. The box had spoken in tones that he recalled all too well—it must have been a gift from her. He felt a sudden lump in his throat. "You might have warned me, Mahsi," he whispered.

He opened the lid. A small amber light came on. Inside, nestled in velvet, was a tiny recorder and the thin silver wires of a full-sensory feedback relay. Zeke reached in and took out the mesh, unfolding the wires into a small headband. He placed it over his head and fastened the sticky pads of the leads on either temple. As he did so, the recorded voice of his mother spoke again, sounding amused. "Speak well of me, love," she said.

For a minute, Zeke simply sat there on his bed. He felt like a stranger listening to an intimate conversation. His mother's gift, his father's life . . . He could hear the hiss of static in his ears and a flickering of light played behind his closed eyes. Then he took a deep breath.

"Playback," he said.

For the next few hours, Zeke relived a part of Leo Bones's life as his father remembered it.

CHAPTER 5

His father's voice was younger, less husky than the one Zeke knew. Through the nervelink connections, Zeke could sense the outlines of his father's emotions at that time, tugging at Zeke's own soul like ghostly fingers: anticipation, longing, and even a tinge of fear. The recorder overlaid the scenery that had surrounded Leo Bones as he'd begun this entry over Zeke's vision of his room. Zeke closed his eyes to see better what Leo had seen: a ship's suite, he thought. His father glanced down, and Zeke seemed to see the recorder sitting on his own lap, held in hands that felt like his own but were his father's stroking the wooden surface. It was an eerie sensation.

Leo Bones began to talk. Zeke touched his own throat, for it seemed to be his voice.

"I thought I'd better bring things up to date, since I haven't used this thing in several days. I have to say I'm excited about what's happened; excited and maybe a little nervous, too. The *Oglivie T. MacPherson* arrived (in one piece, which confirms the experimental data we had on the new drive) last month from the deuterium mining operation at Luyten 726–B. The *MacPherson* had been in that binary star system mining the ice comets. We thought at first she'd returned because 726–B A, a flare star, had erupted again. I was rather angry with Captain Monroe, as the *MacPherson*'s arrival back on Earth after only a few months could easily have tipped off a careful observer that she was outfitted with the invariance overdrive system instead of the standard drive—we're still years away from marketing *that*. It should have taken her eight years . . . But I let the reporters have 'leaked' information that there'd been trouble aboard the *MacPherson*—an epidemic. We let them think that she'd never made Luyten 726 at all, but had turned around quickly on the voyage out. We kept the crew incommunicado under the epidemic pretext."

Here Zeke caught a glimpse of the *MacPherson* as "his" hands came up before his face holding a holocube of the ship. "I'm going to splice in here the images Captain Monroe brought back from Luyten. There should be a record of them someplace; this journal will do for the time being, until we decide how to handle the situation."

There was a brief burst of static, and then Zeke was looking at the Luyten system. The flare star was a spot too bright to look at to the left side of his vision; before him he could see the curve of the magnetic accelerator frame, where the shepherded comet would be vaporized and the ionized gases passed through the collectors, the valuable elements—especially deuterium— separated out. "Okay, what do I need to say here to that future Leo listening to this? Well, my future self, Monroe pointed out (to show her own lack of guilt in this accident, I suppose) that the waste beam from the accelerator is a death ray—stripped and highly accelerated particles. Following regulations, BEC miners are careful to aim the beam into the local sun. Luyten's a binary system; its planets travel in eccentric and wild orbits, and flare stars are never safe to be near. I can understand how this happened, though the courts are going to howl 'Negligence!' if they ever find out. The damages that could result, the fines and punishments . . ."

Leo sighed as the camera view began to zoom in toward a misshappen, mottled sphere orbiting close to the flare star. "Details? They're simple enough to give. It really seems to be a total accident. The sphere I'm viewing now is the problem. At first, everyone assumed it was a drifter. No one cared when it wandered into the accelerator beam—that happens sometimes, and with no life out here to worry about, no one cares. Too bad. Listen . . ." Over the nervelinks came a quick squirt of high-frequency sound. "That's what happened when this supposed asteroid hit the beam—a burst of microwave signals. Monroe claims that it's still not negligence that the accelerator wasn't shut down at that moment, though I hope our lawyers haven't had to prove it in court since I've recorded this—that isn't why you're listening to this again, is it, old future-Leo? Anyway, Monroe says that sometimes there's natural radio interferencce when something intersects the beam. She claims it looks and and sounds just like this. So the accelerator stayed on, frying the moon or asteroid or whatever with hyper-fast particles and radiation. Then we got this—"

The vision of the planetoid shifted—evidently recorded

from a different camera. There was a flashing on the surface, a seemingly random pattern of off-and-on flickerings. "Optical laser signals," Leo explained. "Monroe says that within an hour of someone seeing those and deciding they were too regular to be sun sparking off some rock outcropping, the accelerator was shut down. She seems genuinely horrified at what happened—I hope she can keep that sincerity in court if this comes out. God knows we'll need all the sympathy we can get.

"And I suppose it's good she's a BEC employee all the way. She ran home with *MacPherson* after the station was unable to contact anything or anyone on the planet with radio or laser signals of our own. She says nothing could have survived—the thing's in a close orbit around the red dwarf; its surface is molten in places. The likelihood is that anything there is fried already. Let's cross our fingers on this one and hope everyone's read it wrong."

A burst of static indicated that the recording had stopped at that point. Zeke touched a contact and the machine fast-forwarded to the next selection.

The next entry had been done by an obviously tired and terse Leo Bones. "These are scenes from a survey craft I ordered sent out on arrival at the station. It seemed a good idea—Monroe's pretty edgy; it seems the flare star's about ready to go again. We might only have a day or two here before the eruption. There's not enough time. Okay, splicing them in now."

The first scene showed a closeup view of the wanderer. Lakes of molten material moved sluggishly across the surface, and here and there were the remnants of structures. "She's about a quarter the size of Earth's moon," Leo's voice said over the images, "too small to have collapsed into a sphere by herself. And those structures are obviously artificial. Let me zoom in . . ." The camera seemed to dive toward the surface to show a grainy image of a tripodal structure facing a snoutlike projection. "That's obviously the mirrored aiming system for a laser, now sagging under the heat. That's probably what the Luytens —which is what the miners here are calling them—used to signal. You can see circular depressions that might have been radio antennae, and this trio of mountains may have been the drive system. If so, the Luytens weren't using anything that indicates FTL drive. The ship configuration, the spectroscopic analysis of metals, and a review of the signals received don't indicate that it's anything seen before. Radiation levels are pretty damned high, but I'm going to ask for volunteers to see if we can find an entrance into the place." The film of the alien ship ended abruptly, and Zeke/Leo was looking into a mirror at his haggard face. "God, I'm tired. This is so frustrating—nothing we do seems to get any response from the Luytens. I'm convinced they're dead, but I have to check, if only to cover BEC's ass for later lawsuits. That's it for now. I've got to get some sleep before tomorrow. Later."

Static again. Then: a helmet seemed to come over Zeke's head. He ducked instinctively, then heard his/his father's voice saying in a muffled tone. "This working? Okay. An experiment, then—let's see how this thing works in the field." He was standing before the port of a ship, several other people in bulky BEC radiation suits around him. The port dilated suddenly, and he was looking out at a landscape of hell. A red star filled the sky, impossibly close, and the horizon of this crimson world seemed too near. He hopped/jumped outside in the incredibly light gravity. "Careful," he heard himself say. "You could probably hit escape velocity if you tried hard. Stay low, move slow. Spread out."

Static again. A new recording, as he looked out again at the hellish surface with a BEC shuttle craft perched nearby. "Can't find a damn way in. Set off some mild explosives on the surface, and the sonics tell us that there's large open spaces below, but no frigging ports. Monroe says we only have hours to get back to the station before the flare star erupts and this thing's gone—"

"Mr. Bones!" He heard the call over the radio, felt his head move around to see a suited figure waving frantically several meters away. "I've got something!"

The alien landscape bobbed and swayed as he loped toward the gesturing miner. He saw what seemed to be a triangular airlock set in the shadow of a crystalline outcropping. "Can you get it open?" he said.

"Looks like the mechanism's melted," the man replied. A gloved hand reached down and pulled—the airlock cover bent like taffy. "There's room for someone to slip inside."

"Out of the way," Leo said. The image in Zeke's head showed his hands lifting the airlock door and dropping into the space beyond. It looked to be a launching area, built to some miniature scale—a meter away, he could see what was obviously a small-scale landing craft. He went over to it. The craft had no place that seemed suited for a man or any other kind of creature to pilot it. There was one small hatch halfway down its flank. He touched a spot on the fuselage and the hatchway slowly opened to reveal a cargo area. The interior glinted in the lights of his helmet. Zeke heard his father's intake of breath, matched by his own.

The star seed sat there, pulsating with light.

"Mr. Bones!" The shout pulled him from reverie. "Mr. Bones!"

"Yes?" He didn't take his eyes off the gem.

"Captain Monroe says we have to leave. Now. The flare star's about to go. We have to get behind the station's radiation shielding."

"All right," Leo said, and Zeke could hear the reluctance in his voice. His hand reached out, grasped the star seed and placed it in the pouch of his suit. "There's nothing here anyway," he said. "I'm coming."

Static.

The last scene showed the flare star in eruption. Heavily filtered, the ferocious energies of the star reached out in its periodic consumption of the Luyten system. Zeke knew that somewhere in that furious corona, the mysterious ship that had carried the seed was gone, lost in a moment of light and energy. "No evidence," Leo was saying over the view of the flare star. "It's all gone, except in the minds of the miners, and none of them want to face a shri judge or the Galactic Council. I talked with Monroe and the crew leaders. We all agree that nothing happened here. There was no wandering planet, or if there was, it gave no signals that it was anything other than a piece of empty rock. It's better that way. After all, none of them were really to blame. It was all an accident, and for all we know, there weren't any Luytens on that ship—she might have been entirely automatic, for all we saw." Leo's hands came in front of Zeke's vision. Cupped in his palms, he could see the star seed, now dull and quiet. "As for this, I'll keep it as a souvenir. It's pretty enough, I suppose. I'll be home soon, Mary, though I daresay I'll never let you see this recording. Home to you and little Ezekiel.

"This was crazy. I think I'll make sure that, to the Galactic Counsel and everyone else, it never happened. That's best for BEC, certainly, and thus best for us. End."

Static.

CHAPTER 6

Zeke sat on the bed with the hissing of static in his ears, with the ghost of his father's memories before his open, staring eyes. Unconsciously, his hands went to the star seed that was in his hip pocket. *So that's what you are. That's where you came from.* There was no answer from the seed, only a bare, sad pulsing at the edges of his mind.

•Memory/Sadness. Task interrupted•

Zeke took a trembling breath. Then, with a sudden burst of anger, he ripped the contacts away and stuffed them into the recorder. He slammed the wooden box shut and stalked from his room.

Mahsi glanced up appraisingly as Zeke stormed into the Bantu's small quarters in the lower level of the Bones' house. Zeke half-threw the recorder at Mahsi, who took it and laid it calmly on his desk, to one side of the espresso server set there. The old man's gentle eyes were full of reproach.

"You're all sons of bitches," Zeke spat out. "All of you, everyone who works for the Bones. Damn it, Mahsi, why'd you give me that thing?" Zeke gestured harshly at the recorder. His anger filled him—he'd never cursed at Mahsi before; the fear of Mahsi's reproach had always kept such words away before. But now all the vitriol tumbled out, and Zeke didn't care— didn't care that Mahsi's face crumpled with sorrow, didn't care that Mahsi's distaste showed openly, didn't care that the Bantu seemed suddenly to withdraw from Zeke.

Shadows stirred in the back of the room, and a form, which Zeke hadn't noticed in his rage, stepped out: Leo Bones, holding a cup in one hand. "That's what I was asking Mahsi," Zeke's father said softly, glancing from the Bantu to Zeke. But he couldn't hold his son's challenging stare; his eyes skittered away guiltily after a moment—that in itself was so unlike his father that Zeke shook his head. "I noticed it gone a few hours ago," Leo said.

"The boy needed to know," Mahsi insisted, and Zeke could tell by his tone that he was continuing an interrupted discussion. "He needed to be told the truth."

"The truth?" Zeke scoffed, his gaze going from one to the other. "I needed to know that my father would cover up the destruction of an unknown ship, that he'd steal artifacts from it and a hundred other worlds and keep them all for himself? That BEC and the people that run it are concerned only with keeping their wealth? I didn't need to know that, Mahsi. I knew it already—everyone in the Academy told me what kind of bastards we Boneses were." He snorted self-mockingly. "And I always told them they were wrong."

Leo had flushed at his son's attack, his neck growing ruddy. Now he set the cup down and jabbed a forefinger in Zeke's direction. "That's enough, young man. What I did was for the good of everyone."

"You did it for yourself," Zeke shot back. "You kept the seed like you kept all the rest of the smuggled stuff in the gallery. What's the matter, father? Did you begin to worry that I'd tell someone about it? Were you afraid that I wouldn't keep the horrible Bones secret?"

Leo's face had gone beet red. His face was a mask of fury. "You don't know *anything* about that gallery," Leo shouted in return. "Listen to the thief accusing the owner."

The remark stung Zeke more than he cared to admit. Guiltily, his fingers moved toward the hidden star seed, but he stopped himself. He glanced at Mahsi, who shrugged, his dark face unreadable.

"Then let's give it back," Zeke said. "Give it *all* back, every last piece. Let's correct some of the wrongs we've done. Let's share the technology and the riches. The *MacPherson*'s obviously equipped with a new FTL drive—why keep hiding it? Share the knowledge."

Muscles worked in Leo's face, pulling the lines of his face into tautness. "That's stupid," he said to his son. "That's BEC money in the research. Years of work—share it and we lose all chance to recoup that expense. That would destroy everything I've done for the Bones family. That would destroy BEC."

"Then maybe it should be destroyed," Zeke retorted, not caring what he said, just letting the words tumble out. "Maybe we should all be punished for thinking we were above everyone else."

"No!" Leo shouted, and his hand swung back and forward, cuffing Zeke sharply across the cheek. The blow snapped Zeke's head back, made the room dance before his eyes as he stumbled backward. He could taste blood in his mouth. For a moment, Zeke was back at the Academy, with Devon Charles and his friends gathered around, taunting. He remembered the pushing and shoving; the casual elbows that would jostle him; the fights when the upperclassmen weren't looking. Zeke shouted wordlessly as he surged back up, his fists doubled to strike back at his father.

Mahsi suddenly stood up. The Bantu's muscles rippled strongly over his wide chest; he seemed the incarnation of one of the warriors who'd roamed the plains outside the house. "Enough!" he roared. When both the Bones, wide-mouthed, stared at him, he shook his massive head in grave sadness. "Look at yourselves," he said. "You prattle on like children, each blaming the other. You fight without knowing what you fight for. *I* gave Zeke the recorder on my own initiative, because I thought he needed to know. *I* knew that he'd taken the star seed when he left here four years ago and *I* let him go. You both have the Bones stubbornness; neither of you will see the other's faults for merely being something that we all have. You both expect perfection. Well, you can't have it. You can't *ever* have it, not with any people or race or society."

"We can work for it," Zeke insisted. "We can do our best. That's all I want."

"You're no better than me," Leo muttered. "You've had Academy idealism pumped into you, that's all, the damn shri mentality. It's a fake, too. *You* kept the seed, didn't you, boy? You kept it to yourself. I know; I had people watching, all the time. All the time, you had your own guilty secrets, just like me."

"No," Zeke denied, but he stopped, knowing that there was truth in what his father had said. Leo Bones saw the realization in his son's face and he laughed.

"Yes, you see. Like father, like son. Just the same."

"I'm not the same," Zeke insisted. "I don't want what you want. I want change. I want BEC to be *more* than a money-making industry. There's changes we can make. That's what I came back hoping to be able to do. That's what I want to work toward."

"To salve your guilty conscience?"

"Maybe," Zeke admitted. "What's it matter, so long as it happens?"

"Well, it's not going to happen. I tell you that now. Not while I'm in control."

"Then I don't want anything to do with it—with BEC, *or* with you." The anger made his words more forceful than they might have been. Zeke saw the flush deepen in his father's face. He clenched his own jaw in response, daring his father to argue more, daring him to reconsider what he'd just said.

He should have known, he would think later. He should have known what his father would say.

"Fine," Leo replied. Then again, more softly. "Fine. Consider yourself disowned, Ezekiel. Consider yourself without a father or a home. If that's the way you want it, you're old enough to make your own decision, the same way I've had to make mine. Maybe it's time you learned that decisions have consequences." Leo gritted out the words, pain in his voice.

With a glance at Mahsi, he stalked past Zeke and went to the door. He looked at Zeke for a moment, who stood with a hand up to his injured cheek, a thin line of blood coming from his mouth. Neither of them said anything. Then Leo stalked out. The door barely had time to dilate before he shoved through it.

"Damn the Bones stubbornness," Mahsi muttered softly.

Zeke walked through the house and into his own room in a scarlet haze of pain and unvented fury. He stood for a moment in the middle of the room, breathing heavily as he glanced unseeing at the room he remembered so well—the shelves full of equipment, half-built servos, and microfiche references, the bed that had usually been rumpled but was now neatly remade from Academy reflex. He saw none of it. He saw only the thoughts inside his head. He could taste his frustrations, like some horrible bile at the back of his throat.

His father hated him. His fellows at the Academy hated him. He could do nothing at BEC.

In his pocket, the seed trilled in his mind in sympathy. •Alternatives? Think/compare•

"The Academy? Finish it out?" Even as he said it, Zeke knew that it wasn't what he wanted. The last shreds of his dreams with the Academy had been dissolved by his return home. He didn't want to go back to Mars, didn't want to see Devon Charles and the rest of his classmates again. Commander

Blaine had said it: Zeke wasn't really officer material. He'd hate the regimentation of the navy, its endless regulations, and the politics that went with it.

So what else? •**Think/compare**•

Zeke smiled grimly. He nodded. "You're right," he said to the seed.

On the table by his bed was a long metallic servo in the shape of a beetle. Zeke touched one of the antennae, and the mechanical creature stirred into life, fluttering its wings softly, the small head rising to look at him. "Ezekiel," it said. "The number?"

"I don't know the number," Zeke told it. "I want the Legion of Ares Earth office."

"I will check." The creature blinked its eyes, which became bright as the video relays there locked on Zeke's face. Down the back, a serried row of LEDs blinked. "Dialing," it said, and the wings raised high on its back, fanning out to become a small screen, pulsing green as Zeke heard the phone ringing. The screen shimmered and Zeke was looking at a hovering shri. The alien looked like a huge jellyfish in the beetle's screen, the thick mound of its body glimmering with shimmering iridescent patterns that Zeke knew identified status to others of its kind. Muscular, thick tendrils hung down from the many-colored mantle that hung over the clear gasbag; one of them now inclined toward Zeke, and he could see the shri's mouth moving at the end. "Legion of Ares, Sergeant Khiel speaking," the creature said curtly. The voice had an odd, breathy accent that lengthened and softened all the vowels. It sounded female, though Zeke knew that the shri were hermaphroditic. The shri's eyestalks narrowed as s/he saw Zeke. "What's your business with the Legion?" s/he asked.

"I . . ." Almost, Zeke couldn't say the words. He swallowed hard. "I want to join," he said more forcefully.

His'er gaze was almost mocking. "Why should *we* want *you*, stripling?"

"You always need bodies, don't you?" Zeke answered. "I can handle a weapon, Sergeant."

The shri scoffed. His'er mantle flickered with a bluish cast that disappeared quickly. "On my world, there's a dozen semi-intelligent species that can be taught to handle a weapon. If all the Legion needed were spear carriers, we could recruit them, build androids, or use enhanced-intelligence apes and never recruit again. Bodies we have, stripling. Do you have brains to go with it?"

His'er attitude fed fuel to Zeke's angry mood. His eyebrows lowered and his hands fisted at his sides. "Yes," he snapped back at the shri. "Better than most. I was top academically at the Academy. Easily."

His'er eyes widened in what might have been mockery. "Ooh, a *washout*, eh? What's the matter, stripling, did your intelligence mean that you couldn't learn to cooperate or to take orders?" The shri's tentacles began to move purposefully as s/he floated nearer the camera. An eyestalk remained on Zeke, but another swayed and bent to look below the screen. Two more tentacles began to move as if the shri were typing something on a terminal Zeke could not see. He heard the rattle of the keyboard. "What's your name, stripling?"

"I thought the Legion only used first names. Your records are supposed to be confidential."

"They are—once you join, stripling. Enter the Legion, and you may be called whatever you like. You may disappear from sight if you desire. But I need to know your name now, to check your credentials."

"Ezekiel Bones," he said. Zeke waited for a reaction—surely the invocation of the Bones name would cause even a shri to say something. Even the shri knew BEC. But the sergeant only typed the name in as if Zeke had given him'er the name Smith. There was a faint *bleep;* the shri's mantle shivered and rippled; tentacles retracted back under the colorful mass of flesh.

The star seed touched the edges of Zeke's awareness; intent on the screen, Zeke ignored its mental voice. The shri had stopped typing; the dangling eyestalks all glanced at Zeke again.

"Stripling, I've checked with the central databanks. Your story checks out. If you're who you say you are, regulations say I must make any senior Academy washout an offer." His'er mantle flushed red. Zeke wished that he could read the language of hues. It was like listening to a completely flat voice without a face—it was difficult to read anything past the bare words. "Here is that offer," the shri continued. "You can report to this office anytime within the next two days. If you don't show, there is no problem—we'll record that and you'll be forever barred from joining the Legion. You're already a failure, so we're taking enough of a chance. If you *do* show, you'll be run through our tests. Maybe we'll take you. Probably not.

The next move's yours, stripling. You have forty-eight hours to report."

The shri broke the contact abruptly, so that the screen shimmered and dissolved before Zeke could say another word. The beetle's eyes dimmed; the LEDs went red. "Reinitiate?" it asked.

"No. I'm done," Zeke said. "Deactivate, please."

With a whirr, the beetle's wings lowered and folded over its back once more. The beetle stumped over to its place on the desk and retracted its legs. A motor whined softly once and was silent.

•**Awareness**• The star seed imposed itself on Zeke's consciousness once more. •**Other/Presence**•

"Going to the Legion is an irrevocable decision, young master."

Zeke whirled around at the sound of that deep voice to find Mahsi standing in the doorway.

"How . . . ?" Zeke began.

Mahsi held out his hand, palm up. There were two warning servos there on the lined, dark bronze skin. "I found your loose board years ago," Mahsi told Zeke. "As for the servos—what one man can hide, another can find. You of all people should know that. And you've given me years to find all your warning devices. Even so, I thought I might have missed some. You were a very clever child." Mahsi smiled; Zeke couldn't help but smile back.

"How much did you hear?" he asked.

"Enough," Mahsi replied. Zeke watched the old man's face, but the Bantu was almost as hard to read as the shri. "Will you be leaving? Will you go with the Legion?"

"What would you do?"

Mahsi seemed to consider that for a moment. Then he shrugged. He tapped the BEC insignia on the breast pocket of his uniform shirt. "I made a promise to your father years ago," he resonant voice said. "I told your father that I would always watch out for you. And I did."

"I know," Zeke told him. "Mahsi . . ." Zeke took a deep breath. "Mahsi, sometimes I thought you were more my father than my father. Sometimes I think I've been shaped more by you than him."

With that, Mahsi gathered Zeke to him. They hugged each other for long seconds, then Mahsi held Zeke at arm's length.

"You're not a boy any more. The boy left here long ago; you came back, and I don't know you as well as I knew that boy. It's your decision, Zeke."

"My father will hate me, won't he?"

"He won't like it. He'll shout and scream; he'd tell me I should have stopped you. He may even fire me—he sent me here now to see that you don't do anything rash. But he won't hate you, Ezekiel Bones."

"Are *you* going to try to stop me?"

Mahsi let go of Zeke's arms. He leaned back against the wall near the doorway. He looked at the false wall that hid Zeke's old laboratory, at the shelves of things Zeke had made. "That depends," he said slowly. "Are you reacting out of anger, or do you know what you're doing?" There seemed to be some deeper trouble in Mahsi's face, and Zeke's brow knitted under his blond hair.

"Mahsi, you're holding something back. What is it?"

"Tell me your decision first," Mahsi answered.

Zeke shrugged. He took a long breath. His hand went into his pocket and found the crystalline warmth of the star seed. "Graduating from the Academy doesn't mean anything by itself —that's just a stepping-stone to a naval career, and I don't think I want that; not anymore. I can't do anything with BEC at all, at least not from the outside. I have knowledge that could hurt the organization and my father, but that. . . ." Zeke's thin shoulders lifted again. "The Legion feels right, at least for the moment. I think I need to get away from here, to see what life is like without being a Bones, without being where BEC or my father can affect things." Zeke laughed, but there was no amusement in the sound. "Maybe I'm just running away. Now, tell me the rest of it."

"Devon Charles is dead."

"What!" Zeke shouted. "You're mistaken. You must be."

Mahsi shook his head. "No. There was an accident on the ship he took home—a problem with the drive system and an explosion. Twenty people aboard are dead; Devon was killed when his cabin bulkhead failed. I just heard."

"And that's also why my father sent you in here." Zeke was stunned. Yes, he'd detested Devon about as much as he could anyone, but he would never have wished him dead. "My God, Mahsi, Devon took a later ship home because he had to stay longer at the Academy. Because of me." Zeke's face had gone pale. "If I hadn't commanded the other ship on the exercise, he might have been able to leave earlier. Commander Blaine said . . ."

Mahsi shook his head. "No," he said forcefully. "You can't blame yourself for that, Zeke. It was an accident. Fate." Mahsi was quiet for a moment. One thick finger kneaded his head. He plucked out the little servo Zeke had fixed and looked at it. "It means you could go back to the Academy, perhaps. Devon Charles would not be there."

Zeke looked up. "No," he said. His fingers tingled with the touch of the star seed. •Agreement• the gem seemed to say. "I've made my decision. I'll stick with it. Are you going to try to keep me from going?"

Mahsi said nothing, still leaning against the wall near the door.

"You wouldn't be able to stop me," Zeke told him. "I've learned a few tricks at the Academy. I had to. I'll get past you."

"I would very much like to see these tricks," Mahsi said. Muscles rippled under his uniform shirt as he pushed off from the wall, and Zeke saw again just how strong the old man still was. He remembered wrestling with Mahsi, and how he had never been able to break the Bantu's grip if he decided to hold Zeke down. But Mahsi grinned now. "I left the cabinet door by the roof door unlocked. An accident. The keys to the hoverjet are in there. The jet's still on the roof pad."

"I'm legally an adult, Mahsi," Zeke said. "My father can't stop me from leaving if I want to."

"We both know that, young Bones. But sometimes it's best not to count on legalities, especially with one as powerful as your father. By the time he knows you've gone, you'll be in the Legion and untouchable. I will keep your secret, as you keep his."

"Mahsi, you're more devious than any Bones." Zeke shook his head. "What will happen?"

"We're never allowed to see the future," the Bantu replied. "So I would not worry about it."

"I'll miss you most of all."

Mahsi smiled sadly. "That makes me both very happy and sad, Ezekiel. I'm touched that you would feel that way about me, and very proud. And I'm also disturbed that it would be that way. No son should feel that way about his father." He shook his head. "Go," he said.

Zeke hugged Mahsi once more, tightly. "Goodbye, Mahsi.

Take care of him. He needs you, no matter what he tells you."

"I know that. Now go, please. There's nothing here that you need—will you leave the star seed for him?"

Zeke shook his head. "No," he said flatly.

Mahsi nodded. "Then you're taking all you need with you."

It fell to Tomas Hindemuth, the personal secretary of Bart Charles, to give the Great Man (as he thought of him) the sad news of the accident that had cost Devon his life. Tomas wasn't certain how he expected the old man to react. As Tomas haltingly told Bart Charles what he'd learned, he saw Charles blanch and wither before his eyes. Charles had never looked his age—he'd always been active and forceful for a man of his advanced years. Bart Charles had lived for Devon, who'd come late to him. Especially after the death of his wife, the elder Charles had spoken many times of the pride he would feel when Devon took his place at the shareholders' meetings of BEC. Tomas had never much cared for Devon himself, who to Tomas's mind was a spoiled and indulgent man-child who could never achieve his father's greatness, but the elder Charles had a father's blindness to the faults of his only child.

Now Tomas watched as his news tore at the Great Man. Charles sat behind his desk as if every word ripped a ragged hole in his very being. The blood drained from his face and left his timeworn skin ghostly pale. His fists clenched white-knuckled on the oaken desk. He seemed to slump over.

Then, as Tomas stuttered to a confused halt, Charles rose from his seat, his eyes glaring and his voice choked. "He should have been here sooner," Charles grated out. "He never should have been on that ship, Tomas."

"Sir?"

"I spoke with Commander Blaine last week. He told me why Devon had to stay behind while Bones got *his* son back. This is Bones's fault," Charles declared. He slammed his fist back to the desk with such force that Tomas heard a sickening *crack* and knew that Charles had broken his hand. But the old man paid no attention to the pain he must have felt. His entire body was twisted with surging grief and fury; his empty stare horrified Tomas with its intensity and madness. He'd never seen his employer so shaken—he wondered if he should call the family physician.

"It's Bones's fault," Charles repeated, so softly that Tomas had to lean forward to hear the words. "It should've been Leo's son that was on that ship, not mine. And I'll make them pay for that. I'm a patient man, Tomas."

That was all he would ever say—at the funeral, as his friends gave him their condolences. "I am a patient man."

CHAPTER 7

Legion ships smelled. It was something Zeke had never managed to get used to in the nine standard years he'd been in the Legion. They reeked with the accumulated sweat and various bodily odors of the four sentient races that crewed the Legion battleships. They reeked because the ships themselves were old and battleworn and the odors had transmuted themselves into the very steel of the decks. They reeked because, well, because that was the way the Legion ships smelled.

The infirmary stank worst of all. Somehow the disinfectants and deodorizers used there, hopefully, to dampen the stench, instead lent their distinct pungency to the general aroma. It didn't help that the shri Reelys was the usual officer in charge of the infirmary and kept the concentration of CO_2 so high that Zeke sometimes felt faint. Zeke's nose twitched the entire time he was in the infirmary, and he was looking forward to being returned to active duty. Xi Pyxis 2, the latest world to hire the Legion, was still two weeks away; by that time, Zeke would be fit again and ready for whatever action awaited him there.

It was Zeke's abused nose that first was aware of the new presence aboard the ship as they accelerated away from the black hole transfer station that would send them somewhere in the general vicinity of Xi Pyxis. Zeke sniffed, wrinkling his brow, and sat up on the diagnostic slab, overturning a servo that, like a small armadillo, was crawing over his bare, gaunt chest, its sensors taking readings as it moved. Reelys, an ancient shri who was also the ship's chief medical officer, deflated slightly with a reprimanding loud huff of air from his'er gasbag, and drifted over to the table, one of his'er manipulative tendrils picking up the servo—which chirped angrily—another more muscular one forcing Zeke back down on the cold surface.

"Ezekiel, you must lie still if I'm to get any accurate readings at all," s/he said with the aspirant tones of the shri.

Before Zeke could protest, three hovering globes bobbed through the open doorway to the small lab. The spheres glittered with oil lenses and fluttered colorful, small butterfly wings. Zeke recognized the strange instruments as holocameras, flitting about in the shaped magnetic field that suspended them, the fanciful and certainly redundant wings grotesquely out of place on the Legion cruiser. The cameras were followed by a woman with long, dark hair and almond eyes, the control webbing for a set of holocameras strapped around her thin waist. A fragrance of jasmine escorted her into the infirmary. Even as old Reelys flicked an eyestalk around in midair to glance at her, s/he found his'erself confronting the phalanx of lenses. Reelys bobbed slowly backward as the woman entered. His'er mantle, usually a mottled, cool green and blue, changed hues rapidly with an effect that Zeke had learned meant consternation. "Who—?" Reelys protested airily, his'er tentacles waving in agitation below the purpling mantle. S/he widened the mantle, presenting a more formidable image.

"Sylvie Pharr," the woman answered curtly, without a smile. With the pretty-winged holocameras, Zeke had assumed that the woman controlling them would be as frivolous, but there was a harshness in her voice that belied that thought. Her voice was low and somehow distant; she confronted the shri with a challenging stare. "I came aboard at the transfer station. Check with Captain Huff or Pyrotechnics Officer Kagak!za if you want; they're going to tell you that I've the right to be here. I'm filming a documentary on the Legion. My presence is by explicit permission of General DeVorne of the Legion. What's the matter with him?" The woman indicated Zeke with a slight inclination of her head. Glossy black hair swayed with the motion. Graceful fingers moved over the contacts of the camera netting; the holocameras panned smoothly over to Zeke.

Reelys's mantle flushed deep blue, the gasbag inflating even more as s/he rose, drifting in the air above Zeke like a huge, maternal man-o-war. Reelys was flustered and uncertain; his'er voice was more asthmatic-sounding than usual. "He suffers from an inability to metabolize food properly," Reelys said, obviously gaining confidence once on the familiar ground of things medical. "On the surface, I would have thought it to be a simple enzyme imbalance, easily corrected by the introduction of the proper bacteria into the digestive tract and the addition of substances to aid in the breakdown of ingested materials. But that solution works only for limited times with Zeke. The new bacteria are inevitably attacked and killed. Any enzymes given to him lose effectiveness. I suspect a viral infection, one that mutates constantly to defeat any new steps we take—"

"He's going to die," Sylvie interrupted sharply.

The shri seemed to take deep offense at the sudden remark. The mantle rippled with metallic colors; s/he moved slowly down to come pointedly between Zeke and the holocams. "I did not say that," the shri hissed. "The last countermeasures kept him under control for over a year and a half; the new ones just introduced will, hopefully, do as well. In time, we'll find a way to attack the virus itself."

"Everyone dies," Zeke said, looking at Sylvie through the mass of Reelys's tendrils. "I wouldn't think there's anything newsworthy in my own eventual death. And I don't enjoy being talked about like a specimen under glass."

She looked at him directly with a disconcerting intensity. Zeke fought the inclination to look away and thought for a moment that the ghost of a smile flickered across her lips.

"I know you," Zeke said suddenly—her name had sparked a dim remembrance of some shaky film footage and a tearful commentary. "You're the one who covered the wreck of the *Dahlem* on Devonia." He saw an old sadness come across her face at that, and he remembered one other thing: the nineteen-year-old woman who had recorded that awful scene as the liner collided with a chunk of orbital debris had also lost her parents in that same accident. "I'm sorry," Zeke said belatedly.

She gave him an unconvincing shrug. "Everyone dies," she told him. The words stung him like a whip.

"You're going to be filming on Xi Pyxis 2?" Zeke asked, trying to salvage something from the fiasco.

Sylvie nodded. "Among other things. I want to get a taste of the daily life of the Legion and its members—though right now it looks like most of the crew's still in deepsleep. The potential fighting's part of it, yes, but I'm after more than that. I want the gestalt, the whole life. It won't be easy, since three-quarters of the Legionnaires don't seem to want their faces on film. You see, my interest is in all of life, not just the ending of it." Her dark gaze regarded him with the same challenge she'd given Reelys. "I'd like to film while you finish your tests on him," she said, looking back at Reelys. The release of her stare was like a physical blow.

One of the shri's eyestalks stared at Zeke; another looked toward Sylvie. "It's up to my patient," Reelys said. "He's a Legionnaire; he's allowed his privacy."

"I've no objection, as long as you're not going to embarrass me, Reelys," Zeke said. He found himself intrigued by Sylvie, oddly drawn by the vulnerability she masked with steel.

The shri's eyestalk had retracted back up under the mantle as if slapped. The mouth-tentacle wriggled as the faintest hint of brown colored the mantle.

"You humans are too easily offended by the sight of your own body parts," s/he retorted. "But you needn't worry, Zeke. I wouldn't dream of displaying your shortcomings."

Zeke colored in his own turn. He thought of answering, but it was the star seed hidden in the pouch on his belt that had the last word. Even as Zeke lay back on the table, he could feel the pull of the seed's voice. •**Empathy/Trust**• it told him, and he knew the seed referred to Sylvie.

Zeke closed his eyes and pretended not to notice her presence as Reelys returned to his'er ministrations.

Sylvie Pharr's presence caused some (probably inevitable) changes in the behavior of all the crewmembers. Especially for the first several days, the appearance of her holocams would cause everyone to stiffen. And Zeke was not the only one who found Sylvie intriguing. Most of the humans aboard began to act in strange fashions; some of the most slovenly of them became oddly fastidious with their uniforms. The few women crewmembers generally ignored her, even when it became apparent that Sylvie had no romantic designs on anyone—if anything, Sylvie openly and rudely rebuffed the several advances made toward her. Still, the attempts persisted, though Zeke himself hung back, a strategy with which the star seed seemed to concur.

Whenever Sylvie's cameras were seen, speech became stilted and overdramatic. Humans pulled in their stomachs and did their best to look intent and almost comically serious; the !xaka! rattled their metallic ornaments and clashed the hard segments of their carapaces in threatening display; even Reelys, the lone shri on board, flashed deep, rich hues across his fully inflated mantle.

Only Marty, one of the dwarfish hlidskji and perhaps Zeke's closest friend aboard the ship, seemed immune to the spell Sylvie seemed to cast. Marty would glower at her from the depths of his utterly black eyes, the stark white pupils fixing on her. The short, plump being—one of a race that dwelt in the weighty gravity of massive planets—would rub his silvery skin, muttering and shaking his head. "This is better entertainment than the 'vids. You're disgusting, Zeke, the way you idiots preen yourselves whenever she's around. Dogs in heat, that's what you are." Marty leaned his head back and howled. Then he grinned at Zeke. "I'm telling you, that one's not interested in any of you beyond the film. She's dead inside, all closed up and boarded shut. Nobody home."

"When did you become an expert on human relations, dwarf?" Zeke scoffed as they strode down the corridor toward the ship's shuttle bay, which doubled as a meeting room. "Your idea of a perfect mate looks like a beer barrel wrapped in aluminum foil."

As Zeke had known the stubby alien would do, Marty grimaced sourly and planted himself firmly in front of Zeke, his long fingers on wide hips. All his hilarity had gone. The gaze of the hlidskji's brilliant, strange eyes bored into him. *"You,"* Marty declared, "are simply blind to true beauty, or you wouldn't insult the hlidskji females that way. You demonstrate once again that the only reason you're still alive is because you're lucky." Manty glanced pointedly at the pouch at Zeke's belt—everyone knew Zeke kept some kind of lucky piece there. But the one thing that any Legionnaire respected was another's right to privacy. They often didn't even know each other's full names, or went by pseudonyms; if Zeke didn't want to say what the charm was, that was his business. "Since you were obviously dropped on your head in youth and suffered permanent brain damage, I won't take offense if you apologize. *Now,* Zeke."

Zeke grinned. The star seed in its pouch sent him a faint reprimand: •Shame/Humiliation• Zeke ignored it. "And what if I insist that the hlidskji women still look faintly like glittering tree trunks?"

Marty rumpled deep in his ample stomach. Large muscles slid under that deceptively flabby, silver exterior. "Then I'd be forced to defend the honor of my race by pounding you into the hull. It would be messy and unpleasant, but I'd try to derive as little pleasure as possible from your pain, in remembrance of our former friendship."

The hlidskji didn't move. He waited, hands on hips, as he stared unblinkingly up at Zeke. A servo waddled by them, skirting the confrontation. "All crewmembers report immediately to the shuttle bay," it chirruped as it passed.

Marty ignored it. "Well?" he demanded.

Zeke burst out in helpless laughter, spreading his hands wide. "All right, Marty. I apologize. The hlidskji women are among the most beautiful sights in the entire known universe. The radiance of their skins must light up the night sky. Passing ships must wonder at the aching brilliance that comes from them. They are a beacon—"

"That's enough, Zeke," Marty grunted. "I wouldn't want to think you were being sarcastic. And you're not, are you?"

"Of course not."

Marty seemed only vaguely mollified. "Ezekiel, if you're any example of your race, I'm surprised that any of you managed to survive beyond the nuclear age. You must all carry charms. I fail to understand the joy you get from baiting me."

"I just wanted to show you that hlidskji have their foibles and weaknesses, too. Sylvie Pharr pushes some of the right buttons for us, that's all. Find the right place to push, and anyone of any race will shove right back."

Especially the hlidskji, Zeke thought, but didn't add. Everyone but perhaps the hlidskji themselves knew that the origins of the hlidskji were human. Centuries ago, at the advent of spaceflight, a slowship had gone outward from earth, crewed by robots and laden with biological engineering labs. In frozen compartments on the ship were human eggs and sperm. It was hoped that when, at long last, the slowship found a halfway compatible planet, a new breed of humanity would be engineered to populate that world. The slowship had never been heard from again, and with the discovery of drives and techniques that allowed ships to bypass the tyranny of lightspeed, it had been forgotten.

Until the hlidskji had been found. Their homeworld lay along the path the slowship might have taken. Their history was amazingly short. Their genes, their DNA structure were amazingly similar. Once past the wide, short bodies and silvery skin, they *looked* humanoid, unlike the shri or !xaka!. Admittedly, there was no sign of the slowship anywhere on their homeworld, but that by itself was inconclusive.

The hlidskji pride was like humanity's, as well. The hlidskji loudly denied their kinship to humanity despite all evidence. *We are unique. We are our own*, they declared.

Marty was no different than them in that.

"Hmmph," Marty snorted. "Every time she turns on that camera it's audition time for human male hormones. I think she's trouble, no matter what Huff or the other officers say. We're heading into a fight on Xi Pyxis; we don't need extra distractions and we don't need people trying to be heroes on film. You get killed that way."

"I don't plan on getting killed."

"You're too scrawny to be a good target, Zeke. And it's a damn good thing, too. I've watched you. You have a death wish. You take chances you shouldn't take, charm or no charm. One might think you felt guilty for being alive."

The comment caused Zeke's face to heat with a flush. •Agreement• the star seed whispered. "Shut up, Marty," was all he said.

"Oooh," Marty crooned in reply. *"Now* whose buttons are being pushed?" He gave Zeke a leering grin. With an unconvincing and exaggerated imitation of Sylvie's gait, Marty swung aside and began walking toward the shuttle bay. After a bemused shake of his head and a deep breath, Zeke followed.

"Zeke, Marty, the captain's been waiting for you," the bay doors whispered in the soft, feminine voice of the ship as they scanned the two and swung aside. "The stars always arrive last," Marty commented. "We were busy giving autographs."

Zeke shook his head "Thanks, *Musashi*," Zeke said. "The captain irritated?"

"No more than usual."

The rest of the ship's complement was already gathered under the harsh glare of the bay lights, their voices echoing in the vastness of naked plasteel beams. The crew, newly awakened from deepsleep, was largely human and !xaka!, who for the most part remained segregated—with the long-standing history of strife between the two races, this made sense. Despite some individual cross-race friendships, each preferred their own. The separate units cooperated when they had to and then left each other to their own devices. The hlidskji, their worlds far from the black hole transfer points, were rarer to find in the Legion—solitary and less social than the other sentient races, they formed whatever friendships they wanted and ignored everyone else. As for the shri, to find one such as Reelys— whose mantle fluttered aquamarine by one of the landing craft —was truly an anomaly. Where one shri was found, there were usually several of the gregarious creatures; they seemed to need the company of their kind. Why Reelys stayed apart and alone was something Zeke had yet to understand.

Sylvie Pharr was present as well, though Zeke couldn't see her in the crowd near the bay doors. Her holocams glided smoothly over the heads of the group like a trio of plump birds. For the first time, no one seemed to be paying much attention to them; instead all gazes were on Captain Huff and Kagak!xa, standing in the middle of the circle of crewmembers.

Zeke and Marty moved toward the shri. "Reelys," Zeke said.

An eyestalk twisted and craned around to see them. "Zeke, you're looking better today. Good. And how are you, Marty?"

"Zeke thinks I'm a little short today," the hlidskji answered.

The shri ignored that. "They're about ready to start," s/he said.

One of the more pleasant surprises of Zeke's years in the Legion was being assigned to the ship *Musashi* and finding that she was captained by his old Academy-mate Huff. She seemed less than surprised to find Zeke in the Legion as well. Pyrotechnics Officer Kagak!xa reared up alongside her superior like a ferocious, hard-shelled python about to strike, topping the captain by a good half-meter. Huff clapped her hands together sharply, and the dull roar of conversation stilled. "Now that we're *finally* all here"—that with a significant glance at Zeke and Marty; Marty waved gleefully back—"pay attention. We penetrated the Xi Pyxis system early yesterday and should be in orbit around Pyxis 2 in three days. It's time you all saw what we're up against."

Huff opened a small box Zeke hadn't previously noted. A creature waddled out: leathery wings furled against a thin body covered with russet fur, three-fingered hands ending short arms. The legs were strong, with feet whose clawed toes looked entirely as flexible as the hands; the tail was also muscular and long, prehensile. The beast was about a meter long from snout to tail tip, standing erect. It glanced around the bay, showing all of them a face like that of a ferret, the long snout brandishing serried rows of tiny, needlelike teeth. It held a sharpened wooden spear in one hand, brandishing the weapon as it turned and chattering angrily in a high-pitched voice. With the technology and firepower of the Legion vessel, the thought of fighting one of these seemed laughable: Zeke could hear whispers and chuckling going around the gathered units. The !xaka! especially clicked loudly in their own language. "What are we supposed to do, roll over on them?" one of them commented loudly in standard. "Or just crush them underfoot?"

"That's right, idiots," Kagak!xa rasped. Her voice was harsh and guttural sounding, full of the clattering resonances that made up normal !xaka! speech. "Laugh. Be amused." The officer was two and a half meters long, her body divided into eight mounded segments, each with its own independent double set of legs or arms. The first three segments could lift (as they were raised now) to display the crustaceanlike head and the brilliant purple to pale blue gills surmounting the extended spines under the shell of the carapace. Considering the appearance of the !xaka!, it wasn't all that surprising that humanity had reacted to them with instant and intense dislike. The !xaka! were a living, walking nightmare for any human with the slightest arachniphobia. "Let me tell you about these creatures," Kagak!xa continued. "These pyxies—that's what the locals call them—have killed upwards of a hundred colonists in the last two local years, maybe more in the time we've been traveling to get here. Initially, the local government thought exactly the same things all of you are thinking. The pyxies are only protosentient, aboriginal at best; they should be easy to handle and control. Well, the government was wrong. They had to call *us*. Don't make the same mistake they did."

"Kagak!xa's exactly right," Huff concurred. "I had this servo model built so that you could see them, but *do not* under any circumstances let their appearance lull you. You will die if that happens, and all the other officers and I will tell you is that you richly deserve your death if that happens."

"C'mon, Captain," Marty called out loudly from alongside Zeke. "Those things are ugly enough to be a !xaka!'s pet."

More laughter followed that, but it was tainted now with nervousness. Everyone stared at the servo replica at Huff's feet.

Reelys collapsed his'er airbag slightly and used the vented breath to speak. "Captain, is there any thought that this might be part of lona aggressions spreading out to the other races?"

Huff shook her head. "It's a purely local affair, from all indications. This is what happened, briefly," Huff continued. "You should know from the hypnotapes that Xi Pyxis 2 is a primary supplier of glitter-pods, which we in turn use for natural polymer fibers. Economically, this is a world with great potential. The colonists are contracted to the commercial industries who own rights to exploit the world. The conglomerate of commercial interests, under pressure from the Galactic Council, first signed a treaty with the pyxies before they were allowed to establish their contractees here. By the terms of that treaty, the glitter-pod farms would supply the pyxies with a portion of the harvest, which they eat. In return, the pyxies agreed to give us land and stay off the plantations.

"But not long after the plantations were established, the pyxie population underwent explosive and uncontrolled growth. The new flocks refused to recognize the old treaties. They ravaged the plantations. The local board, whose interests are mostly those of the companies and *not* the people living there, responded harshly after repeated episodes, finally killing several of the pyxies. They literally started a war, and they learned that the pyxies were something more than pushovers. Ms. Pharr was kind enough to arrange for us to get hold of some documentary footage through United Communications. It will speak more convincingly than me. . . ."

The shutters for the bay lights began to close, the room darkened. A holocube lit above them—Sylvie's holocameras swooped down to record the film as well. "This was recorded several months ago, after things had become heated. *Musashi?*"

"The film's ready, Captain," the ship answered. "Coming up now."

The holocube flickered and then they were looking at a landscape dominated by the long, chest-high rows of glitter-pods. A man in steel fiber armor stood in front of the camera, waving a field-stunner toward the camera with a grin. "A real pyxie-stopper, huh, Jack?" he said to the camera operator. He brandished the stunner, thumped the armor with a fist. "We'll show those idiots in South Isle how to handle 'em."

The camera panned jerkily, catching a blur of dark specks against the sky, panning in to show the flight of pyxies moving toward them. There were appreciative whistles from the crewmembers—even in this poor recording, they could see that the pyxies flew far more quickly than they would have thought possible, darting about with a rapidity that left only blurs in the holotank. Even before the camera could fully pan back, they dove. They saw the field-stunner come up, saw it fire. Four or five of the pyxie flock fell to earth. But the others. . . . They attacked with motions almost too fast to be seen. The man screamed shrilly, dropping the stunner and trying vainly to cover his face with his hands. The pyxies were a deadly swarm around him, a killing cloud. When they moved away a few seconds later, the armor was shredded and bloody. They could see bones in the shapeless mass on the ground in the instant it took the pyxie swarm to regroup. A hovering pyxie looked directly into the camera, seeming to stare at the crewmembers themselves. It pointed, and the swarm moved as one with that awful speed. They could hear the scream as the cameraman dropped his recording equipment. The holotank tumbled with images of sky and earth; the soundtrack was loud with a horror-filled, thin, and continuous shrilling which was even more horrible when it stopped. A hand dropped in front of the lens. They could all see the blood on the lifeless fingers.

The film ended in stark whiteness.

Human, !xaka!, or otherwise, they all looked at the replica in a sudden, respectful silence. A faint, knowing smile played at the edge of Captain Huff's lips. "Any doubters still left? Marty, you have any more comments to make? No? Then Kagak!xa will fill you in on the details of the operation."

CHAPTER 8

"Zeke, Marty! A moment."

Kagak!xa's summons brought Zeke's head around as he was about to board the shuttle to go downworld. He glanced over his shoulder to see the !xaka! gesturing with a second segment arm. Sylvie Pharr stood alongside her, the holocameras settled around her shoulders like some exotic pet. Marty sighed alongside Zeke as they walked quickly over to the officer.

Kagak!xa's rows of compound eyes gleamed under the hooded first segment. "Ms. Pharr will be accompanying us, in our squad. She wishes to film some of the action." A series of dry, loud clickings accompanied the word: the language of the !xaka!. Zeke knew the pyrotechnics officer well enough to know that she sometimes emphasized orders with the !xaka! clicks when she knew that they would be unpopular. The clicks lent them an insistence that the other !xaka! understood implicitly; the humans understood their significance if not their meaning.

Zeke knew that Marty understood this as well. Marty simply chose to ignore it. "I'm supposed to charge extra for babysitting," he said flatly in his usual basso growl.

"This isn't a subject for discussion," Kagak!xa said forcefully. She raised high on her third segment, towering over both of them. Her gill stalks lifted and fanned out; pale blue. "It's Captain Huff's wish."

"I've already got one liability trying to hold gung ho Bones back. Bring her along and he'll be tripping over his tongue like all the rest of 'em," Marty persisted. "I'm not going to get killed so she can get some footage."

"This is an order, Marty, not a suggestion."

"Kagak!xa," Sylvie interrupted holding up her hand. Zeke noticed that she used glottal stops in a way that sounded almost

like the !xaka! themselves, her tongue clucking in imitation of
the harsh clicks. "Let me speak, please." Sylvie turned to Marty
and Zeke. "I've taken two slugs from a projectile thrower on
Epsilon Eridani, covering an underworld rivalry. I've carried
twenty kilos of equipment *plus* my own backpack up Mt.
StormBringer on Tau Ceti. I've run a heavy-grav marathon just
to get footage of the people running with me. I'm in shape. In
fact, hlidskji, I'm more worried about losing you than about
falling behind. And *if* I do, you have my permission to keep
going. I don't want a nursemaid or a babysitter, and I'm perfectly capable of taking care of myself."

Marty's mouth had dropped open. "Zeke," he protested,
looking for support. But Zeke only shrugged his shoulders as
Sylvie's gaze caught his eyes. There was challenge in those
dark eyes, in the set of her fine-boned face; he found himself
nodding. "I don't know," he said automatically, and felt the
insistence of the star seed in its pouch under his body armor.
•Empathy/Trust•

"Kagak!xa told me that you'd be best to follow," she said.
Her voice was pitched low and vibrant; she continued to stare at
him with the slightest tilt of her head dropping a curtain of hair
over her cheeks. "I trust her judgment—she says that she
always likes to have luck in her squad, and that you're lucky.
You should trust her judgment too; she wouldn't let me go with
her if she thought I were a burden."

"I have known Sylvie for some time," Kagak!xa confirmed.
Her gill stalks dropped slightly. "This is a well-considered decision, not a whim. I recommended her to Captain Huff."

"*And* it's a damn order," Marty reminded the !xaka!.

Kagak!xa's huge armored head swiveled toward the hlidskji,
looking down at the small, wide alien. "It is a good thing you're
in the Legion, which tolerates a certain amount of insubordina-
tion, or I'd have Huff ship you out the airlock. If you want off
the squad, I'll make the arrangements."

"It's okay, Kagak!xa," Sylvie said softly. "I won't go unless
they're willing to have me. There are other teams I can find
room with." She still looked at Zeke, and the open vulnerability
in her face surprised him. It was as if she'd let him see into the
parts of her she kept hidden away. Zeke nodded again; he
smiled at her and was glad to see her return the gesture—it was
the first time he'd seen her smile.

"She can go with us, Kagak!xa," Zeke said. With the words,

he saw Sylvie's face close up again, becoming only the seasoned, hard reporter once more. The rest of her was hidden
away, gone as if it had never been there in the first place. She
looked at Zeke as if he were simply something in her camera
lens. He almost regretted his decision.

"Zeke! You're listening to your hormones."

"She'll be all right, Marty." But he was no longer so sure.

The hlidskji snorted derisively. "She'd better be. Some time,
Zeke, you'll learn to think with your head rather than lower
down."

The hlidskji turned his back and trudged toward the lander.
Zeke fell into step with Sylvie.

"You always use your looks to get what you want?" he asked
her. "I thought for a second that I might be able to like you." He
kept his eyes forward, but he heard her quick intake of breath.

"Is that what you think I was doing?" she said softly.

"Isn't it?" He regretted the words, regretted the impulse that
had made him accuse her, but it was too late. •**Annoyance/Dis-
appointment**• the star seed yammered in his mind.

She didn't say anything for a moment, until they were about
to swing up the field ladder into the lander. She tossed the
control webbing for the holocameras into the craft. "Sorry that I
disappointed you," she said without looking back at him. She
put her hand on the ladder and then turned around. Her gaze
was harsh and angry. "Are you irritated with me for doing it, or
with yourself for falling for it?"

She swung up the ladder before he could answer.

In many ways, it was a typical Legion operation. The Legion
of Ares had never been noted for either subtlety or timidity.
Operating under license to the government of Mars may have
given the mercenary force the thinnest veneer of respectability,
but in truth the Legion was a simple instrument of brute force,
employed by governments and agencies when other methods
had either not worked, seemed unfeasible, or would take too
long to implement. When the miners of Diane 4 had decided to
revolt—because of dangerous working conditions, poor standards of living, and miserly wages, against the corporation/gov-
ernment that owned their contracts—the corporate officers had
not called in the Galactic Council negotiations teams, they'd
hired the Legion. The result had been bloody violence and too
many deaths, in which Zeke himself had taken part. Still, the
revolt had been broken far more quickly than the Council teams

(headed by shri) would have managed it; with the deaths of the leaders, the rest of the miners filed meekly back to work. Working conditions remained hideous, there was no change in living standards or wages—if anything, those became worse in retaliation. But the Legion's client was satisfied. The problem had been solved with the usual Legion display of simple force and without the possible danger of "concessions," that word the corporation dreaded more than any other.

That was the way of the Legion. It was not a place for idealists. Zeke had always told himself that he didn't care. He told himself that all his idealism had been burnt out of him by his Bones background. BEC and its minions didn't breed idealists but pragmatists. If the nightmares he suffered seemed to imply something different, if he sometimes wondered whether there wasn't a certain just punishment in the disease that occasionally struck him weak and helpless, Zeke didn't say. If the star seed throbbed with such an emotional matrix, Zeke ignored it. He did what the Legion told him to do.

Xy Pyxis 2 had its similarities to the situation on Diane 4. This world of steaming, trackless jungles was also governed by a corporate body, in this case a conglomeration of smaller companies that owned the various glitter-pod plantations in the equatorial regions. The "colonists" were mostly under contract to the conglomerate, and by that contract were little more than indentured servants. The conglomerate had paid for their transportation here, had paid for their houses and the necessary supplies that had to be shipped here from other worlds. Until their debts were paid back, the colonists were owned by the corporation, with very few individual rights. When the pyxie problems erupted, the conglomerate at first did nothing. The loss of a few colonists meant nothing. It wasn't until they saw that the whole plantation system was threatened—until they saw that their pocketbooks were being directly endangered—that the conglomerate chose the Legion as the simplest, most cost-effective solution. It would also be the most damaging to the world and the society the colonists had built up, and certainly to the pyxies. Yes, as a protosentient race, the pyxies were entitled to protection from the Galactic Council. They had certain rights. But the corporation lawyers argued that legally the pyxies had abrogated those rights by breaking the treaty. It would be touch and go in court if the Galactic Council decided to press charges, but the corporation thought there was at least an even chance of winning. In any case, any judgement could be delayed by appeals—it might be decades before any fines were levied.

Economics ruled. The only instruction to the Legion from the corporation was this: take care of the problem.

Three Legion cruisers were involved in the action—a total of some five thousand mercenaries. The first stage was orbital bombardment of the deep jungles which hid the largest flocks. This would drive the pyxies out from the places where they could most easily hide and bring them out into the open. If this had been a naval operation, if the conglomerate had cared about the people living on the planet, they would have first evacuated as many as possible. They didn't. Lasers raked the tangled jungle; defoliant bombs left the trees skeletal and dying; sonic missiles screeched like banshees as they plowed into known colonies of pyxies, their shrill vibrations bursting blood vessels and killing not only pyxies but much of the rest of the mammalian wildlife near them. Even as the squads began to arc down from the orbiting cruisers, the pyxies spilled from their jungle strongholds to attack the plantations and the hated human colonists. Zeke and the rest emerged into a running, chaotic battle.

Zeke's squad, commanded by Kagak!xa, consisted of himself, Marty, and one other !xaka!, Hgax!ki. Huff had decided that the mixed !xaka! and human squads were best here. The !xaka! needed no extra armoring; their excretory spinnerets from the fifth segment's stomach could produce organic cellulose webs to snare the pyxies, and the other stomachs could produce a wide array of organic acids from their anal openings, all of which would be effective. The humans and hlidskji wore powered armor that gave them greater mobility and carried a good variety of weaponry themselves, including the hand laser weapons for which humanity was best known. Considering the pyxies, both !xaka! and human were supplied with sonic grenades and tanglefoot bombs in hopes of being able to deal with the mass attacks.

But despite the weaponry, despite the films they'd seen, none of them seemed to be taking the pyxies entirely seriously. They were too small, too backward.

The lander hit its retros hard about a hundred meters above the surface, snapping everyone back into the acceleration couches with a groan. "Deployment sequence initialized," the lander noted redundantly. "Good luck, everyone." The plastic heat shield peeled back; explosive bolts jettisoned the retros and the remnants of the shields. They slammed into the ground hard as they got their first view of blue sky and emerald jungle. The moist breeze was laden with the smell of wet earth and a thousand unidentified underscents.

A sudden squall threw sheets of water over them. "Why is it always raining?" Marty complained. "Every damn time. And I forgot my umbrella. Couldn't you pick a dry spot for us, Kagak!xa?" The hlidskji threw his restraint harness aside and bounded from the crumpled, expandable lander. The others followed.

Kagak!xa lifted high in the air and swiveled her head about. She pointed with a third-segment arm. "That way. Some of the plantation housing is afire. Move!" She followed the order with a burst of percussive clicks, and plowed into the jungle like an animated tank. The squad began to run. Sylvie followed, shrugging into her webbing and sending the holocameras circling out in front of the group. "Trust a !xaka! to head for the smoke," Marty commented.

They ran through thick undergrowth, awash with bright tropical colors. It seemed a pretty world. It seemed pastoral and safe, especially when they burst from the jungle and into the cultivated rows of pods.

Then the pyxies hit them.

They came from the left side, where Hgax!ki held the flank. Zeke could not have counted how many there were—a hundred, maybe more. They moved with blinding speed and a unity that suggested to Zeke that they might have some type of hive group-mind. Their tactics were brilliant—puzzlingly so, since they could not have previously seen !xaka!. The mass of pyxies flew low. Heedless of their losses, they simply rammed Hgax!ki, the momentum of their combined blows tumbling the !xaka! onto his back. The pyxies swarmed over Hgax!ki as he struck at them, spewing a thick stream of acid that burned the creatures wherever it touched. But the pyxies continued to attack, piercing the vulnerable underbelly of the !xaka! with their spears, with teeth and claws. Hgax!ki writhed in agony, his many legs flailing. Zeke swept the field laser over the pyxies above his companion's struggling body; Kagak!xa's spinnerets tangled them in webbing. But there were too many, and they couldn't fire into the mass of them, not with Hgax!ki underneath.

Hgax!ki stopped moving at all. Kagak!xa bellowed like an amplified snare drum. Marty tossed a tanglefoot bomb beside Hgax!ki's body; Kagak!xa spewed acid over the trapped pyxies as Zeke burned them. The few that escaped fled.

"Hgax!ki!" Marty flung pyxie bodies aside. After a moment, Zeke moved to help him as Kagak!xa kept close watch around them. Even through their filters, there was a horrible stench of burned flesh mingling with the sharp odor of !xaka!ian acid. "Forget it, Marty," Zeke said after a moment. The ruin revealed under the mound of pyxie bodies left no doubt.

Kagak!xa clicked sadly. "He was !xaka!. This is the way he would have preferred to die."

Zeke had seen companions die before in the Legion. He knew he would see it again. Still, the losses always bothered him deeply. Death dug its hooked claws in his soul, making Zeke want to shout with the pain. He gazed down at the torn mound of the !xaka!, the rain sheeting over the transparent hood of his body armor, the carnage spread around his feet as he let his laser droop at his side. He stood there, unmoving, until a flicker of motion brought him from the reverie. He saw Sylvie's holocams hovering directly in front of his empty, savage stare. Zeke gestured angrily. "Get those out of my face!" he said.

"Let's move," Kagak!xa ordered. "There may still be people in those houses. Sylvie, I'll call for pickup for you. Stay under one of the lander sheets and you should be safe."

"No," the woman insisted. She looked at Zeke, at Kagak!xa, at Marty. "I'm staying."

Kagak!xa seemed to sigh. Then she lowered herself down until the first segment was barely raised. "Fine. Let's go—carefully, but quickly."

The dwellings—battered and dingy plastic sheets over a domed framework—were built on a small knoll overlooking the fields. The main dome was engulfed in flame, casting a pall of noxious black smoke over the area. "Stay together," Kagak!xa said. "There's more of the pyxies around: I can feel them."

"Did everyone leave here?" Marty whispered beside Zeke. The hlidskji gripped his laser rifle with white-knuckled fingers, hunkered down on the ground as they surveyed the scene. "Or are they all dead?"

A scream answered him. "Over there!" Zeke pointed to a smaller dome set a bit apart from the others. They could see a blur of pyxies around it; the scream, a woman's high-pitched distress, sounded again. Zeke began to run, followed closely by Marty, Kagak!xa, and Sylvie—her holocams kept pace with Zeke.

The door was dilated open. It was also blocked by a swarm of pyxies. Zeke, yelling, brought his laser rifle to bear, swinging the beam about as pyxies tumbled to the ground. The swarm turned to attack Zeke in a bunched mass, but were stopped by a fine spray of acid from Kagak!xa, catching them in midair. Untouched, Zeke swept past the dying creatures.

He had a brief glimpse of the interior. The few pieces of furniture were plain and well worn; there was a chessboard set up in mid-game in a central recreation area. A large keyboard instrument sat against one wall, a synthguitar leaned against another—obviously the home of someone who enjoyed music.

And it was literally alive with pyxies. The main bunch was concentrated to the rear of the structure. There, Zeke could see a trio of humans struggling under the crush of small attackers—a woman, a man, a young boy. Of the three, only the boy was as yet relatively free of pyxies. He wielded an iron bar double-fisted in his strong hands, swinging it with deadly accuracy as his dark-skinned, muscular arms moved nearly as quickly as the pyxies. The boy's face was locked in a ferocious grimace as he flailed at them. The woman screamed again under the biting, gouging pyxies and went down. The boy's mouth opened in an agonized wail: "Mother!" He began to charge toward her; the pyxies turned to meet him.

"Get back!" Zeke shouted. "Back!"

Zeke underhanded a tanglefoot grenade to the wall between the boy and his stricken mother. The device exploded as it touched, spraying a wide, sticky net over the pyxies. From the edges of his peripheral vision, Zeke saw the man go down. Moving toward the son, Zeke grabbed him by an arm as the pyxies swarmed over the adults, as Kagak!xa and then Marty slid cautiously through the door. He saw the shadow of the holocams as well. "I've got the kid," he cried to them. "It's too late for the others. Get out and let's torch this place!" He gripped the boy's arm and started to pull him with him, retreating.

"No!" the boy screamed, his eyes wide and panicked. He was surprisingly strong; Zeke could not hold him as he pulled away. "I can't. My folks—"

"They're dead," Zeke said brutally, spitting the words out as if they burned his tongue. "We will be too, if we stay." He reached for the kid once more.

Too late. The pyxies lifted as one from the bodies on the floor, the sound of their wings a horrible drone. Zeke bellowed a warning and shoved the boy away as he swung his rifle around. The swarm split around him, the bulk moving toward

Marty and Kagak!xa and pushing them back out of the dome, isolating Zeke.

"Zeke!" Marty shouted. The hlidskji was firing wildly, forced to retreat outside. Kagak!xa's huge form splintered plastic as she made a leap for open ground. Zeke pulled the boy up from the floor and tried to get through the door himself in the momentary clear spot created by Kagak!xa, but the swarm was too fast. They turned and came for him.

Then there was nothing but chaos.

Wooden spears prodded the metal-woven cloth around him, claws dug at the faceplate, tiny hands plucked at the seams of the body armor, tearing with hideous tenacity. He was surrounded, seeing nothing but the blur of leathery wings and the tiny, snarling faces of the pyxies. Zeke came as close to complete panic as he had ever come. It was only the star seed that saved him: Zeke's luck. He could feel it warm under his armor, could hear its small voice in his mind.

•NO: Fear/Panic. Calm/Think• Zeke wanted nothing more than to drop his laser and beat at the things with his own hands. It felt as if a thousand tiny needles were stabbing at him and he knew that in a few moments, one of them would get through the weak points of the armor. He forced himself to remain calm, taking a shuddering, deep breath. He threw an incendiary into a corner of the house. The device exploded in a gout of orange flame, washing him with heat. Deliberately, Zeke plucked one of the pyxies from his chest and flung the beast into the fire—it squawled piteously and then crumpled. Zeke found the boy in the confusion, pulled him up by arm. "Go toward the fire!" Zeke told him. "Slowly but steadily."

"You're crazy," the boy shouted back, his eyes wide, beating at the pyxies, which for the most part ignored him for Zeke.

"You want to live? Do it!"

Zeke began to walk nearer the inferno that had now engulfed the rear of the house. He could feel the pulsing waves of heat even through the body armor. He pulled another pyxie from himself, threw it into the blaze, and immediately grabbed another, then another. The pyxies had stopped attacking him, though they clung everywhere on his body. Another step closer, and sweat had begun to roll in beads into Zeke's eyes. Another step, with the flames flickering wildly before Zeke's face.

At once, as if they'd all made a simultaneous decision, the pyxies howled and tried to flee the house. Outside, a grenade exploded, a laser whined. Zeke immediately brought his own rifle up and at full power, sliced a doorway through the thin sheeting of the dome. Grabbing the boy, Zeke ran like a madman, shouldering his way through the sticky, half-melted plastic and into the open. He rolled in the grass as the entire dome erupted. Through the scratched and pitted faceplate of his armor, he could see Sylvie's holocams on him, could see Marty and Kagak!xa mopping up the remnant of the pyxies.

"You okay, kid?" Zeke asked, kneeling groggily in the rough grass. Waves of heat from the burning dome buffeted him. The boy (Zeke thought he must be about fifteen) stared wide-eyed. He was burned, but he would live. "Kid?" Zeke said again, and the word broke the stasis that held the boy. He suddenly began to sob; huge, aching gulps of grief—his body shook with them. "I . . . I couldn't. . . . couldn't *help* them," he gasped. He spread his hands wide. "I should have died with them."

Zeke pulled the boy to him, hugging him tightly. "You did what you could," Zeke whispered. "They wouldn't have wanted you to die. They were your parents. They loved you." He stroked the tight, black curls. "You fought for them as well as you could."

Even as he said them, even as he hugged the boy tighter, he wondered at his own words.

CHAPTER 9

The residents of Xi Pyxis 2 would afterward refer to that week as the War of the Pyxies. It more resembled wholesale slaughter. After the initial assault, the Legion shifted its strategy, relying more heavily on orbital bombardment and larger squads outfitted with broadbeam weapons better suited for the pyxies' massed, suicidal attacks. Zeke's information that the pyxies possessed a rudimentary telepathy aided the Legion greatly; with Zeke's help Kagak!xa devised a small transmitter to scramble the neural pathways of the creatures. Disorganized, suddenly unable to effectively communicate, the pyxies were smart enough to realize that they were being pushed to the brink of extinction. The so-called War of the Pyxies was a brutal and quick thing. Within three local days, it was estimated that the Legion had killed half of the pyxie population; within a week, the scattered remnants of the pyxie flocks had surrendered meekly. The survivors were gathered and transported en masse to a continent far removed from the equatorial plantations.

The Legion had lost one hundred twenty-five of its troops, almost all of those casualties coming during that initial assault. Zeke's own wounds were light—some relatively minor cuts and second-degree burns wherever the pyxies had managed to damage his armor—but they were enough to keep Zeke out of the remainder of the combat. Instead, he battled the shri Reelys to be allowed to leave the hospital unit. "Reelys, I'm fine. Honest."

The shri stared at Zeke with one eyestalk while other tentacles fiddled with an array of trays on the table below him'er. The shri had focused the oil-filled diaphragm of his'er mantle on a tissue sample and was studying it under strong ultraviolet light. "You still have a slight infection and fever. That's not *fine.*"

"It's no worse than a cold."

The old shri's mantle deflated slightly with what sounded like a wheezing sigh. S/he rotated in midair. "What makes you so anxious to leave, Ezekiel?" The eyestalk blinked, retracted up into the mantle. "Ah," the shri breathed. "It's that boy, the one whose parents were killed. He's being sent downworld today—is that your hurry?"

Zeke shrugged. "I wouldn't mind being the one to escort him down."

Reelys pulled all his'er tendrils up into the mass dangling from the airbag. The mouthstalk came back down slowly as the shri mulled over Zeke's request. "You puzzle me, Ezekiel," s/he said. "Kagak!xa insists that she thought you dead once you were trapped inside the dome. Yet you managed to escape with that boy. And you've been fortunate in similar ways before."

"Luck," Zeke replied. "That's all. We all have our charms." The lie made him uneasy, but he forced himself to show nothing. *Not luck at all. It's the star seed. It keeps me calm; it makes me think when I might otherwise just rush into things. The star seed is my luck—my luck for the last decade.*

Reelys dipped low, then inflated his'erself fully. S/he turned back to the tissue samples. "All right, Ezekiel," s/he said. "If I release you now, will you promise to come back here tomorrow for a checkup before we leave?"

"My word of honor, Reelys. And thank you."

Reelys exhaled forcefully. His'er mantle purpled. "You should not be in the Legion, Ezekiel. You've a sensitivity in you that it is killing, slowly but surely. Too many of us are here because we're running from something. Let me tell you, Ezekiel—none of them ever find what they're looking for here. Instead, they often lose themselves."

Zeke stared at the shri thoughtfully. He'd never heard old Reelys sound so pensive or bitter. He wondered if he should say something, but no words came. The shri kept his'er attention on his'er work, none of the various sensory tendrils paying any attention to Zeke at all. Finally Zeke shook his head, sighed, and swung down from his cot.

"I'll take him downworld," Zeke said. "We ship out tomorrow anyway. I want to make sure the locals are going to take care of him."

"I've never understood the human parental distinctions. It's much simpler when you don't have a sexual stereotype to worry about," Reelys commented obliquely. "You're not his father, Zeke."

Unintentional or not, the words stung. "Yeah," Zeke answered. "I'm not. *Nobody* is. That's the trouble."

Xi Pyxis Port looked like every other port Zeke had seen in his years in the Legion: dingy, run-down, full of the stink of fuel, machinery, and close-packed living. Once away from the huge cradles for the orbital shuttles, the wide street narrowed and became dark as the lighting slid from glaring to dim. Bars and cheap hotels replaced warehouses and offices. Glaring signs advertised the deathfights that were popular in the backwaters of the human empire, each bar touting its current champion; prostitutes of both sexes called out from doorways and open windows. It was nothing like the pastoral emptiness of most of the world. This was a piece of filthy, crowded Earth transported elsewhere.

The boy walked quietly between Zeke and Marty. Zeke had learned little about the boy other than the fact that his name was Jackson Franks, and that he had little enthusiasm for returning to Xi Pyxis.

"You ever been to the port before?" Zeke asked Jackson, trying to prod the boy from his sullen, bitter silence. Jackson shook his head, mumbling something unintelligible. "Give it up, Zeke," Marty said. "The kid's got all the gratitude of a rock. You should've let the corporation wardens bring him in."

"Marty—"

"Well, damn it, it's the truth, Zeke. He'd've been dead if you hadn't dragged him out, and I haven't even heard him say thank you. Hell, he probably doesn't even know your name." The hlidskji's satiny skin gleamed under the sparse port lighting; his black eyes appeared more shadowed than usual. He swung his arm wide, hitting Jackson just above the waist with a massive hand. "Why don't you tell the man how happy you are to be alive, huh?"

That brought Jackson wheeling around. He spun and confronted Marty, jabbing a finger at the hlidskji's nose. Jackson topped Marty by a quarter-meter, and muscles made hard by field work rippled along mahogany arms. "I'm not exactly happy, dwarf. At least the man understands that and leaves me alone. Why don't you just do the same? And his name's Ezekiel—I asked. They also told me that if he wanted me to know the rest of it, he'd tell me himself. I respect his privacy."

"You got a lot of excuses and nothing else. I'm tempted to beat some manners into your thick skull," Marty drawled with deceptive casualness. The hlidskji's wide body braced; Zeke saw Marty's hands tightening into fists. The crowds along the street halted, making a rough circle around the three of them. "Deathfight," someone uttered, and the word flashed through the onlookers, a harsh whisper—a few even began to make bets. Jackson heard the word too, for Zeke saw the boy tense and knew that in a moment he'd fling himself at the hlidskji, thinking it was something he had to do.

"You want it here or in the pits, hlidskji?" Jackson said through clenched teeth.

"Stop it!" Zeke thrust his way between the two antagonists. He placed himself squarely between them. At the same moment, he noticed a trio of holocams hovering above in the shadow of an alleyway. They fluttered Sylvie's distinctive wings. Zeke muttered an obscenity. "Marty, back off—the kid thinks you're challenging him to deathfight. We didn't drag him out of the dome to do that."

Marty grimaced. His hands relaxed; he backed up a step. "All right," he rumbled. "You'd think I was some kind of hot-head, the way you're acting. All right, you can get out of the way. I'd've broken him like the stick he is anyway, if we'd gotten into the fight." Marty glared, but he relaxed.

"Thanks, Marty," Zeke said, then: "Pharr! You might as well come out of hiding."

She was already pushing her way through the front rank of the crowd, which gave way reluctantly. "I don't hide," she told Zeke angrily. There was a flush of color high on her cheek-bones. She swept her hair back from her face with a swipe of her hand as the holocams dipped over the heads of the people around them.

"Then why didn't I notice you on the shuttle?"

"I was already downworld, that's why. I was getting some stock footage of the port when I noticed you. I just hadn't had a chance to catch—hey, the kid!"

Zeke peered back over his shoulder. Jackson was gone, the circle of onlookers closing back in where he'd shoved his way past them. "Jackson!" Zeke shouted after him. There was no answer. Zeke pushed into the crowd. Marty grabbed at him.

"Let him go, Zeke," he said. "He knows this place a hell of

a lot better than you. You're not going to find him if he doesn't want to be found."

"I said I'd get him to the authorities. He's only a kid."

"They'll find him if they want to, then. We're gone tomorrow." Marty tugged at his friend. "Zeke. Let him go. It's what he wanted, or he would've stayed."

From the pouch on his belt, Zeke felt the star seed whispering agreement. He shrugged off Marty's restraining hand with an angry motion, his thin face twisted with the conflicting emotions inside. "Zeke," Sylvie said behind him. Zeke spun around to confront her.

"What?" he spat out. "He's just a kid, and he's all torn up."

"Are you going to stay behind when your cruiser leaves? Are you going to adopt him?"

"You're awfully blunt."

"Am I wrong?"

"No," Zeke admitted. A rage hammered inside him. "I can't."

"Then let him go now. Take Marty's advice: let him go. That's the best help you can give him at the moment. I know this government; they don't care about him at all. He's better off using his own brains to survive."

"It's cruel."

Sylvie stared at him, a strange sympathy in her eyes. "I'd think a mercenary would be used to cruelty by now," she said.

Marty gripped Zeke's arm, giving it a momentary squeeze. "I hate to admit it, but the woman's right, Zeke." Zeke shook his head in denial, but he didn't move. He saw the faces still watching them and gestured harshly.

"Get out of here!" he shouted at them. "Move! Go on!"

They muttered, but they dispersed, walking swiftly away from the gaunt apparition in the Legion uniform. Zeke began walking down the narrow, trash-filled street, hoping that he'd see Jackson waiting for them ahead and knowing he would not. He paid little attention to Sylvie and Marty alongside him.

"I'm going to be using the footage from when you rescued the kid," Sylvie told him. "It was some of the best I've gotten. I thought you should know."

"Could I stop you from showing it?"

Zeke could feel her shrug, though he didn't turn to look as he peered into shadowy entrances and down night-wrapped streets. "No," she said firmly. "I've Huff's permission; if I don't get yours, I'll just hide the face. The scene's too powerful a drama to waste. If you'd like I can preview it for you."

Zeke glanced at her sharply. "You don't use my name. I won't let you use my name."

Sylvie recoiled from the intensity of his stare. She shivered as if suddenly cold. "I'm aware of Legion policy," she told him, narrowing her eyes. "No names unless specific permission is granted. Hey, I don't even *know* your last name, since you didn't list it."

"Then leave it that way." Zeke continued walking aimlessly down the port streets.

Sylvie persisted. "Listen. I thought I might pay you back for letting me go along with Kagak!xa's squad. Can I buy the two of you dinner, at least?"

"There's not much drama in dinner, I'd think," Zeke said coldly.

Sylvie's boots scraped pavement. She halted. After a moment, Zeke did the same. He turned slowly, feeling the silent remonstrance of Marty, feeling the disappointment of the star seed. Somehow that only made his unfocused anger all the more deep. The vulnerability was back in Sylvie's face, in her posture. He knew that with a word he could dissolve some of the hostility between them—none of it was her fault anyway. He might even be able to make the first step toward a friendship. He stood balanced on the edge.

"Why don't you go find a nice deathfight to film? I'll bet they're powerful, too," he said.

Sylvie stepped back as if slapped. She blinked, and the sympathy in her eyes was utterly gone. Zeke could almost see her mind closing up, cutting herself off from him. "You can go ahead and pretend you're all hard and tough if you want," she said. "You keep doing that, and one day you're going to find that you've succeeded. Then you'll only hate yourself. I can tell you that because I know. I know."

Her chin was lifted in defiance. She stared at him a moment longer. Then she turned her back to Zeke and strode swiftly away. The holocams turned tardily with her, drifting slowly behind.

"You've such a gentle, romantic hand with women," Marty said. "The charm just *oozes* from every pore."

"Thought you didn't like her, Marty."

"I don't," Marty grunted. "But I thought *you* did."

"Then maybe we were both wrong." Zeke exhaled sharply. He plunged his hands into his pockets and glanced at their gloomy surroundings. "Let's get back to the ship. We're wasting our time here."

Zeke thought that was the end of it. He thought that was the last he would hear of Jackson, and of Xi Pyxis 2.

He was wrong in that, too.

The recording of the Legion assault on Xi Pyxis 2 took six months to reach Earth. UCI used Sylvie's recordings as a backdrop to commentary on the Galactic Council's investigation of the War of the Pyxies. There were those on the Council, notably the shri, who found the Legion's treatment of the native race of Xi Pyxis 2 harsh and unconscionable. But then the Council had never cared for the Legion. The shri holdings were already under attack by the lona, the Council said, and that war threatened at any moment to spill over into the human, hlidskji, and !xaka! empires as well. This simply demonstrates to the lona and any other race that we can't be trusted. We signal to any watching race that we are aggressive and warlike, that we'll kill rather than seek more reasonable solutions. Is this the portrait we wish to paint?

Sylvie's documentary, in particular her more sympathetic treatment of individual Legion members, tended to be spectacular in light of the Council investigation. For that reason, it received a fair amount of airplay. The rescue of Jackson Franks was used by the Legion itself as propaganda.

Given that, it probably wasn't all that surprising that Tomas would burst into his employer's inner office one morning, breathless from the run up the marble staircase. He threw a holodot down on Bart Charles's desk. "Sir, you must see this. I just viewed it myself."

A servo skittered from Charles's ear where it had been whispering a financial report, down the large man's shoulder and into its compartment on the desk. Charles leaned back in his chair, waving at the holocube in the center of the room. Another servo, like a colorful beetle, scampered over to the holodot, and from the desk to the holocube. Inserting itself in the viewing mechanism, the servo activated the cube. The top of the cube suddenly lit with a jungle scene. A domed structure sat in a clearing, around which an ill-defined struggle was going on between a !xaka!, a hlidskji, and several flying animals. A woman's voice provided commentary too soft to hear. Suddenly the rear of the dome began billowing black smoke and flame. A moment later, a human dressed in Legion battle armor plowed through a glowing hole in the dome, a young black man in tow. The two collapsed on the ground outside the dome as the dome flashed into an inferno, as the cameras zoomed in toward the two. The mercenary cradled the injured boy in his arms, taking off his scratched visor. The camera view expanded until the soldier's face filled the viewing area, anguish and concern etched on his thin, long face.

"Hold that!" Charles grated, and the rushing scene came to a halt. Tomas looked at his employer with a grin of triumph on his face. Charles had risen from his seat, leaning over the desk as he stared at the frozen moment of time. "That's Bones's son Ezekiel," Charles said. "No wonder Bones couldn't find him—he's joined the Legion."

"That was my thought, sir. This was taken on Xi Pyxis 2. You've heard about the investigation by the Galactic Council."

Charles nodded. "And Ezekiel Bones was there." He sat back down, rubbing his chin between thumb and forefinger and swiveling in his seat to look out at the gardens of his estate. After a few minutes he turned back around. He studied the face of the soldier, who gazed at the boy in his arms with grave concern. Charles nodded.

"Tomas, I'll be going to Xi Pyxis 2 myself."

"Sir?" Tomas questioned. "Bones will be long gone from there by now."

"I know. I'm not sure what I'll find there, but. . . ." Charles shrugged. "You've done well to bring this to me, Tomas. Please make the arrangements."

For a long time after Tomas had left, Charles stared at the image of Ezekiel Bones.

CHAPTER 10

"You're Mack the Crack?"

Startled, Mack peered at the apparition standing at the door to his dingy office in Xi Pyxis Port. "Yeah, I'm him," he said uneasily, sliding a hand cautiously under the edge of his desk to a contact there. He pressed the button, pressed it again.

"That won't do you any good," the apparition said. "I've taken care of your security outside. No one's going to bother us for a few minutes, and that's all the time of yours I need." Whoever the apparition was, he didn't want to be recognized. A servo fashioned like a silver python was draped around his neck, and its shimmering scales sent a pulsing screen of light around the man's face that hid his features. Nor could Mack be entirely certain it was even a man, for the person wore bulky clothes and the voice was filtered, probably also via the python servo. The hands were gloved, the clothing plain. About all Mack could be certain of was that the apparition was human. The servo hidden in the matted, multicolored hair that cascaded over Mack's shoulder told him that the pheromones were definitely of that race.

Mack himself was hlidskji; short, wide, and bulky. He pressed his call button once more, then let his hand drop. He thought for a moment of whistling the three-note figure that would activate the automatic pulse-laser hidden behind the ceiling panels, then decided that it wouldn't hurt to hear a little more. If the apparition had wanted to kill him, it would have been easy enough to do from the doorway before Mack had seen him. He could afford a little patience.

"All right. You've got my attention. Now what?"

"You represent a deathfighter named Jackson Franks." There was no question in the filtered voice—it was a flat statement of fact. Mack shrugged acceptance. "He fights tonight," the apparition continued.

"If you know all that, why are you bothering me? I manage the guy—and a dozen others like him. I don't make bets. You want to make book on the fight, I'll send you to someone I know."

"How much is Jackson Franks worth to you?"

Mack's interest perked up. So that was it—the guy had heavy bets against Franks, who had become the overwhelming favorite of the crowds in the year and more he'd been fighting. The kid was good, good enough to withstand the no-holds-barred punishment he took weekly in the deathfight rings. Good enough to avoid serious injury thus far, good enough to stay alive. And this joker wanted Mack to make sure that Franks took a fall. Mack could do it; he'd done it before. Anything could be bought for the right price. "It's not exactly in my interests to fix a deathfight, mister..." Mack paused, but the apparition volunteered no name. Mack shrugged. "Especially with Franks. He's thirty points ahead of the next best guy. He's good, and he's honest. He won't take a cheap dive, not for me or anyone. When a fighter won't take a dive, then you have to make sure it just *happens,* and there's a good chance Franks is gonna get killed in the process. I lose a damn good fighter then." Mack waited, his hands behind his head. A finger touched another servo where the apparition could not see the motion—its miniature snout lifted, sniffed the air. "A hand laser right side," it chirped softly. "Outside, two more people: projectile weapons, heavy beam weapons. Call the cavalry."

Mack grimaced slightly. Bad news—a good thing he hadn't tried to burn him. He'd better hope snakeman here didn't have a grudge.

"I don't want Franks to lose, necessarily," the apparition said. The python-servo shifted slightly; the haze around his head shimmered with azure sparks. "I want him damaged but not dead. Can you do that?"

"Sounds like either way I lose my best fighter." Mack shook his head slowly.

The apparition moved his hand, very slowly so that Mack could follow the motion. Deliberately, the man reached into a pocket of his dark cloak. Mack stiffened, ready to reach for his own weapon, but the apparition pulled out a thick cloth-wrapped bundle. He placed it on the desk. "Open it."

Mack looked at it very carefully before doing so, lifting the edges of the cloth cautiously, then more eagerly. His eyes narrowed with greed when he saw the pile of scrip. He touched them unbelievingly.

"Shri notes of account," the apparition confirmed. "Payable to the bearer, no questions asked, at any bank in the United Worlds. Best currency anywhere. There's enough there to make you a very wealthy man. Should I keep talking, or must I take that and go elsewhere? I appreciate your obvious concern for your fighter, but I hope it won't stand in the way of my needs."

Mack's hand slammed down atop the bills. The hlidskji grinned up at the apparition. "Talk," he said eagerly. "I think I can accommodate your request."

Jackson fought at the Black Dome, the largest and most expensive of the deathfight bars. The deathpit there sat at the bottom of tiered rows of tables that could seat over a thousand people. Bets were handled in-house for a small handling fee, and a circular bar at the top of the pit was kept busy every sixth day, when the big fights were scheduled. There were bigger establishments on other worlds, but on Xi Pyxis 2, the Black Dome was unrivaled. "Getting to the Dome" was the dream of every deathfighter on the strip. "Holding the Pit" there for even a month was a fantasy. Jackson Franks had held the Dome's pit for six long and grueling months. He intended to hold it for another six.

His body showed the toll exacted by that intention. Stripped to the waist and laying on a table in the dressing rooms below the pit, his skin was a network of scars, ugly furrows of lightness in his dark skin. A quartet of servos crawled over his back, laying a glistening track of oils as they massaged his muscles. In his fourteen months of fighting, he'd gained bulk and size. He was a robust seventeen, nearly six and a half feet tall and muscular, with a young man's confidence that he could not be beaten.

The door to his dressing room opened without a knock. Mack the Crack strode into the room followed by the screams of the audience as they cheered the preliminary fight. "How'ya doing, kid?" Mack asked. The hlidskji grinned, as usual, sighing as he placed his rotund body on a short stool alongside the table.

"I'm ready," Jackson said, lifting up slightly from the table. "Is Bushorn?"

Mack shrugged. He glanced at the door. "You ain't fighting Bushorn tonight. There's been a scheduling change. Martin scratched; he says he's not ready for you. So I got you matched with McStevens."

Jackson shrugged, laying his head back down on his arms as the servos gently stroked his back. "McStevens, Bushorn, what's the difference," he said. "So what should I watch for with this guy? He fight dirty or clean?"

"Clean as a servo and just as predictable," Mack said. He cracked his knuckles loudly, one at a time. "He's a lefty, so be aware of that. He doesn't like to get close. Rather than grappling, he'll try to stay outside and use his fists and feet. I'd charge him if you get an opening."

"You check him out?"

"Yeah," Mack said. "Just now. My sniffers say he's all tidy. His manager's the Lynx. She'll be in to check you in a minute."

"Sounds like fun."

"Just don't enjoy it too much, kid. As soon as she says you're clean, you'll be going up." Mack hopped down from the stool and moved to the door with the sidewise gait of the hlidskji. "See you in the pit," he said. Just before he went out the door, he paused. "Hey kid, how come you never save any of the money I make you in these fights? How come you always blow it? You think you can fight forever?"

"What do I need money for, Mack? I got you."

Mack shook his head. He left the room.

The pit was a circle of fine sand six meters in diameter and ringed by a repulsor field. Standing in it always gave Jackson a rush of adrenaline. The audience was a noisy presence in the darkness beyond the brilliance of the spotlights overhead. The heat of the lamps baked the sand, made his muscular, gleaming body immediately break out into sweat. Raising his clenched fists high above his head, he pivoted as the crowd gave him an ovation, turning as they gave him their adulation. His face was split in a wide smile. He felt powerful, ready.

Sand spilled as a trapdoor opened and McStevens rose into the glare. Jackson inspected his opponent carefully, arrogantly. The man was a steroid-puffed giant maybe a few years older, who overshadowed even the tall Jackson. He looked to be a bag of muscles about to burst from underneath skin; he also looked like the sheer weight of his beef slowed him down. Jackson nodded—McStevens was a typical enough example of someone who thought they could make it on the deathfight circuit, but who forgot that power didn't mean much if you couldn't utilize it. The seasoned fighters weren't going to be awed by appearances even if the audience sometimes was.

The braying voice of the Dome announcer introduced the fighters and closed the betting as Jackson and McStevens glared at each other across the shimmering transparent curtain of the repulsor field which kept them separated until the beginning of the fight. McStevens was anxious; he pounced right up to the boundary of the field, ready to charge the moment it dropped. Jackson's brow furrowed at that: hadn't Mack said that McStevens didn't like to get close? He examined the face of the fighter—McStevens's eyes; they bothered Jackson too. The pupils were wide, dilated even under the spots, and the man breathed heavily. *Stims,* Jackson realized abruptly. *He's on stims. I thought Mack checked him.* Then, with sudden certainty: *He's set me up, the bastard. McStevens is a ringer.*

It was too late to stop things now. The announcer had finished his spiel, all the house lights had been doused. In a moment, the repulsor curtain would fall and the fight would start. For the first time since his initial fights, Jackson felt a shiver of fear.

A deathfight is a cruel and simple sport. That is perhaps the very reason for its popularity. There's something visceral in the sight of two people, stripped of anything but their own brute power and cunning, locked in combat. It stirs racial, animalistic memories. In a deathfight, there are no breaks; no well-ordered rounds or quarters; no coaches, substitutions, or timeouts for injury. No blows, pins, or holds are illegal; no part of the body is inviolate. The fight ends when one fighter collapses to the sand, at which point a repulsor curtain will separate the fighters once again. If the fallen man gets up before the minute ends, the fight continues. If he stays down, the other fighter has won. Most fights last about ten minutes; a minute or less isn't all that uncommon, half an hour is rare.

It even sounds almost humane, in the sense that you'd think that all a beaten man has to do is sink to the ground and stay there—he'd at least be spared further punishment. But the repulsor fields are slow to push someone back. In that time, most deathfighters do their utmost to ensure that the downed man will not be getting back up. There are deathfighters who say that to die in the pit is the easiest thing. It's easier than living with the pain of broken limbs and cracked skulls or passing the rest of your life under a servo's exoskeleton because your spine was snapped.

A deathfighter's usual fighting life was three or four months. Good ones might last a year before the constant injuries and brutality took their toll. The longest anyone had lasted was "Iron Skin" Geffen at two and a half years. Jackson knew that he was pushing the odds already. And it looked like Mack the Crack had overbalanced the scale.

The curtain dropped with an electronic sizzle.

McStevens rushed Jackson with a scream, his thick legs kicking up the soft sand. It was an easy tactic to counter; Jackson stepped to his right, stooped low, and drop-kicked for McStevens's crotch. He hit McStevens square in his manhood; McStevens only grunted. *NoPain tabs, too. They won't last long, but it may be too long for me.* McStevens sprayed sand as he turned, reaching for Jackson, who backed hurriedly out of the man's reach. He could hear the screams of the crowd, who thought Jackson had missed his kick by a few centimeters. McStevens straightened his stance, his hands curling into fists. He began to stalk Jackson now, ploddingly but steadily. Jackson feinted another kick, then launched an uppercut that hit the man directly on the chin. McStevens's jaw snapped shut, blood began to flow from his mouth, but all he did was shake his head and keep coming.

Jackson knew then that if he wanted to live, he was going to have to kill McStevens. Quickly, before the stim-hyped giant could get a hold on him. Jackson made a run for the nearest edge of the pit, gaining speed as he ran directly into the repulsor field there. It bent under his momentum like elastic, and then *shoved* him back into the pit, adding to his momentum. A smart opponent would have sensed Jackson's strategy and been ready for the sudden reversal. McStevens, instead, was still moving toward Jackson like a ponderous, lumbering bear. Jackson plowed into McStevens feet first, kicking. He felt ribs snap under the impact and more blood began gushing from McStevens's mouth. McStevens went down on his knees, his eyes glazing, and for the first time Jackson felt some hope. Jackson tumbled in the sand, regaining his footing quickly. He moved behind McStevens, taking his head in strong hands, ready to twist it savagely around. But the giant fooled him. He got his own hands on Jackson's arms. The man was *strong,* Jackson realized too late as McStevens twisted around, breaking Jackson's grip. The giant surged up with a roar, his fingers open like claws as he struck at Jackson's face. Jackson screamed shrilly as McStevens gouged at the eyes. The pain was searing, lancing, an agony that made him bellow in fury and surprise. He could feel blood, far too much of it, pouring down his face, and his left eyesocket was in agony. Jackson roared, kicking and punching blindly, and somehow connecting. He staggered back from McStevens, gore covering his face. He could see nothing out of his left eye; the right was covered in a veil of blood. He tried to rush the flooding redness away with a forearm, panic coursing through him. Shock made his skin cold; he wanted to throw up, wanted to just sink down in the sand. *No! Do that and you'll stay there forever. You have to see. You have to think.*

McStevens was up, unsteady. He had to be close to collapse himself, Jackson knew. The ribs would have punctured the lung —he had to be losing blood worse than Jackson himself. Anyone else would have already gone down. McStevens shook himself like a wet dog, and began stumbling toward Jackson. Jackson waited for him.

One blow. That's all you have. You can't see him well enough, and you're going to go down yourself in a minute. You have to take him now. His breath was ragged; he could taste the salty sweetness of his own blood filling his mouth. He spat, he wiped again at his right eye. As McStevens approached, he crouched down, obviously leading with his left leg. *Let him think you're going to kick. When he goes to block it, make your move.* When McStevens kept coming, Jackson let fly a slow, looping kick to the knee, which McStevens blocked with a forearm chop to the knee that nearly bent it backward. But with the same motion, Jackson had come up, his hands locked together. He screamed as he struck at McStevens, striking directly at the man's throat. Jackson felt the windpipe collapse even as McStevens's fingers caught his arms. Jackson felt his forearm snap under the desperate grasp. McStevens tried to cough, tried to draw air through his ruined trachea.

His grip on Jackson loosened. He toppled to the sand.

The hardest thing Jackson ever did was retaining consciousness for the next minute.

He remembered drifting moments of coherence: someone cursing monotonously as they hauled him to his feet; the voice of a doctor calling his name over and over; some cool salve being lathed over his forehead; the smell of disinfectant and the sour taste of his mouth.

He heard, he felt. He tasted, he smelled. But in none of those moments did he ever see anything.

Jackson remembered that as he slowly came back to awareness. He could feel cool sheets underneath him and the sway of a gelbed as he shifted position slightly. He could hear his own harsh breathing. And he was afraid. He was afraid to try to open his eyes. He was afraid that they were already open.

"Jackson?" A man's voice. Jackson turned his head toward it.

"I . . . I can't see," he said.

"Here." Jackson felt someone take his hand. His fingers touched something slick and warm swathing his head. "Paraflesh dressing," the voice explained. "!Xaka! stuff, actually. It's supposed to be excellent for quick healing. You'll see out of the right eye in time. The left. . . ." The voice paused. "I'm sorry, Jackson. The doctors couldn't do anything to save the nerves there."

The news registered slowly. Jackson took a deep, shuddering breath. "I'm going to be blind in one eye . . ." he began. His mouth twitched. "You said 'the doctors couldn't do anything.' Who are *you?*"

"My name's Charles. Bartholomew Charles. I was watching your fight."

His mention of the fight sent a cold rage through Jackson. "Mack set me up," he cried. "The guy was on stims and No-Pain—" As Jackson struggled to sit up, he felt the hand push him back down. He had no strength to resist.

"Rest. Be quiet," the voice said soothingly. "You've been through a lot—you've lost an eye. You've a broken arm, a wrecked knee, and too many cuts and bruises to catalogue. Another man might have died in that pit. You impressed me, Jackson. I came here to make a proposition to you."

"Yeah, I'm sure you're real impressed. I already have a manager." He started to shake his head, remembering what Mack had done, but the stranger had already caught the mistake.

"You *had* a manager. Word on the street is that he wants nothing to do with a crippled fighter."

"Hey, I've had broken arms before. It'll heal. In a month I'll be back in the pits."

"And the first fighter you face will remember that you've lost half your vision. You've a blind side now, Jackson. They'll pick on that weakness and eat you up. Your fighting days are over, son. Forget them."

Jackson lay back. He longed to rip the dressings from his eyes. "Fighting's all I have, Mr. Charles. There are ways to compensate for weaknesses."

"There's another way."

"Your offer?" Jackson sighed. "All right, I'm listening. What else have I got to do?"

He could hear the rustle of clothing, the sound of leather as Charles leaned toward him. The man's voice spoke close to his ear, enticing and promising. "I told you that you impressed me, Jackson. I meant it. You showed me that you've drive and determination, that you can think in a crisis and win even when the odds are against you. That's a rare quality, especially in so young a person. I'd like to see you reach your full potential, Jackson."

"You a philanthropist, or do you just like charity cases, Mr. Charles?" Jackson asked bitterly.

"Neither one," the man said without offense. "I expect value for money. I need a personal assistant, and I can afford to take the time to train the man I think best suited. I expect to get loyalty and hard work from you; a five-year contract should do it. There may even be some fighting involved. It's possible. Rich men have enemies."

"You seem to forget that I'm half-blind. Why should you take a chance on me that Mack the Crack wouldn't take?"

"Come with me and you won't be blind. The eye can be replaced with a servo. I'll pay for the operation if you'll come back to Earth with me."

Jackson felt a sudden upsurge of hope, breaking up the despair that was settling around him. He forced the optimism down. "I don't get it," he said. "You give me my eye back, you take me to Earth, train me, and all I have to do in return is work for you for five years. It doesn't exactly sound like an even bargain. What are you holding back, Charles?"

"Nothing."

"I'm not a fool, mister."

"If you were, I wouldn't be here. Are you willing?"

Jackson said nothing. After a minute, Charles sighed. Jackson heard him get to his feet and walk across the room. "My ship leaves in a few hours," Charles told him. "If I leave here now, the offer's void. Ask yourself this: can you afford to pay for an eye servo yourself? Do you think you'll live past your next fight when they know that you can't see from the left side? Are you even going to be able to make your living expenses until you recover, or pay for this hospital stay? Mack the Crack won't touch you or help you—are you going to go back to the dives to fight for a few lousy credits?"

Jackson reached up to touch the dressings over his eyes once more. He stared at the darkness inside his head.

"Okay," he said. "You've got a deal."

CHAPTER 11

Legion ships are fast by sub-lightspeed standards, accelerating quickly to a substantial percentage of that mythical barrier with massive deuterium drive engines. From a distance of a kilometer or so, the Legion ships appear to consist almost entirely of the drive systems and fuel tanks, with the life-support pod glued on as an afterthought. They are energy hogs with one purpose: move a large number of troops and equipment as quickly as possible from one transfer point to another. The Legion had made no concessions to budget or economy with the cruisers. For that reason, they responded more quickly to a call than the shri sail-liners, the !xaka! planet-crackers, or the human navy.

Of course, that requires a payment to the God of Relativity in the form of severe time dilation for those aboard. Einstein's curse—the closer you approach light speed, the slower time seems to pass for you. This was compounded by the fact that the crew spent much of the time between points in deepsleep. To Leo Bones and Mahsi, Zeke had been gone from their lives for the past decade: local standard time. For Zeke, he had experienced a very full three years: proper time. For all intents and purposes, Zeke now was possessed of two ages. Measured from the viewpoint of a static observer on Earth, Zeke was twenty-eight; in Zeke's own mind and body, he was a much younger twenty-one.

So it is with travel through the vast distance between the United Worlds. The jumps through the relativistic gateways of the black hole transfer stations might be instantaneous, but one still had to move at sub-light speeds between the widely separated points that linked the tenuous empire together.

Thus it was that to Zeke and his companions, the War of the

Pyxies was only a month old in their minds at the moment that Jackson Franks lay blinded in a hospital room paid for by Bart Charles.

Three years in the Legion could still be a long time. To that previously mentioned observer on Earth, the Legion may streak into bloody action once every standard year or so. To the mercenaries on board those ships, it often seemed that each month contained a new call, a new crisis, and new deaths. Zeke's three years had been packed full. He'd made and lost friends. Three years could scrape away at a person's idealism and leave him bitter and confused.

"The Legion doesn't have morals. That's what bothers me the most. We do whatever we're paid to do. We don't worry about it being right or wrong."

Zeke, Reelys, Kagak!xa, and Marty had gathered in one of the cruiser lounges midway between human and !xaka! territories of the ship. It was mostly empty—most of the crew had gone to the deepsleep chambers after a week or so of ship time. Reelys had brought along "supper"—a ring-shaped ultraviolet lamp under which she basked, his'er photosynthetic mantle spread out to catch as much of the glare as possible. The usual purplish markings seemed a phosphorescent green under the light. Kagak!xa had also brought along a meal. Like all !xaka!, Kagak!xa preferred her daily dose of minerals straight from the source, and had piled an odd collection of small rocks on the floor in front of her. Marty and Zeke sipped on drinks from the dispensary.

Zeke's comment elicited only an abrasive clatter from Kagak!xa.

"We're not paid to have morals. We're paid to take care of problems."

"Usually by blowing them up," Zeke retorted.

"If we're lucky," Kagak!xa answered with no trace of sarcasm. The pyrotechnics officer sounded pleased at the thought. "The incendiaries worked well with the pyxies. I've always thought that smoke, flame, and a good loud bang have a psychological effect on your enemy that is as important as the actual physical damage." A segmented, hard-shelled arm reached out, plucked up a pebble, and tossed it into her undermouth. "Don't you agree, Reelys? Certainly the shri fear the percussive effect of explosives."

The shri wriggled tendrils, his'er mantle fluttering. His'er mouthstalk uncurled. "I think you misunderstand what our young human is saying."

"She understands perfectly," Marty snorted. "She just thinks that an explosion is the next best thing to an orgasm. To a !xaka!, there's only two types of beings in the universe. Those with power—who can have fun blowing things up—and those underneath—who have to take whatever's given them."

Kagak!xa reared up on her first two segments with a distinctive hiss. Her gills spread out like angry plumes on their stalks as glittering compound eyes fixed on the hlidskji. Mandibles clashed together with some phrase in her own language before she switched to universal pidgin. "And hlidskji make stupid assumptions about other races. Another !xaka! might think you were serious about what you just said and issue challenge. Another !xaka! might think that a hlidskji was just an overgrown liver fluke and squash him before he could demonstrate any signs of intelligence."

Marty laughed scoffingly, but he also turned away, shutting his mouth abruptly. Kagak!xa expelled breath in what might have been satisfaction and returned to her pile of stones.

"That's exactly what I'm talking about," Zeke told them. He rubbed at his forearms, scratching at the itchy skin grafts Reelys had placed over the burns he'd suffered rescuing Jackson. "Whenever the Legion gets called in to take care of a problem, we solve it by throwing all our available firepower at it."

"It works," Kagak!xa said firmly.

"Maybe. But what if there might be other solutions? What if there might be better ways? What if we could solve the same problem with more time but at a lesser cost in lives?"

"You're not being paid to think," Marty said sullenly. "And seeing the way you act sometimes, Zeke, it's a damned good thing; you'd never make any money. We're being paid to do what Huff and her superiors want us to do: that's it."

Reelys drifted up toward the lamp. His'er sibilant voice was understanding. "My sympathies are with Zeke," s/he said. "There are times when I regret my decision to be here. But there's nothing you can do about it, Ezekiel. At least, nothing beyond resigning."

Zeke sighed. "Still—" he began, then noticed that Sylvie Pharr, sans holocams, had approached the group and was listening to the conversation. He bit off the rest of his remark, looking at her. The others became aware of her at the same time. Reelys was the first to move. One tendril flipped up and touched the contact of the ultraviolet lamp; the filament flickered off and the lamps collapsed into an improbably small package. S/he waved the mass of tentacles hanging from his'er mantle in the intricate patterns of polite shri leavetaking. "I'll see the rest of you later. I need to check some samples in the lab." The shri collapsed his'er mantle, shrinking the airbag until s/he rested at neutral buoyancy a meter above the floor. His'er muscular gripping tendrils dropped, touching the floor plates. S/he "walked" away. Kagak!xa, watching the shri depart, shoveled rocks into her undermouth, then dropped all eight segments to the floor.

"I need to be certain that the fuses for the replacement incendiaries have been retimed," she said. "Why don't you come with me, hlidskji?" she suggested pointedly. "I could show you what kind of argument explosives can make."

"Why the hell should I care about—" Marty started to protest, then scowled. "Oh," he said, glancing at Sylvie. "Yeah, I guess I might do that, huh? Let's leave love to work its magic." The hlidskji groaned to his feet, shaking his head. The dwarf followed the massive bulk of the !xaka! out of the room.

"Your friends certainly are subtle."

Zeke shrugged. "I guess they thought we had something to talk about," he said as noncommitally as he could.

"I couldn't help overhearing part of the conversation."

"I'd think that overhearing things would be part of your job description."

Sylvie came and stood in front of Zeke, her hands on her slender waist, her head canted to one side so that the mass of dark hair hung over one shoulder. "You and I got off on the wrong foot from the start. Part of it's my fault, and I'm sorry for that. I think maybe we both misunderstand one another. I'd like to begin again."

Zeke could feel the star seed warming in its pouch. He knew that the crystal was trying to tell him to listen to her. He forced himself to keep that still voice out of his mind. *I don't need a damn conscience. I already have one that's too large.* "Why?" he asked. At the last moment he softened his tone, so that the query sounded less harsh than it might have.

"Can I sit?"

Zeke nodded and she pulled a chair up from the floor, leaning forward as she spoke. "When I first started this assignment, I talked to several of your companions. Most of them I find to be totally uninteresting—they have one motivation: they're here to make money, and they don't care how they're doing it. Most of them never even question their actions. It wouldn't occur to them to think about morals and ethics. I came to *Musashi* because I knew Kagak!xa—met her on an earlier assignment. She knew that I'd be concentrating on the humans aboard; she suggested you, said you were different. She's right. I saw a sensitivity and concern in you, especially in the moments after you pulled that boy from the dome. You care, Zeke. That's too rare. It made me sorry that you didn't seem to like me. It made me sorry that I was coming off as the hard-as-nails journalist instead of being just me."

She shrugged, looking down at her hands folded in her lap. "It made me want to come here now and see if we can't tear down the wall we're building between us *now*. Before it gets any higher." She looked over to him. She spread her hands wide. "What do you think?"

Her honesty destroyed any thought he might have had of keeping her distant from him. He didn't need the small, insistent murmur of the star seed. For the first time in what seemed ages, he smiled. "Okay," he said. "We'll start over."

She returned his smile. The warmth of it seemed almost palpable. She reached out to brush his hand gently with her fingers: a soft touch. "Then I have another request, Zeke. Please say no if it bothers you at all. I'll understand and I won't press it further."

"What's that?" Zeke asked.

"I want your permission to film you again. I was going to leave at the next transfer point. I thought that would be the last opportunity to work on this Legion documentary out in the field. But Captain Huff just told me that she's just received a relayed distress call. You'll be moving from this transfer right into another situation."

She could see the strain lines deepen on his boyish, drawn face. Zeke seemed weary and exhausted, suddenly. "Where this time?" he asked.

"A BEC installation—ice miners. Some place called Luyten 726-B."

She certainly had not expected the reaction that news got her. Zeke jumped up from his chair. He seemed almost frightened, his light eyes wide. "What?!" he cried. And then he rushed off, leaving her to stare dumbfounded.

"Now what did I say?" she wondered aloud.

• • •

Jackson Franks found that the training Bart Charles had spoken of was as bizarre as the offer the man had made in the first place. The Charles estate was set in the still-extensive Amazonian jungle of South America, about as remote a place as you could find on Earth. Charles himself would be absent from the estate for weeks at a time, off to New York or Nairobi for business, taking a shuttle to the moon or the asteroid belt to oversee some BEC installation or dealing with other board members. Jackson was left alone with the hundred or more servants that Charles employed to keep his estate in order, and with his instructors. The series of tutors was long, none of them staying more than six months at a time. Jackson was not someone to fail to take advantage of a good situation—he'd learned in the deathpits that an advantage not seized was one lost forever. The intense grind of study was more a joy for him than a burden. The courses included mathematics and languages, physics and chemistry. He learned the strange mores of shri society, was given glimpses of the labyrinth of bureaucracy that the gossamerlike, floating creatures seemed to revel in. He learned the ways of the !xaka!. He learned to understand their harsh, brutal caste system and the effect it had on the creatures. He learned to read some of their subtle body language, if not truly to enjoy the look of the !xaka! themselves.

He rediscovered music. Jackson's parents had been accomplished amateur musicians; he himself had a good deal of natural talent, which grew under the hands of his tutors. He was encouraged to play chess—a game he had always loved—for the insights a game of pure strategy would give him in the art of looking ahead.

Nor was his body neglected for his mind. Among the teachers who lived on the estate for a time were those who taught him karate, tai kwando, jeet-kune, wing-chun, kendo, fencing, archery, and marksmanship. He learned tricks that he'd wished he'd known before, and he learned just how amateur the deathfights were—had he had this knowledge before, there would have been no serious challenge to him in the deathpits. At the same time, with such knowledge, he would never have ventured into them.

Charles had kept his promise. On arrival at Earth Jackson had been given an artificial eye. The servo that replaced his natural eye was sharper and more sensitive than the original, and looked only slightly different from its companion. He was told to expect that the servo would, for some time to come, give him occasional debilitating headaches, and it did—it seemed a small price to pay for the return of full vision, indeed for the *enhanced* vision of the new eye, which could see higher into ultraviolet and lower into infrared, which could zoom in to view distant scenes or magnify tiny objects held in his hand.

His mind was pumped full of information. His body was conditioned and trained. Jackson grew sleek and powerful and perhaps somewhat arrogant. And one other thing he learned was nobody was going to tell him exactly what all this work was for. Bart Charles, when he was at the estate, would only say that Jackson would be his personal assistant, or simply smile and say something vague about great things in store. "Take advantage of what I'm giving you," he said to his protegé. "Don't question it—just accept it."

For two years, Jackson did exactly that.

It was on the second anniversary of Jackson's arrival at the estate that Bart Charles, after the sumptuous dinner had been cleared away and all the servants dismissed, took a bottle of brandy from the shelf and poured some into a snifter set before Jackson. He waited. Jackson started to raise the glass to his lips, then stopped. He took a minuscule servo from the pocket of his dinner jacket, held it for a moment over the snifter's rim. It blinked green and chirped once like a cricket. Jackson took the snifter in hand as Charles grinned.

"Good, Jackson. That's exactly the precautions you should learn to take. Trust no one, not even me."

"I trust you, Mr. Charles."

"Bart, please."

"Bart, then. I trust you. But it would have been easy for someone to have slipped a poison into the decanter without your knowing it. Checking it had nothing to do with you."

Charles simply smiled. He filled his snifter, and checked it with his own servo. "Good, again. I don't trust any of the servants myself, not even Tomas, who's been with me for years. A toast, Jackson. A toast to two years of intensive study, to two years of hard work." He held out his snifter, and Jackson touched the rim gently with the base of his own. Glass chimed. They sipped. "I'm very proud of you, Jackson," Bart said. "And very attached to you, as well. I know I haven't been around as often as I'd like to be, but I do keep in touch with your progress. I have reports sent me every few days, along with holofilms. I feel I know you very well."

He set his brandy down on the table, going over to an ornate fireplace. There was a picture of Devon Charles set on the mantel. Bart Charles brushed his fingers over it as he spoke. "I know you've wondered what it is I've been grooming you for. I think it's time to tell you, Jackson. So," he said, looking back at the young man, "what do you know about BEC and its corporate structure?"

Jackson took another sip of the brandy, relishing its fire. He liked everything about his new life, the elegant surroundings, the feel of the new clothes, the sense that for once he was at the top of the power structure instead of the bottom. "I know that it's closely held in Bones family hands, though that's split somewhat over the years. No one has outright control of a majority of shares. Leo Bones, as the direct descendant of Oliver, holds the largest block—but what will happen with his shares when he dies is unclear, since his estranged son has dropped from sight for the last several years. You received your shares through your mother—I think her great-aunt was Oliver Bones's sister, is that right?" Charles nodded. "And you're one of the largest of the minority stockholders, followed closely by the Chrysanthis, the banking family. A loan was involved with their shares, if I'm not mistaken."

"Correct again," Leo Bones told him, speaking more to the picture of Devon than to Jackson. "Manoli Chrysanthi personally loaned Anthony Bones the funds to develop the first antimatter separator—personally, mind you, not through the bank. As security, he accepted a third of Anthony's block of shares in BEC. The loan was never paid back. Peter Chrysanthi holds those shares now. That's important, Jackson. Very important."

He left the fireplace and sat at the table, very near Jackson. "Snoop!" he called softly.

A servo skittered from an unnoticed niche in the wainscotting. Mouselike, it parked itself at Charles' feet, the fine wire antennae of its "whiskers" quivering. "Reporting," it said.

"Privacy request," Charles said.

"Clear. Scramblers on." The servo scampered back to its niche once more.

"I wouldn't care to have anyone else hear this, Jackson. I think I can trust you, or I wouldn't be saying this now. You want to know why I've been grooming you. I'll tell you. I intend to take control of BEC, to wrest it away from Leo Bones. Our young Peter Chrysanthi is, umm, *persuadable*. He can be swayed, because he's made himself vulnerable. If he can be made to vote his shares with mine, I can take control. I can make BEC mine. *Ours,* Jackson."

"I still don't understand."

"It's simple enough. Peter is a compulsive gambler—never on simple games of chance, mind you, but on anything where skill and judgement enter into the equation, especially physical contests. He gambles only with those he considers to be his peers, socially and intellectually. But he *is* compulsive. My sources tell me that four years ago, he managed to lose much of his family stocks and securities to a rival financier. Two days afterward, the financier's yacht was found abandoned off Tahiti. His body washed up a week later, what was left of it. The incident was dismissed as an accident—there'd been a convenient storm the night the yacht overturned. But I also know that similar things have happened in the past with Chrysanthi. Is it becoming clearer to you now?"

Jackson tugged at the sleeve of his silk jacket. He swirled amber liquid in his snifter. "I'm your bait," he said. "I have the sophistication and the connections—via you—to get Chrysanthi to deal with me. *And* I have the physical skills needed to stay alive if Chrysanthi tried to do something afterward."

Bart Charles looked very pleased. "You understand perfectly," he said. "And how do you feel about it?"

"I'm beginning to get the feeling that there are deathpits in every level of society, wherever I go." His eyes caught those of Charles. His dark, handsome face was fierce. "I never ran away from the pits before," he said in a throaty rumble. "I don't intend to start now."

Charles laughed. He held his snifter out to Jackson in salute, drained the contents, and flung the snifter into the fireplace. The crystal shattered against marble. After a moment, the shards of Jackson's glass mingled with them.

CHAPTER 12

As Zeke remembered from his father's journal, Luyten 726–B was not a convenient place to get to. Far from any of the normal transfer stations, the distress call routed through the Nemesis black hole to Earth took a standard year to reach Earth. By the time the Legionnaires received their orders and rerouted to that area, the crisis was nearly three standard years old.

What they knew was precious little, for the ice miners' visual communications link had been sheared off in the first attack. All information had been relayed by a compressed data burst from the sole remaining antenna. The Legion was aware that the ice miners in the comet cloud had been attacked without warning by an extremely large ship using laser and particle beam weapons. Beyond that—nothing. For all the Legion knew, the miners might be long dead, they might have beaten off the attack by themselves, or perhaps the attacking ship had been joined by an armada—they couldn't know. It was not a pleasant thought.

For Zeke's cruiser, it was a two-month trip under deepsleep and some occasional uncomfortable acceleration. The cruiser shuttled through the Xi Pyxis transfer station directly to Nemesis, the black hole companion of Sol that had been humanity's first link to the stars. From there they plunged through the event horizon to within a few light weeks of Luyten. The cruiser's sensors probed the interstellar reaches and relayed back a scene that surpassed anything they might have expected.

Captain Huff had called a small group together in her quarters to view the first relays from the sensors. As Pyrotechnics Officer, Kagak!xa was a natural choice—few beings had her expertise in long-range weaponry. Reelys was present as the sole representative of the shri, Marty had been chosen as a nod to the hlidskji. Zeke was present as well. As Huff had explained to the gathering when they arrived, Zeke "had some experience with mining stations." Huff had glanced at Sylvie Pharr when she'd said that and had given Zeke a knowing wink—Huff was following Legion rules concerning privacy. Zeke was there because he was a Bones and this was a BEC installation, though Huff had no suspicion that Zeke was as intimately involved with Luyten 726–B as he was.

"Visual link initiated, Captain," *Musashi* said. "Relaying them to your screen."

In a way, the visuals that filled the wallscreen behind Captain Huff were beautiful except for the violence and energy that they portrayed. In the enhanced color of the sensors, the comet mining station was a framework of boxes and spheres around the pulse-rings of the accelerators. What should have been pristine and gleaming steel was instead pitted and scarred from three years of bombardment. The deflector and radiation screens created a faint blue nimbus around the station; the accelerator beam—a fiery, speckled orange—blazed against the background of stars as it lanced outward to the intruder. Over the station swept a wavering beam from the attacking ship, the deadly swath a hideous blue-purple that sparked where it touched the screens.

The image panned back to include the intruder ship and everyone present gasped. The intruder was indeed huge, a globe as large as a moon, its craters the blackened opening for lasers and stripped-particle beams, studded with an array of smaller turrets and sling gantries. She glowed incandescently, as if alive with fire and heat, her own defensive screens up against the station's counterattack. Lasers cut fine, achingly blue lacework lines around her, firing repeatedly on the mining station.

"By any god you care to name, *that's* been going on for three years?" Marty uttered reverently, too awed to utter one of his usual sarcasms. "How could anyone survive a siege like that?"

Reelys had reacted to the sight of the visitor as if to an apparition of Death itself. His'er mantle had gone dull and splotchy, shrinking as s/he backed into a corner as if to get as far away as possible from the vision on the screen. "Lona," s/he said. "One of their machines of destruction. I saw a fleet of them attack my homeworld. The Iona war has come to other races at last."

"This ship must agree with you, Reelys," *Musashi* replied—

for the first time, Zeke realized that she sounded suspiciously like Huff. "I would not care to approach that machine too closely, though of course that's *your* decision, Captain."

"Thank you," Huff said drily. She turned back to the others. "We may have walked into something more important than anyone had thought. Zeke, anything you can add? What about the miners? Do you think they're still alive?"

Zeke shook himself into belated awareness. The scene had doubly mesmerized him—once because it was etched in his memory from his father's journal, and also because the instant the lona ship had flashed on the screen, the star seed had given a wordless mental cry. Zeke could feel the heat of the crystal even through the pouch of his belt. He knew it would be glowing brilliantly; he was almost surprised that its radiance didn't penetrate the leather around it.

•Recognition•

"You can see that the miners have altered the mass spectrometers and the accelerators into beam weapons," he said at last. "The shielding on a BEC station is extensive enough to withstand the flare star's periodic eruptions, so they should have gotten decent protection, especially after the first attack. There should be two ore ships tethered to the station ports, but I don't see them. I hope they didn't try to escape—from the looks of that lona ship, it would fry anything that left the protection of the station's shields." He could feel Sylvie's holocams focused on him—he forced himself not to look that way. He hadn't seen Sylvie since the last, abrupt conversation. When he'd gone to see her the next day, she'd already reported for deepsleep.

"Someone must be there," Marty grumbled. "They're still firing."

"Could be slaved automatics—the computer system directing the fight," Kagak!xa pointed out. She clicked several times for emphasis. "A !xaka! would set that up—we would not simply give up, even if we were dying."

Zeke nodded in agreement. "No way of telling, and all the external communications gear have been destroyed. There's not even any of the running lights left."

"There'd be enough food for the miners for three years?" Huff asked.

Zeke nodded. "They'd have a lot in frozen storage, plus they should be able to synthesize from the protein tanks—the stations have extensive laboratories. They'd be okay that way."

Huff tapped her foot, staring at the mesmerizing slow ballet of the battle. She spoke to the cruiser. "Can our screens hold up against that energy?" she asked.

"My most optimistic projections are measured in minutes, Captain," the ship answered. "The station has far heavier shields."

•**Recognition**• The prodding from the crystal was insistent. •**Sadness/Incomplete**• Zeke found himself yearning to talk to someone about it. At that wishful thought, the crystal suddenly added its own reinforcement. •**Affirmation/Enhanced. Consult**• Fine, Zeke thought, but with whom? Kagak!xa, Marty? Sylvie? The answer struck him then. If the crystal recognized the lona ship, then it very likely was something made by that race—and of the races here, only the shri had had contact with the lona.

Zeke had the feeling that he'd finally come full circle. He had fled Leo Bones because of his sins and the sins of these miners. Now retribution had come to them, and Zeke had been one of those summoned to rescue them.

"Damn." Huff prowled the deck, her hands behind her back. "We haven't too many choices. To try to take that machine with one cruiser is suicide. We can wait for other Legion cruisers to arrive, but that will take time. On the other hand . . ." She shook her head. "Let me think about it," she said. "Anyone else have anything to add? No? Good, you're dismissed."

Most of them filed out quickly. Sylvie started to remain behind, but a motion of Huff's head and her scowl convinced the reporter to head for the corridor with the rest. Zeke turned to follow her and saw Reelys still huddled in the corner, his'er eyestalks riveted on the screen and the siege of the mining station. "Reelys?" S/he ignored Zeke. "Reelys?" he said a little louder. One eyestalk turned slowly toward him. "I'd like to talk with you. Please."

"All right, Ezekiel," s/he said. A shudder seemed to pass through his'er mantle. "It's not good for me to watch this without the comfort of others."

"Come on, then." As Reelys drifted past Zeke, his hand brushed the pouch in which the star seed sat. The leather was almost searingly hot.

Reelys's rooms were unlike anything in the rest of the cruiser. The air was heavy with CO_2, almost making Zeke giddy. The light was glaring and direct, the air almost hot. A perpetual fog seemed to drift in the air, and what little furniture there was looked as if it had been blown from glass. Everything floated in the random currents of the room—the furniture, a colorful transparent chest that looked as if it contained tools, a rack of beverages in various containers for the several races aboard. Zeke, despite being underweight, still felt ponderous and heavy there.

Reelys had gone to the beverage rack, hovering over it as tendrils played with the containers there. "May I offer refreshment?" s/he asked. "After seeing the lona machine . . ."

"Nothing, Reelys. Thanks."

An eyestalk curled to glance back at him. "You're having trouble metabolizing your food again . . . ?" Reelys began, but Zeke waved a hand.

"No. Your last treatment's still holding up." Zeke took a deep breath. His resolve held. "I . . . I want to show you something. I think it might be important." Zeke touched the pouch in which the star seed, silent now, was cooling.

The eyestalk widened, and Reelys shifted his'er mantle so that the fluid lens inside it was also directed that way. "Your luckpiece, Ezekiel?"

Zeke nodded. "Yes."

"I've often wondered what it was."

"Then let me show you." Zeke put his hand in the pouch, cupping the star seed and bringing it out. Holding out his hand, he uncurled his fingers to reveal the gem in his palm.

The reaction was far greater than he expected. Reelys whistled shrilly, and his'er mantle flared out further than he'd ever seen, the purple splotches widening and growing more brilliant. His'er tentacles danced below the dirigible of the gasbag, a volley of shri excitement in which Zeke caught a few familiar signs. It was nearly half a minute before Reelys could speak in words Zeke could understand.

"A star seed!" Reelys exclaimed. "I have been searching . . . ! Ezekiel! Do you realize—? Where did you get it?"

"You know what this is, then? You know what this does?"

"I know more about them than you might believe, Ezekiel. The star seeds have been the study of myself and my podmates since the three were found. I knew that there must be another, all along."

"You've talked to the other three star seeds?"

"Talked? Of course not . . ." Reelys drew his'er mantle back. "You can do that with yours? What does it say?"

"Nothing. Not in words, anyway. It's a long story, Reelys, fifteen standard years or so long. Let me tell you . . ." With that, Zeke unburdened himself to the shri. He'd forgotten how good it could feel to share himself with someone else, to speak of problems with a sympathetic friend. There'd been no one since his mother, since Mahsi. Zeke told Reelys about his father's discovery of the seed, about the emanations he'd felt in his mind when he'd first found it, about how, in times of crisis, the seed sometimes led Zeke along the right intuitive path. Reelys listened patiently, not interrupting until the tale was finished. Afterward, Reelys bobbed silently before Zeke.

"Ezekiel," s/he said at last. "I'm honored that you consider me enough of a friend to say these things to me. A friend should match confidence with confidence—and I have my own tale to give you in return for yours. How well do you know shri culture—have you heard the name Reelys before?"

"Some hero in a shri epic, isn't s/he?"

Reelys gave a hiss of acknowledgement. "Yes. And Reelys is not my name, but one borrowed in the same way my mantle pattern is borrowed. Once I wore the red pattern of the High Ones, until it was decided that I would mingle for a time with the other races. You see, Ezekiel, I knew that there must be at least one more star seed. They are pieces of a larger machine, I think. They were meant to function together—not a surprising thing when you consider that the three were found nearly simultaneously. We've always suspected that the seed's emissions were meaningful, though no one has ever been able to decipher them."

"They're crystalline, like the Iona. The Iona build from stone and crystal. My crystal recognized that ship."

"And we're currently at war with the Iona," Reelys added.

Zeke curled his fingers tightly around the star seed, feeling its warm pulsations. "Then that wasn't a wandering planet or some unknown race that the mining station destroyed years ago. It was a Iona ship, one carrying a star seed. And this war machine attacking the station now—it could be retribution. The timing, though . . ."

"It would be right, Ezekiel. The shri have shared worlds with the Iona before, if man has not. We take the sky, they the ground. We have studied them but learned very little—we don't know their language, their culture, not even the way they reproduce. That they are sentient is inarguable, for they build relay satellites and powerful ships. Those ships travel only at sub-light speed—they ignore the black hole stations. Given that, it would be about right." Reelys whistled once again.

•**Affirmation**• The crystal radiated the thought to Zeke. •**Implications?**• Zeke shook his head. "What implications?" he began, then his eyes widened. "My God," he exclaimed. "Reelys, we have some math to check . We know the star seeds were found simultaneously and independently. Let's surmise they came from the lona homeworld. Given the lag time for response and sending out the lona attack fleets, could it be that the lona war began first against your race because your worlds are closer to the lona homeworld? The attack here, even if years after the first attacks on the shri, could be part of the same wave."

Reelys's excitement was apparent in movement of his'er body. Tendrils waved. S/he touched the wall with a manipulative tentacle—colors and symbols raced across it. She tapped the wall, finally. "You are right, Ezekiel," s/he said. "The correspondence is very close—the lona attacks on the shri began at nearly the same time your father took the star seed from the lona ship."

Dressed in his black dogi, a belt of matching color knotted around his waist, Jackson watched his new martial arts teacher —or *sensei*—enter the dojo Charles had built for Jackson's tutoring. The Sensei Moroshiba didn't impress Jackson at all. He was a slight, elderly Japanese man, his sparse hair and beard white with age and his body stooped. He wore a white dogi, frayed around the edges though immaculately clean, and his legs were swathed in a black *hakama,* the ancient, loose trouser-skirt of the Japanese samurai. He bowed before entering the dojo, glanced once at Jackson standing on the tatami mats, and delicately removed his sandals, placing them beside the mat. He bowed to Jackson. "Sensei Moroshiba," Jackson said.

"Mr. Franks," Moroshiba answered. "Mr. Charles, your employer, wishes me to teach you aikido. I tried to persuade him that I know very little, but he is a difficult man with whom to argue."

Jackson smiled at that. "He is that."

Moroshiba "hmmed" under his breath. He bowed again, stepping onto the mats. He groaned as he sat, folding his legs underneath him in the formal seiza posture. "So, young man, tell me. What have you studied before?"

Jackson folded his arms over his muscular chest. "Almost

everything. I've had several senseis in various arts. I hold black belts in karate, tae kwando, wing-chun. I've studied kendo."

"You seem very confident. I'm surprised that you need me or my small art. What made you look for aikido?"

"I had nothing to do with it. My employer's a completist. He wants me to know everything, so he brought you here."

Moroshiba nodded. "Then show me what you know."

For the next half-hour, Jackson went through kata after kata, performing moves from all the various disciplines he knew. His thunderous *kiai* brought dust from the ceiling, his massive hands and feet flashed out with powerful thrusts and cuts, the cloth of his dogi snapped with each kick or punch. Through it all, Moroshiba watched, impassive, sitting motionless in *seiza*. Finally, Moroshiba clapped his hands sharply, and Jackson came to a stop, sweat pouring from his body, his breath still regular and deep. He matched Moroshiba's examining stare. Moroshiba looked away first.

"You know much," the little man said. "You are very good."

Jackson nodded. "I'm not worried about defending myself, or about taking anyone else out."

"Bring my bag to me," the sensei told Jackson. "Then sit here." He patted the mat in front of him. Jackson did as Moroshiba asked, and watched as Moroshiba pulled a pipe and a pouch of tobacco from the bag. "A filthy habit," the sensei told Jackson. "One which a student should not emulate. That is the first lesson—no matter who your teacher is, there are parts of him which are not you. No master is perfect." Moroshiba began packing tobacco into the pipe, talking all the time.

"You know much," he said again, his fingers tamping tobacco down and reaching for more of the fragrant herb. "You have a great physical gift. Your body knows by itself what way to move, how to retain balance, how to get the greatest force behind a blow. You would stand before an opponent utterly unafraid, ready to let him break himself against you." His fingers dipped into the pouch again. Jackson watched, puzzled, for the bowl of the pipe was packed full. But Moroshiba, his eyes not on the pipe but on Jackson, continued to try to place more tobacco in it. Strands fell into his lap, onto the tatami. "You're aware of how strong you are, of how much you know. Your teachers have shown you all the correct moves to make."

Again Moroshiba dipped into the pouch. More tobacco spilled. Finally, Jackson shook his head. "Sensei, the pipe—it's full. You can't get any more in the bowl."

Moroshiba gave Jackson the slightest smile. "So it is with *you*, Jackson. You did not seek me out. For you, your head is full enough. You've no more room for anything else, and if I tried to put it into your head, it would just fall out, like my tobacco. You must first learn to approach your life with an empty bowl. Be receptive to new knowledge."

"You teach Zen riddles, then."

Moroshiba gazed at him sidewise. Then the little man placed his pipe carefully on the edge of the mat and rose, his joints creaking. He motioned for Jackson to stand; he towered over the sensei. "Hit me," Moroshiba said.

"Sensei?"

"Do it!" Moroshiba barked suddenly, and the command in his voice was so compelling that Jackson obeyed, his right hand moving like a lightning strike toward Moroshiba's face.

Jackson wasn't quite sure how it happened. He should have felt his fist strike the man, should have heard the snap of the nose being broken and seen blood. But he struck only air, and then suddenly he was being flipped, landing awkwardly on his back. Jackson grunted, and got to his feet quickly, his defenses now up. Moroshiba was standing a few feet away, smiling at him. "You're angry," he told Jackson. "Good. I want you angry so that your attacks are real and not feigned. Strike at me again," he said. "Now!"

With a shout, Jackson rushed the little man, intending to grab him. But Moroshiba simply wasn't there. Jackson felt hands on his shoulders, impossibly heavy, and then his legs flipped out from under him with the momentum of his attack and he was on his back on the mat again. He got to his feet in a second, and this time tried a side kick to the ribs. Moroshiba pivoted, moving inside the circle of the kick gracefully and pushing up and out—once more, Jackson went flying. A red haze was before his eyes now. He wanted nothing more than to land a kick or punch, to grapple the sensei and drag him down on the mat. Moroshiba seemed to grin mockingly. Jackson roared and charged.

And slammed into the mat once more. Again and again. Moroshiba was never *there*. He would be on Jackson's side, suddenly, or even behind. There would be a quick grab, a turn of the hips and Jackson would be airborne once more. It lasted for what seemed to be hours but was probably only fifteen minutes or so. At the end, Jackson was bruised and out of breath. His body ached in a hundred places, and his left shoulder throbbed from hyperextended tendons. Moroshiba seemed to have barely broken a sweat. His breathing was even and calm. He smiled serenely as Jackson dropped to his knees and bowed deeply to him. "Sensei," he said. "Would you teach me?"

Suddenly Moroshiba looked very serious. "Aikido is the way of harmonious energy," Moroshiba told him. "One blends with the energy of the attacker and becomes a part of him for a moment. In that moment, the energy is redirected and reenforced. What happens is that the attacker hurts only himself with his aggressiveness. That is what happened to you. You hurt only yourself with your anger."

"I understand that, sensei. I still want to learn."

The sternness etched lines on the sensei's face. "Your former teachers—they taught you only what to do with your body. I can't do that and still teach you aikido. I can't teach you the art without also teaching you the mind that you must have to go with it. It is not the mind that I see in you now. It is not the mind that I saw in your Mr. Charles, and I think that he would disapprove of it if he knew. He knows nothing of aikido beyond that it is a martial art and he wishes you to know the martial arts. Aikido is *harmony*. Aikido strives to bring conflicting elements together."

"I would still study with you."

Moroshiba sighed. He looked around the dojo and out the windows to the estate. "All right," he said. "I will stay until I'm asked to leave." He went back to the edge of the mat and sat *seiza* once more. "The first thing you must do is learn how to move. Let me see you walk across the mat."

"Sensei?" Jackson asked questioningly.

"Empty your bowl of knowledge, student. You must begin from the beginning—there's no other place to start. Now, walk."

CHAPTER 13

Captain Huff's decision wasn't surprising given the gung ho attitude of the Legion. The Legion was used to attacking problems head on. To do differently would have been a radical departure. It's safe to say that no one felt particularly surprised when Huff asked for volunteers for a commando raid on the Iona war machine. She stood in front of the ship's complement in the shuttle bay, looking out over the mercenaries from a small platform.

"I've run the scenario through *Musashi*'s tactical program three times. Given the speed and maneuverability of the shuttle, she thinks she can get you on-surface without a loss."

"Ninety percent probability," chimed *Musashi* herself.

"You mean it's ten percent we get fried before we even get there," Marty called out from the crowd around the dais. He stood next to Zeke in the middle of the human Legionnaires. As usual, Sylvie's holocams flitted over the bay near the ceiling girders.

"In the best scenario," the ship added. She imitated Marty's sarcastic tones. "Don't be *too* optimistic."

Huff ignored the interplay. "The Iona ship, from our examination of it, seems to have most of its offensive capabilities directed toward ship-to-ship combat," she continued. "There are smaller laser installations on the surface around the entrance ports and Reelys informs me that the war machines that attacked the shri also had some offensive surface vehicles. I'll need two groups. The smaller unit will attack the Iona machine itself, trying to see if you can disable it or at least get us more information about its capabilities and weaknesses. You'll be in the most danger, of course. But at the same time, you'll be providing a diversion for the second group, which will be going to the BEC station to pick up any survivors there. Hopefully, if the first unit can keep the Iona at least partially occupied with fending off their attack, the second unit's task will be that much easier."

Huff, from her dais in the central meeting area of the ship, looked out over the Legionnaires. "All right, then. I need volunteers for the first unit." Various appendages rose in the air. Huff pointed to them. "Kagak!xa—good. We'll need an expert in explosives. Please, would you choose ten !xaka! from the volunteers to join you. Marty—you too, short stuff? You're thinking you'll be too little for 'em to hit, huh?" As rough laughter filled the room, she peered toward the human contingent. "Zeke? We'll need luck, won't we? I want you to command the unit, with Kagak!xa directly under you. Pick another dozen from the human volunteers to join you. Okay. The second unit, then . . ."

It went that quickly. It may not have been a good plan, but it was typical Legion strategy—when in doubt, charge. When that doesn't work, try it with twice as many people. The only thing that Zeke fought—unsuccessfully—was Huff's permission to allow Sylvie to accompany them. His protest netted only a shrug from Huff. "She signed the release. It's her life," was all the captain would say.

"Stay by me, then," Zeke told Sylvie.

She looked at him oddly. "There's worse things I could do, I suppose."

An hour later, the twenty-five members of the commando group met in the bay once more and boarded one of the armored shuttles. The Legionnaires were strapped tightly into high-gee acceleration couches. "Good luck," the ship told them via the com-link, and then the shuttle hurtled from the bay. They were shoved back against the padded seats of the couches, as if an incredible weight had been set on their chests that was slowly pressing the life from them. They could barely breathe as the shuttle canted first one way and then the other, all at incredible speeds. The momentary gee forces flirted with the safety tolerances of the couches.

It was one of the feats of daring which the Legion touted (in their recruiting brochures) as routine. The shuttle dove headfirst into an offensive barrage from the Iona war machine. Small, highly maneuverable, and extremely fast, it depended on those features more than armoring to protect its cargo. Armor and shields would only have slowed it down and drained the energy that fed the overlarge drive system, and they would not have helped in any event. The massive pulse lasers that shot out at the craft would have sliced through the best shielding like a hot knife through butter; the sandcasters that threw particles in their projected path would have ripped the shuttle open and spilled out the broken bodies of those inside. No—better to trust to stealth, to clench your teeth and ride the monster down, like some harrowing roller coaster in death's amusement park.

No pilot—human, !xaka!, or otherwise—could have handled the shuttle. The gee forces were simply too massive. Hands would have been wrenched off controls, blood would have pooled in the brain and blacked them out, and no race's reflexes would have been fast enough for the war machine's multipronged attack. No—*Musashi* herself directed the ship, using the nanosecond responses of her gigantic artificial intelligence. Initially, *Musashi* relied on the shuttle's great speed plus electronic counter-measures to render the little craft "invisible"—coated with a molecule-thick silicon coating and shaped so as to present no flat surfaces, the shuttle was nearly invisible to normal detection devices such as radar, scattering the beam to send back almost no echo. For the first minute or so of approach, it was more a blindingly fast chess game between *Musashi* and the lona machine, as measures, counter-measures, and counter-counter-measures were exchanged in an effort to foil the lona machine's defenses. The endgame was a brilliant display to those who watched from *Musashi*'s screens. The war machine's laser stitched the sky; bright explosions left fading afterimages as the little shuttle dodged and weaved.

And somehow she made it. The landing wasn't pretty, kicking up a long plume of dust as the shuttle nearly canted and overturned. She ground to a halt, battered and scorched, but intact. The doors opened as the couch webbing fell open. Zeke leaped to his feet, shouting into the communicator of his battle helmet. "Move it! Go, go, go!"

They spilled out onto the pitted crystalline surface of the war machine.

The machine realized that it was under intimate attack. The Legionnaires' plan had been to make for the nearest port into the machine, make a foray into the interior and then return to the shuttle. The !xaka!, at Zeke's hand motion to Kagak!xa, immediately loosed a barrage from their hand launchers toward the nearest laser turrets. Had there been air, it would have been deafening—Zeke could feel the shock waves trembling the "ground" under his feet. The rest of the unit had readied the portable shield generators and thrown up a defensive screen.

None too soon—the screens began sparking and shrieking almost immediately as the war machine directed intense laser fire on the group. They returned fire, trying to take out as many of the lasers as they could, ready to make the dash for the opening into the machine, several meters away.

They waited for Zeke to give them the command. Sylvie's holocams were focused tightly on him, expectant. But Zeke did nothing. "Zeke?" Marty's voice came over the intercom.

He paid no attention. He listened instead to an inner voice.

After the initial burst of recognition on seeing the war machine, the star seed had remained strangely, disquietingly silent. Zeke had been bothered by that—after all, listening to the seed had been one reason Zeke had survived his years in the Legion, and now it seemed that the seed had gone dead on him. There had been nothing from it, not after he had talked with Reelys, not during the preparations or the hectic flight down. Only now it had come back to life. It thrummed in his mind, wordlessly, imperiously. Zeke reached into the high pouch of the tight battle-armor and pulled out the seed. It glowed strongly against the steel-woven cloth of his glove, a pulsing orange flare. Unexpectedly, high-frequency vibrations burst from it—all around him, Legionnaires clapped hands helplessly to their helmets as the shrill wailing screamed over the full communications band; !xaka! moaned and rumbled.

Sylvie was the first to notice. "The shields! Look, the machine's stopped firing on us."

It was true—the shields no longer flared. They shimmered, nearly invisible and undisturbed.

•Comfort/Peace• The feeling came strongly to Zeke through the crystal. •Aggression/End•

"Back to the shuttle," Zeke ordered, still holding out the glowing crystal in his palm. His companions stared at him strangely, as if he were some ghost, an apparition. He could hear whispered comments.

Kagak!xa reared up on her back segments, gesturing toward the now-undefended opening into the war machine. "No!" she clicked. "Forward and attack!" The !xaka! started to move past the shields, but Zeke laid down a blistering line of laser fire at the ground before them.

"That's an order," Zeke said more strongly. He gestured with the laser. "I'm the commander here. Go back to the shuttle and strap in."

Reluctantly, they obeyed, backing away with their weapons

till out and ready. The war machine's turrets tracked their retreat but remained still. Zeke waited until most of them were in the craft before he too moved away. Sylvie was waiting by the hatchway. "Go on," she said. "I want to get a shot as you enter—you know, the last commando to leave."

"Get inside," he told her harshly, gesturing. "Get inside or I'll leave you here."

Sylvie sighed audibly, but she obeyed. As she passed Zeke, she thought she saw him cant his head to the side, as if he were listening to some ghostly voice that only he could hear. The impression lasted only a moment, then Zeke clambered aboard the shuttle and strapped himself into the webbing of his couch. "*Musashi*, get us out of here," he said. "Quickly."

"Ready for evasive tactics," she told him.

"Cancel that," Zeke told the ship. "Just take us back to the ship. Directly."

Huff's voice came on at that. "Zeke, what's going on?"

"Trust me," he said. "Get us out of here now. *Musashi*?"

"Initiating," the ship answered.

The shuttle growled with the sound of her engines, and then they were slammed back against the seats once more. As the shuttle streaked away from the lona war machine, the huge structure remained silent and motionless. Then, as the shuttle made its approach to *Musashi*'s bay, the lona machine's immense antimatter engines flared into life.

The huge vessel rotated with an improbable grace, accelerating as it moved away from the *Musashi*, away from the BEC mining station and Luyten 726–B.

"You'd damn well better explain yourself, Zeke. What the hell happened out there? What was that in your hand?"

Captain Huff met them in the shuttle bay as the commando unit emerged from their craft. She confronted Zeke, hands on hips, as the others filed past, muttering to themselves.

"What's the problem, Captain?" Zeke asked. His own stance matched hers, and his light eyes were challenging.

"You know damn well what the problem is. I want to know what happened."

"What happened is that the lona war machine has left. You can send a shuttle over to the mining station and pick up the survivors. We're done here."

"*I'm* not done. Not until I know what went on. I'll ask you again. What did you have in your hand?"

"My luck, Captain," Zeke answered shortly. "That's all."

"It's not enough."

"It has to be."

"You're under my command, mister."

Zeke shook his head. "Not any more, Captain. As of this moment, I resign. That's within my rights as a Legionnaire. I resign. I'll leave the ship at the next transfer."

"Don't be stupid, Zeke," Huff said, not unkindly. "I'm not asking for the world. Just tell me what happened."

"I can't, Captain. I'm sorry. Do you remember once, long ago, telling me that it was no good to keep beating your head against a wall. Well, that's what I've been doing in the Legion, beating my head against a wall I couldn't even see, doing things I didn't really enjoy doing because I thought that was the way it had to be. I thought that once a mistake had been made, there was nothing to do but hide it, get rid of it. I was wrong. There's always more paths to take than the one you see. The Legion doesn't know that. You might understand, but the commanders wouldn't."

"And if that's not good enough, Captain, you'll take my advice as well," said an airy voice. Huff turned to find Reelys hovering behind her. The shri mantle had changed, his'er patterns now more oval than splotchy, more red than purple. "I'm giving you my resignation at the same time, Captain, and taking up my former responsibilities as a member of the Galactic Council. I take back my true name—Ahnast Jhiila. You don't want to go against the wishes of a Council member, Captain. Your commanders will tell you that if you don't know it already. If you doubt my credentials, please contact the Council offices at the next transfer station."

Huff looked from Reelys to Zeke. She turned on the balls of her feet and strode angrily away.

Jackson didn't actually meet Peter Chrysanthi for several months, when he learned that Bart had decided to throw a party at the South American estate. An invitation from one of the largest stockholders in BEC and one of the wealthier men in the United Worlds was enough to attract most of the influential people in human affairs as well as many of the other races as well. Among the many guests who arrived by hoverflitter that evening was the shri ambassador to Earth and his'er staff, who arrived like a flotilla of gorgeous zeppelins, their mantles glit-

tering with a hundred hues and shades. The !xaka!ian ambassador did not attend in person (as the ambassador did not consider
Bart Charles to be a social equal) but he did send his immediate
assistant, who gleamed with interlaced strands of metallic chain
and pendants. Jackson wondered how the creature managed to
walk under the weight of his ornamentation.

Human, shri, !xaka!, hlidskji, and a few of the minor sentient races who were part of the United Worlds—all of them
were represented. The party filled the house and spilled out into
the gardens surrounding it, where brilliant, particolored follow-
lamps bobbed through the trees, tracing the slow magnetic paths
of their holders. It was a feast of the senses: the servants passed
through the milling crowds carrying trays full of the delicacies
of half a hundred worlds: spinefish from Griynsh, blackfeathers
from Thule, bladderworts from the depths of the Compule Sea
on Nicari.

"This is beyond me, Jackson." Moroshiba had emerged from
the crowd to stand next to his student. Moroshiba was dressed
in traditional garb, a wide-sleeved, lined *awasa* in which his
tiny frame seemed lost.

"Perhaps the pupil can teach the teacher, then," Jackson replied, smiling. "I've had enough tutoring in social mores to
spout off any rule of etiquette you need." He plucked a bladderwort from a tray balanced on the trunk of a servo shaped like a
small elephant. The delicacy looked like kelp crossed with can-
taloupe. "Now, the bladderwort's only edible part is the juice
inside the flotation pods. The meat and rind might taste fine to a
hlidskji, but for humans it's like chewing on parboiled rubber.
But it wouldn't do to let on—after all, some hlidskji diplomat
might be watching. So . . ." Jackson lifted the pod to his mouth,
bit sharply once and let the juice drain into his mouth. He
smiled in delight. "We show our gratitude, and then we continue talking. I place the bladderwort down as if I needed my
hands to adjust my tie—" He did so, played with the knot of his
tie, and then spread his hands wide. "And I can simply pretend
that I've forgotten about the bladderwort in the meantime—one
of the servos will pick it up later. As long as I'm not seen
making a face or throwing it away, no one's feelings are hurt.
You see, it's very simple."

"You play games." Moroshiba's face was neutral. Jackson
couldn't tell whether the sensei found the notion pleasing or
not.

Jackson smiled anyway. After all, this was *his* element. This was what he'd trained for. "I would think that it's good not to hurt someone else's feelings."

"That would depend on the reason for doing so."

"Never offend someone who can hurt you."

Moroshiba nodded. "Ahh," he said. "Then you are polite only if it bestows power."

Jackson glanced at the little man, who stared blandly back. Moroshiba's barbed, flat comments rankled him, and he wanted nothing more than to be somewhere else. He glanced over the heads of those nearest him and caught the eye of one of Charles's associates. Jackson waved. "Excuse me," he said to Moroshiba. "One of the obligations of the host."

"Don't worry," Moroshiba answered, bowing slightly. "You haven't offended me yet."

Away from Moroshiba, Jackson did his best to enjoy the party. At one point, he was in a room with Peter Chrysanthi, who stood in the middle of a circle of admirers. He noticed that Chrysanthi looked his way once and then bent close to one of the men around him. The man looked back to Jackson and then whispered in Peter's ear. Chrysanthi nodded. Jackson loitered nearby for a few minutes, thinking that perhaps Chrysanthi would break away from his conversation or perhaps invite Jackson to join him, but nothing of the sort occurred.

In fact, that was much the way everyone seemed to treat him. They would talk to him politely but coldly if he initiated a conversation, but for the most part the only people who seemed genuinely interested in cultivating Jackson's acquaintance were those clearly inferior to him in social status. For Chrysanthi, for the diplomats and the upper social strata of human society, Jackson was merely another one of Charles's employees, here on sufferance. He would be treated kindly so as not to offend his master, like some type of exotic pet, but he was not an equal.

It was a subtle attitude, one he didn't actually recognize for many hours. Once noticed, it began to wear thin quickly. He knew that Charles's plan would never work. Jackson could not be the bait for Peter Chrysanthi. Chrysanthi would never have anything to do with an underling.

At midnight some invisible osmosis brought most of the guests together in the main drawing room. Charles was there, and he clapped his hands for attention. "Please, everybody. I have an announcement of some importance to make. Please, gather around." Jackson, watching from the edges of the crowd, started to slip away, thinking that he would perhaps seek out Moroshiba once again. Maybe he could cajole the old man into some late-night practice—it would feel good to sweat out his anger. But Bart Charles caught his eye and motioned him forward. "Jackson, please come stand next to me.

"As you know," Charles said when he had everyone's attention, "I lost my son many years ago in a transport accident. Since then, I've often wished that I had other children, that there was someone to carry on the name and traditions of the Charles family. I thought I'd never find such a person. But I'm happy to say that all that has changed in the last three years." With the words, Charles placed an arm around Jackson's broad shoulders, drawing the young black man closer to him. Jackson looked over to the older man, who smiled broadly back at him.

"Three years. When I first met Jackson Franks, I thought that he would make a good personal assistant. My intention was that he would fulfill that function. But over the years, he's come to mean far more to me. I've come to look upon him as a friend, as a confidant, as someone who shares my hopes and aspirations."

Bart Charles looked out on the crowd who now buzzed with speculation. "I suppose most of you have guessed what I'm about to say. Jackson"—Charles held the young man out at arm's length—"I would be proud if you would be the son I thought I would never again have. I have the papers of legal adoption drawn up. All you have to do is say yes, and you'll be Jackson Franks Charles. My son."

Jackson gaped, utterly stunned. Charles had caught him completely off guard. Yes, he'd felt that Charles had some genuine liking for him, but he would never have thought . . . For a moment, the party went dim around him, and Jackson remembered his own family, the warmth and affection he'd had from his mother and father. Maybe he could have that again. Maybe he could feel that closeness and protection.

And then he realized why. He knew why this was being offered him, despite the questioning smile on Charles's face, despite the protestations of love and affection. This would give him the social status he needed to get close to Chrysanthi. It would give him clout. In payment, he would become a Charles. It made sense—after all, Bart Charles had no one to give his wealth to after he was gone. It didn't matter. Jackson might as well have it as anyone else.

It all made sense. Jackson took a breath—he noticed Moro-shiba watching from the doorway, his face stoic. Somehow the disapproval Jackson thought he saw there decided him, strengthened his resolve. He tried to match Bart's smile. "You honor me," he said. Then: "Father."

The crowd broke out into applause and congratulations. He was hugged by Charles, by others. The faces that had looked away from him all evening now suddenly wanted nothing more than to talk to him. They swam by in a blur.

A hand was extended to him. Jackson took it. "Congratula-tions," a deep, resonant voice said. "I'm Peter Chrysanthi."

CHAPTER 14

Coming upon Griynsh was like entering the land of faerie. Seeing the homeworld of the shri made Zeke understand how it was that humans responded so well to the race that had molded the United Worlds. Everything about the shri seemed designed to produce a resonant yearning in the breast of man. The shri floated like diaphanous beings through a landscape of cloud and light, their mantles rippling with glowing colors. Their language was like an intricate ballet, the delicate hand-tendrils swaying and interweaving; when they spoke with words, their voices were quiet whispers, breathy and feminine, almost seductive. And just so that they were not *too* perfect, their short lifespan of forty to forty-five years made them sympathetic to the longer-lived humans.

The shri, developing in the skies of their otherwise hostile world and equipped with the fluid lens in their mantle that provided them with the equivalent of a built-in telescope, had had their minds on the stars and the universe from the beginning. As a consequence, they were as a race inclined to a certain mysticism. The humans who first contacted them found the shri to be contemplative and intelligent. Inept at anything approaching physical combat, they had created a peaceful society with a Byzantine complexity of levels, a bureaucracy that, while benevolent, surpassed anything mankind had imagined in the way of government.

And their architecture, their technologies . . . The shri spacecraft looked like immense sailing ships wafting along the solar winds, the molecule-thin sails spread out over hundreds of kilometers, connected to the plastic, colorful body by thin lines. The shri cities were floating castles, like things glimpsed in dreams or depicted in fantasy. Constructed of plastic polymers, rising in turreted spires and drifting serenely among the clouds as the sun bathed them in light from a deep azure sky, they were awe-inspiring. At night, the brilliant, multicolored stars of the galactic core were dusted across the heavens, reflected in the glossy flanks of the buildings.

As one of the first human visitors to Griynsh is reputed to have said: "The universe insists on balance. In a reality that has made the !xaka! as ugly as something could possibly be, there also had to be the shri."

Zeke found himself just as impressed. The Galactic Museum was mind boggling. It seemed to be as large as a small city, with entire sections devoted to pottery periods or extinct species. Spidery walkways spanned vast areas of open space, leading to doorways set in the midst of clifflike, blindingly white walls. There the ground dwellers walked (and woe betide someone with a fear of heights)—the shri floated majestically through the canyons. In truth, considering the ambitious scope of the museum, the immense structure was actually tiny, for the museum devoted each of the interconnected buildings to one of the United Worlds.

When Zeke could finally speak and relay his awe at the size of the museum, Reelys responded, "A world is an awfully large place. There're inevitably entire cultures that have been missed, vast spans of time that are poorly represented or even ignored. We keep working toward completeness, but it's a vain goal, one that gets further away with each passing year."

"My mother would have loved it," Zeke answered. "She always wanted to come here and study. She never had the chance." With that thought, Zeke remembered the secret gallery his father had constructed. It seemed like such a mean and shabby place in comparison.

The star seeds occupied their own exhibit. Zeke had first realized the extent of Reelys's pull in the shri government when, at the transfer station where they left *Musashi* (along with Sylvie Pharr), s/he contacted Griynsh and ordered the exhibit closed. Now Reelys waved a casual tentacle at the guards around the sealed door and glided through. A tentacle pointed to a case set on a raised platform. "There," s/he said.

Zeke went to the case. Three stars seeds sat there, all slightly different in size and hue, but undeniably kin to the crystal he had carried for so long. At his approach, all three began to glow dimly. "Good, Zeke," Reelys said. "They respond to you. Can you hear them?"

"No," Zeke admitted. "Not like mine."

"Yours?" Reelys chided gently.

Zeke smiled at the shri. "I stand corrected."

"Can you hear the one you carry?"

Zeke listened, shook his head. "No, not since Luyten." That information seemed to excite Reelys. His'er mantle fringe wriggled. Zeke reached out to touch the case, let his finger drift along the edge—he wanted to touch the crystals, to take the star seeds in his hands. "I don't know what to do, Reelys," he said. "You said these sometimes emit sound? The one I carry has never done that. Heat and light, yes, but nothing audible."

Reelys drifted over to the wall, where an explanation of the display was mounted. A tentacle reached out to press a contact there. "Listen," s/he said. "This is a sample."

The sound was a discordant symphony played on quavering chimes, rising and falling with no rhythm and no melody that Zeke could decipher. A holocube display above the case showed the scene as the sounds had been recorded, the crystals glowing and fading as the bursts of sound came from them. "There doesn't seem to be a pattern to it," Zeke commented.

"We've subjected the recordings of the crystals to every kind of test we could think of. Sometimes, I thought I caught a glimmer of a pattern, started to make sense of a little scrap of it, but it always fell apart again. We've raised and lowered the pitches, tried to correlate light and sound patterns, let the computers try to tear it apart and make sense of it. I'm convinced it's a code, Zeke. Several of my pod-mates and I came to the conclusion that we couldn't decipher it because some crucial part was missing from the puzzle. That's why I was on *Musashi*, why others like me are scattered throughout the United Worlds. We were certain that one day one or more additional star seeds would be found."

Zeke listened to the cacophonous song of the seeds. "What do we do now?"

"You said that yours never made audible sounds. Neither did these, until one day they were placed in a room together. We still don't know what triggers them to emit sound, but they *only* do so when together. Usually just one of them sings. Sometimes two. Rarely, all three—the recording is one of those times."

"Crystal does resonate. We've used that property for years in electronic devices—to regulate pitch, frequency, and time. Maybe it's accidental, Reelys." Zeke paused, listening to the alien "music," watching the holocube. "No," he said thoughtfully. "You've noticed that each one has a distinct timbre, even when they're giving out the same pitch? Like different instruments playing the same note . . ."

"Yes," Reelys answered. "That's what makes me think this is deliberate. That's why I think they're parts of a whole." Reelys hissed, moving forward to brush against the case. At his'er touch, the solid front dissolved. "Zeke, put your crystal with the others. Let's see if they make a complete unit."

Zeke came forward slowly, taking the star seed from the pouch it had occupied for so long. He looked at the crystal tenderly—his luck, yes: the reason he'd taken the path he had. The seed was a link with his past, with a father and home that seemed more distant with each passing year. The crystal was utterly cold to his touch, silent. Gingerly, Zeke set it alongside the others, his fingertips brushing each of them in turn. He sighed, straightening and backing away a step.

"Say hello to your friends," he said.

It was as if he'd spoken an incantation. All four of the crystals erupted into bright sound and brilliant light. Zeke threw his hands before his face to protect his eyes from the shifting, diamondlike glare of the star seeds. Reelys drew his'er tentacles up into the mantle reflexively, uttering a shrill whistle. The star seeds pulsed randomly at first. Then they synchronized, the hues and shades pulsing and fading in intricate counterpoint to a music that suddenly had a cadence. The chords formed by that high-pitched series of frequencies were strange and dissonant, the pitches too close together to sound harmonious to human ears, but distinct nonetheless. There was a definite pattern to it: several dissonant chords, then one pulsing, screaming unison note. Another random series of chords, another unison. There seemed to be five series of chords before the cycle began to repeat. "Reelys!" Zeke shouted into the clamor. "We've got to record this!"

"We've been doing that since we entered," Reelys answered. His'er mantle had expanded once again, the lens within focused on the case and the dancing light of the seeds.

The star seeds continued to reproduce that five-cycle pattern until Zeke and Reelys finally left the room. As soon as the door had closed behind them, the recording instruments showed that the crystal lapsed into silence and dullness. Zeke shook his head to the gathering flock of shri around the entrance of the exhibit —from the mantle patterns, most were museum staff. "*That* was incredible," he said reverently.

"And a pattern finally," Reelys said excitedly. "It seems

more and more like a code. There's hope of making sense of it."

But that hope died. Despite the best efforts of Reelys and his'er pod-mates that gathered over the next several days, no sense was made of the emissions. They listened to the tapes over and over, watched the flare of light and sound, heard over and over that insistent five-figure display.

Late one night, Zeke found himself tired of endless repetitions of the tapes. He withdrew from Reelys and his'er fellow researchers and sought out one of the terraces of the museum. The core stars were nearly as bright as moonlight, casting a distinct shadow behind him—Zeke stared at them as if they held the answer. The cold wind of Griynsh's night sky made him shiver; he pulled his coat tighter about him. He didn't know how long he stayed there before light from the room washed over him for a second, blotting out starshadow. He heard the hushing exhalation of shri motion.

"Hello, Reelys."

"Hello, Ezekiel. You seem tired," Reelys said.

"I am tired. The food tonight didn't seem to do anything but burn in my stomach, and I can't sleep—I think the sickness is coming back again."

"I'll have some of our medical experts check you. Ezekiel, I wonder . . . we know that the star seeds emit light and heat and some small amounts of radiation. You carried the seed with you for years. I wonder if perhaps it isn't the source of your cyclical illness."

Zeke knotted his hand on the railing, his face still upturned to the display of distant suns. "Somehow, that doesn't bother me at all, Reelys. My family stole it; *I* stole it. If I've picked up some virus from it, then it only seems just punishment. I deserve worse for keeping it hidden so long—I'm no better than my father in that." Zeke looked down into swirling, starlit cloud. A flotilla of shri passed by several meters below, majestic and graceful. "They're speaking a language, Reelys. I know they are."

"I agree with you," Reelys said. "But we're missing the key. We need to know what they're saying before we can translate it."

"They haven't responded to anything since?"

Behind him, Zeke heard tentacles rustling. "No. They've been silent. Tell me, Zeke, did the seed you held speak to you in words? Human words?"

"No," Zeke answered. "It was more emotions, feelings. I provided the translation."

"But there was definitely an intent to communicate?"

Zeke nodded. "Definitely. In fact, I wonder if all along I wasn't a sort of puppet to the seed, something it was using to try to find its way to the other seeds. Which tells me that communication's the intent of the star seeds as a whole. They're meant to say something to us. But what good's a message you can't read?" Zeke sighed. "Look out there, Reelys. There must be a billion suns out there in my sight right now, with maybe thousands of races that we don't know, that we've yet to meet. What would we say to them if we met?"

Even as he posed that question, Zeke's forehead suddenly furrowed in thought. His knuckles were white, clutching the railing. "We've been so stupid," he said.

He turned to Reelys. "Do you remember when I put the seeds together in the case, Reelys? What did I say? What were the words I used?"

Reelys mantle fluttered in agitation. "I don't remember," s/he said.

"I said 'Say hello to your friends.' *Hello*, Reelys. What is it that I said to you just now—what do any two beings do when they encounter each other? They give greetings. I wonder..." Zeke was suddenly seized with excitement. "C'mon, Reelys. I think we might have found our key."

Back in the seed's display room, Zeke flipped on the sound system and let the five-interval pattern blare out. "One seed was found on a shri world, another by a !xaka!, the third by hlidskji. The fourth talked to me—a human. And we have five distinct patterns being repeated over and over. You're right, Reelys: the seeds are a code machine. Listen!" Zeke set the playback mechanism so that it repeated one of the patterns. "There, this one has four notes. The unison chords are to separate the different languages. What if that's *Hello*, Reelys? And one of the other figures is a basic shri greeting, and the other three !xaka!, hlidskji, and lona."

Reelys's mantle had gone visibly darker, the red hues deepening to a dark scarlet. "If that's right, Zeke, then the star seeds could be a type of Rosetta Stone." Reelys's mantle shrunk, expanded; tentacles literally danced underneath. "Let's try something," s/he said. "I'll start the analysis program with your assumption in mind. Zeke, you're the electronics man. Follow me." With that, the shri abruptly fled the room.

It was several hours before they returned. Zeke carried a cumbersome box that he placed on the floor. A servo link sat on his shoulder like a tame cricket. "Activate," he said, and the box hummed to life. Zeke glanced at Reelys—the shri fluttered restlessly. "Try it," s/he said. "You're the one with the closest link to the seeds. Give your greetings, Zeke."

Zeke took a deep breath. "Hello," he said loudly. With the word, a sequence of dissonant chords emerged from the box— the word not translated, but changed into lona notation. "Hello," Zeke said again.

And the star seeds burst into a long display of sound and light! This "song" was far longer and more complex than the first, Zeke laughed with hearing it, turning to Reelys with a whoop. The shri had flattened his'er mantle out, as if to catch some of the brilliance of the seeds. "That's it, Zeke. With a long enough sequence, the computer should be able to get a full translation. You were right—all we had to do was initiate contact. Say hello."

Within an hour, the results had come back. The lona message was repeated in all five languages: **•The Resonant One speaks to all in friendship. Speak friendship in return if you share that friendship•** With the message were coordinates corresponding to a lona world.

"It's so obvious in retrospect," Zeke said. "Without faster than light travel, the lona sent out the stones at long intervals, timed to arrive nearly simultaneously throughout the United Worlds. But the miners on Luyten 726–B accidentally disabled the lona ship carrying the human star seed. Without the fourth seed, the other three couldn't synchronize the message. We know now that the message demanded a reply. Having received none, the lona assumed we were enemies rather than friends and sent out the war machines. The shri empire is closest to the lona; you even share worlds—therefore you were attacked first."

"But we can send that message now," Reelys said. "We can finally tell them that we are friends."

Reelys's optimism didn't cheer Zeke. He looked at the shri with a face drawn thin with exhaustion and sadness. "I wonder how many people I killed because of my selfishness, Reelys? How many of your people perished in the lona attacks because my father stole the star seed and kept it secret; how many more have been lost in the years that I kept it? I have those lives weighing on my soul, Reelys. I don't know if I can ever make up for that."

"I understand your guilt," Reelys answered. "I can't do anything to lessen it—what you say is true, after all. But at least you have remorse, Ezekiel, and a desire to make what amends you can. What are you going to do?"

"I'm going to make use of what resources I have," Zeke answered after a moment. "BEC and my father began this. The Bones family and BEC will make amends as well. I'm going back to Earth, Reelys. It's time my father and I began to make amends."

CHAPTER **15**

It was almost comically easy to lure Peter Chrysanthi into a bet once the initial contact was made. In the days after the party, Jackson became a companion on several of Peter's expeditions. In Monte Carlo, he watched as Peter ignored the casinos to engage in games of chance he felt involved more "skill"—horse racing, boxing, sports events. As Peter explained to Jackson: "No one can predict the roll of dice or the turn of a card. No one can entirely predict the ways of flesh, either, but the variables are fewer and more controlled. You can look at a horse and see how he's feeling that day; you can check his record and find that he only runs well on a dry, fast track and know not to bet on him when it's rained the night before. You can talk to the jockeys and find that he was sick the day before or that he always runs best from the outside. Cards and dice don't feel. They don't emanate anything. I can *feel* flesh, Jackson. That's the kick. Feeling the flesh and knowing that you saw what would happen."

Jackson saw the kinds of kicks Chrysanthi derived from his contests. He saw the tight smile that Peter didn't bother to hide when a horse went down in Louisville, trampling its rider underneath. He watched Peter applaud when a kickboxer from Taiwan snapped a high kick to his opponent's head and everyone at ringside heard the distinct crack of the man's spine. He saw Peter's eyes close in near-pleasure when a blow from an Irish brawler broke the nose of the challenger and splattered blood over them as they sat in the front ranks of the crowd.

He also saw that Chrysanthi, despite his lectures on "skill" and "research," also cheated if he could. He bribed the jockeys, he'd talk to key players in a game and see if they might be willing to be "sick" for certain considerations. He would find out who was a user and threaten to reveal the drug habit.

When he couldn't trim the odds, he'd still gamble, and he

made bets that were less than smart. If anything, he lost as often as he won. When that happened, Chrysanthi would fly into blind rages. After a favored horse on which Chrysanthi had bet heavily was disqualified for bumping, Chrysanthi went to the owner and bought the horse. He then walked out to the stable and personally broke the gelding's legs.

Chrysanthi gambled for power. His sadism was a part of that lust. Jackson could see how Chrysanthi had managed to lose his fortune for a bet, and how he would be willing to keep it.

Chrysanthi probed Jackson's past as well; Bart Charles had told him to hide nothing. When Peter learned of the deathpits and how Jackson had lost his eye, there was in Peter's face something akin to lust. It appalled Jackson, seeing that raw need exposed there.

Bart Charles had let it be known that Jackson was involved in martial arts training. Peter had watched a workout with Jackson and Moroshiba and hadn't seemed overly impressed with the sensei, who had decided to give Jackson a basic, slow class that day. "That's what you do, huh?" he asked after the session. "Doesn't seem like much—stretching and rolling. I know several fighters who I think would be able to beat that kind of thing." Jackson could hear the speculation in Peter's voice, could see him eyeing Jackson's body as he toweled off.

"Yeah?" Jackson answered. He decided to play arrogant and overly confident. "I doubt it."

The lure was offered, the bait taken. As a fish, Peter seemed remarkably easy to hook. "You wouldn't care to wager on that, would you?" Peter asked.

"I might," Jackson answered. "I might."

All that remained was making sure that the bait wasn't devoured by the fish.

Bart Charles was pleased, but Moroshiba was coldly and obviously disappointed when Jackson told him. He sat *seiza* on the mat and stared into space without looking at Jackson. "You're a puppet dancing on someone else's strings," he said to his pupil. "You haven't learned anything."

"I've learned more moves from more different disciplines than anyone else I can think of," Jackson retorted. Moroshiba's quiet tongue-lashing made him angry. What made the sensei's scorn worse was that he just sat there, composed and unblinking, while Jackson strode around the mat like a dervish. "You're awfully damn self-righteous."

"Don't you listen to anything I say?" Moroshiba questioned him. "How many times have I told you that the student who knows only the moves has learned half the lesson. You must earn the attitude as well."

"I study. I meditate."

"But you have no calmness in you. You rage. You let others control your mind instead of controlling it yourself."

Jackson whirled around at that, confronting Moroshiba in a threatening stance. Moroshiba glanced at him once, and then looked calmly away again. "You're insulting the man who has cared more for me than anyone since my first parents," Jackson shouted. "He named me his son. He has affection for me—I can see it. I owe him my allegiance. He took a chance with me, and I'll take this risk for him. It's what I trained for."

"Then you have been training for the wrong reasons." Moroshiba sighed. He rose to his feet and padded to the edge of the mat, slipping on his sandals as he bowed off. He shouldered the long, thin bag that held his wooden practice weapons: sword, staff, and knife. "I will leave you, Jackson, since I have nothing to teach you that you will learn."

"Sensei," Jackson began, suddenly repentant, but the old man simply shook his head.

"No," he said firmly. "It was a mistake to come here in the beginning. You seem to think that you can only serve yourself by serving others. I tell you that you have it backwards. You have it in your mind that true power comes from outside yourself. You have that backwards, too. I teach blending; you want to learn opposition. Find another teacher for that."

Moroshiba went to the door of the dojo. Jackson watched him go, silently raging on the mat. With sunlight limning him from behind, Moroshiba bowed once more toward the mat. "Your father looks at the universe and thinks that it will only be in harmony when he controls all the instruments that play its song. I feel that the true path is to tune the instrument of self first. Jackson, you won't be happy at the end of this. I guarantee it."

"More homilies, Sensei?" Jackson asked scornfully. "You're awfully close to mixing metaphors."

Moroshiba's face went blank and empty. "No, Jackson," he said. "I have no more words for you. You'll have to fill the emptiness of your soul yourself."

Quietly, Moroshiba shut the door to the dojo. Jackson stood on the mat for several minutes afterward, breathing heavily.

Then, deliberately, he began to go through a *kata*, a series of kicks and punches. He imagined that Sensei Moroshiba was standing there, unable to dodge the rain of blows.

The terms of the wager were exactly what Bart Charles told Jackson he wished them to be—no cost to either one of them. Peter Chrysanthi was an ambitious man, too; he understood what Jackson was asking when he said that if he, Jackson, won the match against Chrysanthi's champion, then Chrysanthi would vote his block of shares with Jackson's father at the next meeting of BEC shareholders. "So," Peter had grinned. "Bartholomew thinks he can oust Leo Bones, eh? Charles isn't content with his tithe of power as a shareholder. Well, your old man doesn't make a move unless he's pretty damn certain. Which means if Bart Charles can be elected Director, so can Peter Chrysanthi. All right, Jackson, we'll wager control of my shares of BEC stock. If you lose, you'll convince your father that it's in his best interests to vote *his* shares my way. Can you do it?"

"I won't have to," Jackson answered.

Chrysanthi had only grinned, a mirthless smile like a shark. "That's not what I asked you, my friend. I expect you to lose. I want to know that when that happens, you can keep your end of the bargain. I don't care how you do it, just do it."

"He dotes on me," Jackson replied. "It won't be a problem. Unless I die."

Chrysanthi's grin had gotten wider at that. "If that happens, I've made other arrangements—as far as the authorities know, it will look like an accident. And if you die, Jackson, I won't expect you to keep your end of the deal. We'll consider the death payment enough, eh?"

Chrysanthi had rented a gymnasium in New York for the contest. Built several centuries before, it was small, dirty, and out of the way. In the seats around the ring that would function as deathpit sat a small group of spectators, most of them wealthy young friends of Chrysanthi. Jackson felt a distinct hostility in the room.

Then a door opened in the rear of the hall. Peter Chrysanthi stepped through, escorting Jackson's opponent. A sudden icy fear settled in the pit of Jackson's stomach as the harsh overhead lighting revealed the shape behind Chrysanthi: a !xaka!. "Chrysanthi!" he called. "You said nothing about using one of them. I'm calling this off."

Peter's face took on a feral aspect. "Do that and you've automatically lost, Charles. You're right, I said nothing about a !xaka!. Neither did you. I'm well within the terms of our agreement, I think. Are you going to fight, or are you giving me control of your father's shares now? Your choice. I don't care, so long as I win," Chrysanthi said as the !xaka! slithered into the ring.

Jackson felt hemmed in, trapped. The faces around him stared without pity, without friendship. "All right," he said at last. "I'll fight."

Chrysanthi almost managed to look disappointed. "You're sure, Charles? Let me introduce you to Hygyk!cil. Are you familiar with !xaka!? No? Well, you can see by his gill plumes that he's low caste—once a slave, in fact. He's used to fighting and killing. He can spray acid from his stomach, he can spin webs thick as ropes to hold you, and those clawed hands . . ." Chrysanthi clucked in mock sympathy. "Why, you couldn't even tell him that you've had enough—I'm afraid he doesn't understand our language at all. I had my good friend the !xaka!ian ambassador explain to Hygyk!cil that he's here to do one thing—to beat you into the mat until you don't get up again. Your last chance, I'm afraid, Charles. Tell me that you've lost, or I'm fairly certain that you'll most likely die here. You should have watched me more closely, Jackson. You know I like the odds in my favor."

That sparked anger and a certain fear in Jackson. Bart Charles had trusted him. No, Charles wasn't the kind of loving father he'd once had, but he was *all* Jackson had at the moment. Bart Charles had trusted him. He had trusted Jackson's talent and training. If he gave up now, all of that would have been for nothing. Jackson suddenly knew with certainty that Bart Charles would disown Jackson as easily as he had claimed him. Win, and he won everything. Lose, and he lost all that he'd gained in the last years.

"I'll fight," he said again.

Peter seemed almost happy. "It's your funeral." He went to his seat and turned to the others. "This is a deathfight," he told them. "It follows the rules our friend Jackson has so graciously outlined for us—the fight will continue until one of them can no longer rise." He sat and faced the ring. "Jackson, Hygyk!cil has already been told the rules. When the houselights go out, he will begin fighting."

In the moments before the fight began, Jackson studied the

!xaka!, trying to fathom its weaknesses. Certainly the armored carapace wasn't vulnerable at all, though perhaps the joints between the eight segments were. Jackson knew little of !xaka! anatomy, and nothing he could see conformed to human standards. Pale blue gill plumes were raised under the hood, compound eyes glittered under the hood of the carapace as the !xaka! lifted its first three segments and clicked its several clawed hands forcefully. He felt with a certainty that this would not be a long fight. This would be like the battle of two samurai that Moroshiba had once spoken of—a long study of the opponent, then a momentary flurry of blades, and one would lie dead. One stroke.

Can't let Mr. Ugly here touch me. He's bigger and stronger; if he gets me in his grasp, I'm gone. Those claws look like they'd snap me in half.

The houselights flickered and died. Charles shifted out of his corner but didn't move toward the !xaka!. Hygyk!cil's top segment, the head, canted slightly as it followed his motion, though the !xaka! remained still otherwise. In fact, the creature seemed to turn a little sidewise to Jackson. He puzzled at that, then heard a faint hiss/click and saw an orifice on the !xaka!'s side suddenly dilate. Jackson leapt to his left as a jet of noxious liquid sprayed the mat where he'd been. The smell of it burned his nostrils, and where the stream touched the ring's surface, the fabric covering steamed and melted. *Acid! I can't even wait, then—it has a weapon to get me at a distance. No choice. No choice—I have to close now.*

Jackson screamed. The !xaka! seemed startled. In the instant that it reared backward, Jackson charged across the room with a flying kick. He aimed directly at the eyes, felt his foot contact a soft, wet surface that gave under his thrusting blow. Hygyk!cil roared with the clamor of a wounded steam engine. Claws raked out blindly at Jackson, tearing as their serrated edges gouged his chest and back. Jackson plunged his open hands into the wound his kick had left, digging and ignoring the frantic convulsions of the !xaka!. He could smell acid, could feel a raging agony as it sprayed over his legs. Claws ripped his shoulder wide open. Jackson ignored it all, plunging his hand back, back through membrane and tissue, tearing as he went. The !xaka! reared, then smashed down, nearly crushing Jackson and driving the breath from him. Once more the creature reared up, green fluid gushing from the horrible wound in its head. Jackson tried to rise and get out of the way, but his legs would not move. He could barely breathe. He waited for death.

But the !xaka! toppled the other way, rolling half on its back. Multiple arms and legs writhed in death throes, and then it was still.

The fight had lasted less than thirty seconds.

Jackson levered himself to a sitting position. Peter Chrysanthi splattered with gore himself, stared at the carnage before him. His gaze came around to Jackson, and there was a hatred in his eyes. "I won," Jackson croaked. "Damn you, I won."

Chrysanthi was on his feet. He shook his head. "No. You lost, Jackson. Didn't you know that? I don't like losing." He gestured to two of his companions. "Edgar, David. Cut open the !xaka!. There's enough fluid in the fifth segment to make it look like poor Jackson here was killed by acid."

"You can't do that," Jackson breathed. He struggled to rise, to run. But his body disobeyed.

Chrysanthi watched and laughed. "What are you going to do?" he asked. "Will you crawl away? Go on!" he said to the others. "You lost, Jackson Charles. Now you'll pay me."

"You're mistaken about that."

The voice came from the back doors of the gymnasium. Bart Charles stood there, several burly-looking guards behind him. "I'm afraid that *you've* lost the bet, Peter. And you'll pay up. You'll pay up or I'll send Jackson after *you*. Do you think that you could keep him away after this?"

Bart Charles came toward the ring. "Father," Jackson said. His face was a mask of pain. "You knew? You knew where, you knew that a !xaka! . . ." He ran out of energy to say more.

"I trusted you," Bart said. He smiled, but he didn't look at Jackson, didn't make a move even to see how badly injured he was. All of Bart Charles's attention was on Chrysanthi.

Finally he turned to Jackson. "Now, let's get you someplace where they can patch you up again." Jackson knew the voice was supposed to sound sympathetic; instead, it sounded condescending, the same way Bart spoke to a favored servant like Tomas. He thought that maybe he'd misunderstood, that the pain was making him read things into his father's tone that simply were't there. Jackson tried to smile back and found that he couldn't. Bart had known. He'd known and he'd let Jackson walk in there.

Through the haze of pain and shock, Jackson was suddenly aware that Bart Charles would have been equally ready if Jackson had died. Bart Charles was someone who would not make a bet unless he was certain he would win. He looked at Peter Chrysanthi and the man he called father, and he could see little difference between them. It was as if they wore the same face.

Then a rolling blackness smothered him and he fell into blissful unconsciousness.

CHAPTER 16

Leo Bones was quiet and uncharacteristically lethargic on the brief flight from Africa to Nairobi. Mahsi, piloting the little four-seater jet, assumed that his employer was worried about the coming board meeting—rumors of a pending power struggle had been rampant for the past month. "Don't worry, sir," Mahsi said over his shoulder, his eyes on the array of instruments before him. "Charles can do nothing; the minority stockholders will side with you, and that will be it."

"I don't know, Mahsi," Leo whispered—Mahsi had never heard Leo sound so despondent. He'd complained of weariness and stomach problems that morning at breakfast, eating very little. Mahsi knew from the servants that Leo had spent a restless, sleepless night, prowling the hallways of the estate, spending a good deal of time in Zeke's old room, just sitting in one of the chairs there and staring at the wall. The years had aged Leo Bones more than Mahsi cared to admit. Given the rumors, Mahsi had been surprised that Leo Bones had seemed so uncaring about the meeting. They had started late and gotten later. When Mahsi had voiced concern that they would not be there in time for the start of the meeting, Leo had simply shrugged his shoulder. "Sharlee knows to start the meeting if I'm not there. Nothing important will happen until the routine business is over. We'll get there in plenty of time for that." And he'd resumed watching some innocuous documentary on the cube. Mahsi had shaken his head and gone up to the rooftop pad to wait.

"Word has it that Charles and Chrysanthi have been plotting," Leo told him now. "Their combined block of shares gives Charles leverage he hasn't had before. If he intends to depose me as Director and have himself elected . . . I don't know. He might be able to pull it off—they don't have to convince many people before they have the votes they need. Some of the smaller holders are wavering, waiting to see what happens."

"Nobody will sit on the fence with this one, that's for certain," Mahsi agreed. "The proxies will all be there. But so will you. You are a Bones—BEC has always listened first to the Boneses, who speak with the wisdom of the founders. They will listen to Charles, and they will listen to you. The vote might be close, but you will prevail. Believe that, sir."

"Profits are down," Leo answered in a despondent voice. "That's the bottom line for many of them. The invariance overdrive units were supposed to be marketed by now, but we're having trouble with them. No profit, no dividends. Maybe they think it's time for a new director."

"Profits have fallen before. They know the market—it's a cyclical fluctuation. You worry too much, sir." Mahsi had not intended to say anything further, but the additional news he carried and the despondency he sensed in Leo made him hint at it. "Take a brighter outlook, sir. Everything may change soon."

There was no answer from Leo Bones in his seat behind Mahsi. Considering the weariness Leo had displayed this morning, Mahsi thought that perhaps he had fallen asleep. Not wanting to wake Leo, he waited a few minutes, then set the jet on autopilot, intending to get a blanket from the overhead compartments and make Leo comfortable. "Auto," he whispered.

"On," replied the board.

Mahsi unbuckled himself and turned around. What he saw made him fall back in his seat, stunned.

"Sir?" he gasped.

But there would never be an answer from those gray lips.

Jackson saw the disturbance ripple across the floor of the BEC boardroom in the middle of the meeting's agenda. The meeting thus far had seemed more like some governmental congress than a shareholder's meeting, and there was some truth in that. Since the late twentieth century, the large corporations had become more and more like part of the government that supposedly ruled them—the corporate structure had shifted as well, with the corporate director having greater freedom of action and control. As corporate influence waxed, that of the actual governing bodies waned. BEC, in many ways, was more responsible for the welfare of humanity than the elected officials with the titles. Parliamentary procedure ruled the meeting, under the capable hands of the assistant director, Sharlee Cooke. Leo Bones had failed to arrive as yet.

Jackson was in the private gallery. Only shareholders and their proxies were actually allowed on the floor, but the gallery was alive with spectators, most of whom were related in one way or another to the shareholders, though there were a number of reporters in evidence—BEC, as one of the largest corporations of the human worlds, attracted a lot of attention, especially when the rumors said that a Bones would no longer be director after today's meeting.

A woman beside Jackson leaned over, whispering. "Some news must have reached them," she said. "Look—see how everyone is suddenly intent on their monitors." Glancing over the brass railing of the gallery, Jackson could see that the woman was right. All over the vast hall, board members were bent over the tiny flatscreens built into their desk or were hurriedly whispering over their hushphones.

The servo at Jackson's right ear bleeped suddenly, and Jackson heard his stepfather's voice. "Jackson—Leo Bones is dead."

"What!" Jackson subvocalized. The woman next to him stared at him strangely.

"Yes." There seemed to be glee in Bart's voice. Jackson looked down at the floor to find Bart, saw him at his desk. He brought the image closer with his artificial eye, until he could see the half-smile on his father's face. It didn't seem that Bart Charles was going to grieve much at the news. "A heart attack on the flight over. Just got the report from Nairobi Hospital. It was too late to save him—a massive coronary. The man had evidently been in bad shape for years and had simply neglected to do anything about it."

"What does that mean for us?"

"I don't know. We'll find out. Without his block of shares voting, no one can stop us, but they might try to adjourn the meeting—in which case our whole attempt here would be lost. Might have to ram our stuff down their throats. We'll see. Just watch. Watch and learn, because one day you'll be the one down here."

Sharlee Cooke, another distant relative of the original Bones, gaveled the meeting back to order. "Mr. Bowers has the floor, please. Mr. Bowers, I'm asking you, however, to please yield the floor back to me as I have an announcement of some importance." Bowers, a thin, tall man with a scraggly beard, nodded to the chair. "I yield," he said.

"Thank you, Mr. Bowers." Cooke was visibly distressed; in

the large holocube that dominated the back of the hall, everyone saw her take a deep breath to compose herself, and her voice shook with emotion as she spoke. "I've just received news that most of you have by now also received through your own sources. I regret to say that I've just received confirmation from UCI. On his way to the meeting today, Leo Bones, Director of BEC, suffered a massive and fatal coronary. Measures to restore his heartbeat, administered by his assistant and later by hospital personnel, failed. He was pronounced dead approximately half an hour ago. In honor of Director Bones's long service to this company, and because I know all of us here are disturbed by the news, I ask that this meeting be adjourned. Are there seconds to that motion?"

Several people did so.

"Objections?" Cooke scanned the monitor in front of her and saw a flashing amber light. "The chair recognizes Bart Charles."

Bart Charles rose to his feet. His face suddenly filled the holocube behind Cooke. "With all due respect, I object to the motion and ask that it be put to a vote."

The cameras flashed back to Cooke. Her face reflected open distaste. "Would Mr. Charles care to explain his reasoning for objecting to such a motion? Surely in such a time of grief, our *personal* ambitions might be put aside." No one in the hall missed the unsubtle inflection. There was assorted nervous laughter and some catcalls from the floor and the gallery. Jackson watched intently.

"With all due respect to Leopold Bones," Charles answered, unflustered, "as everyone here knows, this shareholders' meeting can only be held every five standard years, due to the interstellar distances some of us must travel. If we cancel this meeting for a week, for a month, some of us here may be forced to return to our homeworlds and miss this meeting. Five standard years is a long time. In addition, the rules of this meeting clearly state that if the Director (and I quote) 'is unable to attend *for any reason,* be it personal, health, or otherwise, the Assistant Director shall perform the functions of Director and conduct said meeting.' Ms. Cooke, I ask that you perform those duties now."

Her scowl filled the back wall. "Which is exactly what I am trying to do, Mr. Charles. The functions of the Director include the right to call for adjournment when that seems advisable." She shook her head and glanced down at her monitor. "However, your objection does give you the right to put the motion to a vote. All those in favor of the motion to adjourn this meeting, due to the death of Leopold Bones, please so indicate."

The holocube display went blank for a moment; then names began to scroll across it in blue as those on the floor touched the servos on their desks. "Opposed," Cooke said, and red names appeared alongside, the first to appear that of Bartholomew Charles and Peter Chrysanthi.

"We've lost, then?" Jackson whispered to the servo on his lapel. "The blue list is longer."

His father's voice rasped in his ear. "Not yet. You're forgetting the proportions of shares. The largest blocks of shares are ours and Chrysanthi's. And there *are* a great many shareholders who would find it inconvenient to return at some other time. Wait a moment."

A chart had appeared between the two columns of names. Bars in the appropriate colors began to rise from the baseline, along with a central bar of white. When they had stopped moving, the blue lagged behind by a few percentage points.

"The motion is denied," Cooke said grudgingly.

"You see," Bart's voice came to Jackson. His face was upturned toward the gallery and Jackson in triumph.

"The Director's block hasn't voted," someone noted from the floor. "Is there a proxy who can vote his shares?"

Cooke canted her head to one side, pressing a finger to her ear as she listened to the reedy voice of a servo-link to the central databank. After a moment, she looked back out to the floor. "The control of the Director's shares goes to his heir, Ezekiel Bones. The registered proxy is Mahsi Zabinul, who is not present. As neither heir nor proxy is here, the Director is considered to have abstained. The motion is denied."

Jackson's artificial eye, focused closely on his father, caught the satisfaction that lifted one corner of his thin lips. Charles turned to whisper something to Chrysanthi.

The item calling for dismissal of the current Director of the Board and election of a new one was far down on the agenda. For the next few hours, other items filled the time. The gallery filed in and out, as did the various shareholders, as the discussion and voting continued on the floor. Everyone could see the one vital item on the list come closer and closer for discussion: *Proposed by Peter Chrysanthi: to elect a new Director of the Board for the coming term*. As the items before that proposal grew fewer, an anticipation built in the hall. The buzz of conversation grew so loud at times that Cooke had to gavel the meeting to order. The gallery, at times during the day half-empty, was packed. All the shareholders had returned to their desks by the time the last item before the Chrysanthi proposal was dispensed with.

"The chair recognizes Peter Chrysanthi," Cooke said at last. She gaveled for silence as he rose. The handsome Chrysanthi appeared subdued in the wallcube, uncharacteristically nervous. Once, he glanced up at the gallery. Seeing Jackson there, he swallowed and cleared his throat.

"No one here is more surprised and disappointed at Leopold Bones's unexpected death," he began. "I find myself in an awkward position that I wish I could avoid. I had intended to put before the shareholders the motion that we have a vote of confidence for the current Director, and, should that vote indicate that it was our wish, elect a new Director of the Board for the term following this meeting. Leopold's death has made that intention seem almost cruel."

Chrysanthi paused. He had gained confidence as he had spoken, and the cool actor in him had risen to the surface. There was a glistening in his eyes that was convincing, and his voice held a deep undertone of emotion, as if his grief nearly choked him. "Yet his death makes this proposal all the more crucial. As all of you know from your reports, BEC—while not precisely sinking—is wallowing in the storms of commerce. More than ever, we need a firm hand on the helm. There are crucial and difficult business decisions we must make. We *need* a leader. I propose that we elect him today. I put before the shareholders the motion that a new Director of the Board be elected to replace Leopold Bones."

Cooke's sigh was audible over the hall's sound system. "The motion is before the shareholders. Is there a second?"

Several seconds were shouted from the floor. Bart Charles said nothing.

"The motion is seconded, then. Do we have candidates for the position. Yes, Mr. Chrysanthi? You still have the floor."

Chrysanthi swallowed again. Most of the shareholders no doubt expected that he would place his own name in nomination. Instead Chrysanthi took a breath and said: "I nominate Bartholomew Charles."

Cooke stared at him for a moment, then glanced over to Charles. "Mr. Charles, your name has been placed before me for nomination. Do you accept?"

"With all due humility," Charles answered, "I do."

"It's so recorded, then," Cooke said glumly. "We're open for other nominations."

There were few. One minor shareholder nominated himself, Cooke's name was nominated, but she declined. And Ezekiel Bones was nominated to replace his father.

"He's not here," Jackson noted. On the floor, he watched his father shrug. "It's a ploy," Bart said. "He's been seconded in absentia. If he wins, he'd have to be offered the directorship. Until he's found to accept or decline, Cooke runs the show, and she's Leo's person all down the line. Even if the younger Bones would decline, no new director could be elected until the next shareholders' meeting and Cooke would be in control for this term—because of the time lag in communicating between worlds, the board has full control of BEC until the next election. If nothing else, it would buy time. But it's too late. We were expecting to win even with Bones's shares against him. With that block held back . . ."

The actual voting proceeded slowly. The rules of the corporation gave the shareholders half an hour to cast their votes, but until the final moment the votes were not recorded. Even if they had already voted, a vote could be rescinded and cast elsewhere at any time within that period. The big blocks of shares went up on the wallcube almost immediately: Chrysanthi's and Charles's blocks went predictably to Bart Charles, in red on the wallcube graph. Cooke's and several other smaller blocks went to Zeke, in green. The few other names in nomination were slivers of color barely visible on the graph. The central column of uncast votes was still the largest, but it was already clear that Bart Charles was the leader among the candidates.

After the initial flurry of voting, the string-pulling and leverage began. Bart Charles and Peter Chrysanthi, like Cooke, were on the floor phones constantly, trying to woo and sometimes browbeat the minority shareholders into voting for their side. Small blocks of shares were added to their respective columns of the graph as deals were made and favors called in. With ten minutes to go, the conclusion seemed foregone.

Bart Charles would be the new director.

The greatest bulk of the uncast votes were those of Leo Bones's block, and they all knew that would remain exactly where it was. The minority shareholders who had voted for Ezekiel Bones in the first few minutes began to sense the political wind shift and were defecting despite Cooke's best efforts

—it would not be advisable to be on the new director's bad side. The green column had visibly shrunk from its former heights as the red continued to press higher.

The doors to the hall dilated with a hushed exhalation. The shareholders paused to see who had entered. A tall, very thin young man with blond hair was striding toward the podium where Cooke stood. He walked slowly, as if the effort tired him, and his skin was darkened by the light of a hundred stars. Behind him came a burly black man dressed in BEC coveralls, a shri with the mantle patterns of the Galactic Council, and a woman trailing hovercams. Jackson Charles saw his father's face blanch, and he squinted toward the intruder, letting the servo eye focus on that face.

What he saw made him sit back in utter shock, his mouth gaping helplessly. "No, it couldn't be," he gasped. "It can't be him."

Sharlee Cooke glanced over, and her face in the wallcube broke into a grin. She bent down to speak to the young man for a moment and then spoke into the sound system for all to hear.

"The chair recognizes Ezekiel Bones," she said into the sudden, utter quiet.

Those who had known Leo Bones in his younger, more energetic days before his first wife had died were immediately struck by how much his son resembled him. There was a presence in him, a charisma that made everyone in the hall crane their heads toward him as he spoke.

"All of you knew my father," he said, and though his voice was strong, there was a bright gleam of moisture in his light eyes. "I'm very sorry to say that probably you knew him better than I did. For the last ten years or more, I've . . . well, I've been trying to run away from Leo Bones. I ran because I thought I knew him too well. I'm afraid that all I've found is that I didn't understand him at all. I found that my reasons for running were entirely selfish."

Zeke smiled sadly for a moment. He laughed self-deprecatingly. "I know none of you forgive me; it's been a hectic several hours since I arrived back on Earth, a very emotional time." He glanced back at the wallcube, at the glowing rods of color that indicated the status of the vote. "Sharlee tells me that Mahsi and I can vote my father's shares. She tells me that if I voted for myself, a lot of you might be tempted to side with me. I think that's unfair. I think that's unfair to BEC, to you who are ultimately the controllers of her, and—especially—to the memory of my father, who built his life around the company. My father would have enjoyed this fight, I think. I find that I would rather look for a way to avoid it."

Bart Charles rose with those words. Zeke looked at him, waiting. "I'm sorry for interrupting the procedure of this meeting," Charles said. "But I want to commend the young Mr. Bones on his concern for the goodwill of BEC. Withdrawing his name from nomination is an act of courage that we should all acknowledge—"

"You misunderstand," Zeke broke in. Charles scowled, his face going bright red. "Let me finish, please. What I ask instead is that this vote be forgotten entirely. I propose instead that control of BEC be dispersed into the hands of several people, instead of concentrated so much in that of the Director. I've learned that one person can easily be wrong—it's more difficult for several people to agree, but it is also harder for them to make simple mistakes."

"Ms. Cooke!" Charles blustered, shouting. "This motion is entirely out of order. The motion to take a vote was agreed upon and should be continued. By the rules, Ms. Cooke."

"And I have the floor, Mr. Charles. I know that I don't understand the procedure here. I do know that if you force a vote on me, I will vote for myself. How many would vote with me, Mr. Charles?" Zeke glanced back at the wallcube again. Already the tide of defection had turned—the green column was inching higher as the red fell. "BEC can be a tremendous force in the United Worlds. We can—all of us—make BEC far more than a tool for wealth and power. We can make it also a tool for the betterment of humanity. Force this vote, Mr. Charles, and I will use the directorship to move in the direction I wish BEC to go. As director, it will be harder for you to oppose me. Until the shareholders meet again, I would be able to head the board and move BEC as I wish—you will have lost, as you're losing now. If you'll instead adopt the proposal I have, you'll have lost nothing."

Jackson watched his father consult his monitor, touching his ear to link with the databanks, and then confer quickly with Chrysanthi. He shook his head at something Chrysanthi said, pointing at the wallcube graph. He turned back to Zeke. "What's your proposal, then?" he asked.

"It's very simple," Zeke answered. "First the directorship is to be abolished. In its place, I propose a council of shareholders—including the minority shareholders—to manage the affairs of BEC. I leave it to this gathering to work out the details of that; I know they would have to live here on Earth to be close enough to consult quickly in a crisis, and that might mean hardships for some of them. I withdraw myself from any nomination to that council, and from any future directorship should that council decide to reinstitute the current corporate structure. My block of shares will be linked with the majority rule of the new Council whenever this body meets. As a concession to that, I will take on the task of establishing a foundation under BEC auspices dedicated to the preservation of cultural treasures—something both my father and mother were interested in doing. I would want the BEC experimental ship *MacPherson*—to be renamed the *Ostrom*—as the base for that foundation. She will be outfitted as a field laboratory at BEC expense. I assure you that the research and time that have gone into developing the ship and its drive won't be wasted."

Zeke paused, looking out at the assembled shareholders of his father's company. "My family has run this corporation for centuries. Many of you out there are related in one way or another to me. Listen to our ancestors singing in your mind. They were people who looked outward, who looked beyond themselves. It's time we did the same. That's all I ask."

"Mr. Chrysanthi, it is your motion that is before the shareholders. Do you wish to rescind it?" Sharlee Cooke looked almost exultant as she threw the question into the rising hubbub in the hall. Chrysanthi looked helplessly at Charles, who cast a desperate eye to the graph of the vote. The defection was a rout. He could see defeat written there. He shrugged his shoulders and nodded to Chrysanthi.

"I withdraw the motion," Chrysanthi answered.

In the tumult following the decision, Jackson caught a clear glimpse of Bart Charles's face looking up at him from the floor of the hall. In that stricken despair, there was a clear message that Jackson could read all too well. He didn't need the confirming whisper of the servo by his ear.

"I've trained you for years, son," the servo said in Charles's voice. "Now it's time for you to help me. I want you to kill him, son. I want you to kill Ezekiel Bones."

CHAPTER 17

"I want you to kill him, son. I want you to kill Ezekiel Bones."

The words echoed in Jackson's mind. They mixed with the tumult there: the memory of Zeke pulling him from the burning dome after the pyxies had killed his parents; the appearance of Bart Charles just when it seemed that his entire life was about to collapse; the years of training and support he'd received from the man; the night he'd made Jackson his son and heir; Moroshiba's words that Jackson would never be happy at the end of this path he followed—that seemed to be horribly true.

And most of all, the sudden realization that this enemy of his father's, this hated rival and son of Leo Bones, was none other than the one who had saved his life. Recognizing the face of the person who had saved him in Ezekiel Bones had been a blow from which his mind still staggered. Jackson Charles had left the shareholders' meeting reeling.

"I want you to kill him."

In the deathpits, there was no mercy. There was no friendship. There could be no thought of the other person as anything other than The Enemy. There was only one path. This time the deathpit was a rambling mansion set in the dusty African plains. This time there were no bright lights and the shouts of spectators. There was only the darkness of a moonless night and the spectres in his own mind.

His true father and mother were there, and their reproving silence was louder than any words. Mack the Crack was there, laughing, making rude jokes. Moroshiba was there, sitting stoic as usual, his face stiff.

Servos lined Jackson's collar, their delicate senses reaching out into the night and whispering back to him. "Detection— sonic device ahead. Triggering range, three meters." Jackson halted. He unclipped a servo from the wide belt he wore, set it, and placed it on the ground. A few seconds later it hissed and died, but the short burst from its transmitter had completed its task, disabling the sonic fence around the estate.

Jackson loped forward like a piece of the night himself. His artificial eye let him pierce the murk and see the lone guard walking the perimeter. Jackson hugged the ground, nearly invisible in his night clothing. When the guard walked by him, oblivious, one kick to the knee toppled him. Jackson bent over the man before he could cry out, and sprayed a burst from a canister on his belt. The guard went limp in his arms and began to snore softly. From there it was a quick dash across the wide lawn to the cover of the house itself.

"Anyone?" he whispered.

"No one within range."

"Check for electrical emissions—alarms."

"The front door is shielded. Class One device—stay away."

The front door might have been shielded, but one of the ancient windows yielded to his touch, unlocked. Jackson frowned; such a lapse in security would have never happened on the Charleses' grounds. He sprayed the edges with lubricant and gently eased the window up until there was room for him to slip over the sill. He landed silently on a thick rug in the front room.

Jackson knew from what his father had told him that the place was a maze. He'd been able to give Jackson some idea of where the bedrooms lay, but he couldn't be sure where Zeke might be—in his old room or possibly in his father's, or even somewhere else. The shri that had been with Zeke was staying at the shri embassy in Cairo; the woman, some reporter from UCI, was already offworld on another assignment. Jackson unclipped another of the servos and placed it on the floor. The thing skittered away as Jackson unrolled a flatscreen from his belt. He watched a moving dot on the grid pattern, trying to correlate it to the house. The green dot turned red after a few minutes, blinking twice. Jackson stuffed the flatscreen back in his belt. Two people upstairs then, a little to the east. The servants must have separate quarters. Taking care to make no noise, he moved like a feline up the staircase and to the right.

He saw the old man in the BEC uniform walking slowly toward him, recognizing him from the fiasco at the shareholders' meeting: Mahsi, the longtime Bones retainer. Mahsi was whistling, oblivious to the threat that lay in the night-wrapped shadows. Jackson pressed against the wall. He let the man come abreast of him and then leapt forward. Mahsi barely had time to utter a surprised grunt as the canister hissed and he sucked in the choking fumes. His knees collapsed and he fell. Jackson caught him under the shoulders and noiselessly lowered him to the carpet.

There was light coming from an open doorway just down the hall. He began moving that way.

With his father gone, the old Bones house didn't seem the same at all. It seemed far too big—lonely and haunted by ghosts. It didn't matter that Mahsi was there, that servants bustled through the place. It was empty, and the silence howled with the presence of those who had walked here before him. Even his room seemed strange, a place that had been inhabited by someone else, not Zeke.

Maybe it was simply because he was so tired—that old illness again. Most of the meal he'd eaten the night before he'd thrown up an hour later, his body rejecting it. Reelys had insisted that Zeke put himself under the supervision of experts in human illnesses. He'd promised to check into a hospital soon, see what the doctors could do to patch him together again for a time. But that could wait until after the funeral, after all the arrangements were made.

Zeke whistled a nearly forgotten four-note figure. The false wall dissolved to reveal the old laboratory, now coated with the dust of a decade. Leo Bones had disturbed nothing from the night that Zeke had left. All of it was still in the same place. The protein separator was slightly askew in its holder. Impulsively, Zeke reached out to straighten it. He ran a finger over a rack of vials, leaving a clean trail behind. He blew the dust from his fingertip and watched it spark in the lamplight.

The old warning board squeaked outside his room. "Mahsi?" Zeke called, turning. "Have I been away so long you've forgotten all—" Zeke stopped. He'd expected to see Mahsi there, perhaps with an apologetic smile on his face, but there was no one at the open door to the room. "Mahsi?" Zeke called again, softer this time.

No answer. He instinctively reached for his pouch to touch the star seed, to see if it could tell him something. There was no pouch, no gem. "The Legion's made you paranoid, Ezekiel," he muttered to himself, but still some instinct held him back, made him eye the dark corridor with suspicion.

Zeke rummaged on the lab bench in the pile of servos. Finding the gossamer-wing spy he'd built as a thirteen-year-old, he touched the antennae leads—the eyes winked green, telling him that there was still battery power. The last time he'd used the spy, it had been set to travel to his father's secret gallery. Zeke activated the pre-set program, flipped on the viewer, and let the servo go. The delicate, silken wings beat as the device drifted up from his hand, heading slowly toward the door on a wobbly course. It reached the doorway and turned right down the corridor. Zeke touched the viewer-contact; the servo's camera clicked. A brief still image showed on the screen—the corridor, bright in the spy's infrared eyes; and two figures, one prone on the carpet near the staircase. He knew immediately it was Mahsi, and Zeke's heart beat loudly in his chest, suddenly worried for his old friend. The other figure was pressed against the wall just outside Zeke's door. In the frozen image, the figure by the door was reaching out toward the spy's wide-angled lenses. Zeke triggered the contact again. This time the screen showed nothing but static. Zeke took a deep breath.

"I know you're there," he said loudly. "You might as well come in."

A soft step, and a muscular young black man slipped around the corner, dressed in tight-fitting, dark clothing, a knit mask covering most of his face. He held a knife in one hand, and there was a small impact pistol on his belt. He crouched at ready, relaxing slightly as he saw Zeke standing empty-handed near the workbench. "You'd better not have hurt Mahsi," Zeke said to him. "If you did, then one way or another, I'll make you pay for that."

The slightest smile seemed to pass over the man's lips. "You sound like a Legionnaire, *or* a Bones—making threats. Your man's just out for a while," he said. "No permanent harm done. Too bad the same doesn't apply to you."

"What do you want?"

"You shouldn't even have to think about that. My orders were to kill you," the intruder said flatly.

The words should have horrified Zeke. Perhaps it was the fact he'd seen so much death in the Legion that made him shake his head. "Then why waste your time talking?"

"I thought I'd see if you'd beg first."

Zeke shook his head, forcing himself not to show any of the cold fear he felt. "You're just one man. I've faced worse odds before and come out of it."

"You've never faced me before." The intruder touched the pistol, then seemed to shake his head. "No, I won't need that. Just the knife. Knives are good weapons, don't you think?— quiet, and very personal. Anyone can use a gun; it takes expertise and intent to use a blade."

Zeke had been watching him, his attention on the bunched muscles of the man's legs. When he saw them tense, ready to spring, Zeke whistled again, desperately. The wall collapsed back into place in front of him. If he was lucky, it would hide him from view, maybe confuse the intruder enough that he could make some plan, perhaps signal someone else on the grounds. Despite his bravado, Zeke knew from looking at the man that he was no match physically.

But Zeke had not counted on the intruder's incredible agility. He was already halfway to Zeke when the illusory wall started to coalesce. When it snapped into place, the man was already past, lunging toward Zeke. Zeke swept the microscope from its stand, throwing the heavy instrument at the man, but he dodged with catlike reflexes—the expensive tool smashed against the floor. In desperation, Zeke pulled a vial from a rack, holding it in front of him, ready to throw. "Stay back," he said. "This is acid. I'll burn you if you come any nearer."

"You're bluffing," the man said, but he came no closer. He still smiled, a savage, senseless grin under the mask. One of the eyes seemed to leer at him, unblinkingly. "I'd be on you before you managed to throw that. You'll miss."

"Try me." The intruder took a step. Zeke brandished the vial. "It's not a bluff," he warned him, hoping the man would believe him. He had no idea what was in the vial—it looked like sterile water.

The knife's blade gleamed in his assailant's hands. He held it to one side, making certain that Zeke was watching. "Okay, we'll call it a draw for the moment. I'll sheath the knife if you'll put the vial down," he said. He started to turn the blade.

At the same time, he kicked. The strategem was totally unexpected. Zeke's hand felt as if it had been hit by a hammer; he thought he heard bones snap. The vial went flying to dash harmlessly against the wall, and the man pounced. He threw Zeke onto the floor, and he could feel the keen edge of the knife cold against his throat. Zeke started to cry out, but a gloved hand covered his mouth. The intruder's deep voice whispered in his ear, savage and quick. "Move and you're dead, Bones. I have a proposition for you, one that'll save your life, huh? It's not even asking much. What I want you to notice is how easily I got in here. I can do it again, Bones, just as easily—so when you make that promise, don't think that you can renege on it and stay safe. You'll keep the promise or I'll come back and finish this night's job. You understand?" The man lifted his head slightly to let Zeke reply.

"What do you want?" Zeke managed to grate out.

"Nothing much. Just your word that you'll give up your new scheme for BEC. I want you to go back to the shareholders and tell them that you've changed your mind. Tell them to elect a new Director, and tell them you're not a candidate for that position. That's it. Easy, huh? Nothing much to trade for your life. Just a few words that'll do you no harm at all."

That told Zeke who had hired this assassin—Charles. It had to be Charles, trying to sabotage all Zeke had done. Zeke found that there was no hesitation at all inside himself. The words simply tumbled out of their own accord.

"I won't do it," Zeke said. He knew that he meant the words, no matter what they might cost him. He would not take that way again. He would not live his life for someone else. It would mean following the old ways again.

"What?" The knife pressed hard against his throat. Zeke could feel the warm trickle of blood.

"I said I won't do it. Kill me if that's what you're after, but I won't go back to the shareholders."

Amazingly, the pressure against his throat seemed to ease. The intruder let go of Zeke. As Zeke rubbed unbelievingly at his throat, the intruder took off the mask. Standing before Zeke, he gazed down at him. "Do you know me, Ezekiel Bones?"

Zeke stared at the man. He remembered a younger face, a face wracked by the pain of loss and anger, a face streaked with soot and blistered by fire. "Jackson," he breathed. "I saw you, in the gallery at the shareholders' meeting. You looked familiar, but I couldn't place you . . ."

He put the mask back on. He stared at Zeke for long seconds. "I had to know," he said. "I had to know if you were really different from the rest of them."

Then, with a graceful, quick turn, he nodded and left. Zeke lay there, rubbing the stinging cut on his throat for a long time.

• • •

The next day, before he had decided whether to report the break-in to the authorities, he heard the news reports. "Jackson Charles, adopted son of Bart Charles, one of the principal shareholders of BEC, today denounced his father in a press conference in New York. Saying that his father had opposed the plans of Ezekiel Bones to finance a research vessel using BEC resources, Jackson Charles said he gave his full support to Bones and would do all that he could to bring about the completion of the project."

The scene then switched to a closeup of Jackson. "It's time we listened to our idealism rather than our greed," Jackson said. "If Bones will have me after what my family's done, I'd like to work with him."

Zeke mused on that for the rest of the afternoon, despite Mahsi's protests that the local police should know what had happened. That evening, he sent a message to Jackson. *Our debts to each other are even*, it said. *Now we should pay back the rest. See you on the Ostrom.*

Mahsi rushed into Zeke's room, where he was busily arranging to have supplies placed aboard the newly rechristened *Ostrom* in preparation for her shakedown cruise. The Bantu switched on the wallscreen without a word, signalling to Zeke that he should watch.

Zeke recognized the face on the screen immediately: Sylvie Pharr. She was speaking before a backdrop of a ship that Zeke knew to be a lona war machine, in orbit around some unknown planet. ". . . Council has reported that the lona aggressions have broken off everywhere within the shri empire. We know from sources within the Council that the end of the lona war is due to the deciphering of a message placed within the star seeds in the Galactic Museum on . . ."

Zeke whistled off the screen, almost as if he were annoyed. Mahsi glanced at him quizzically. "You don't want to hear the rest?"

"I've heard all I needed to hear. It's over."

"I thought it would make you feel good."

Zeke looked up and saw the disappointment etched on Mahsi's dark face. Shaking his head, he smiled at Mahsi. He groaned to his feet, going over to give the man an affectionate hug. "I know. It should make me feel that I've accomplished something, but somehow all it makes me feel is guilty for having kept the star seed so long. I've had enough guilt; now it's time to begin making amends."

"Your father would be pleased to hear that, I think. He would approve of what you're doing."

Zeke didn't reply to that. He looked at the wallscreen, as if watching some image there that only he could see. "He would say he's proud of you, Ezekiel. I know he would." After a moment, Mahsi turned and left the room, leaving Zeke to his contemplation.

APPENDIX
THE LONA CODE

We can reproduce the lona chords by using more familiar Western musical notation. The following is how the four-seed arrangement might have shown the word HELLO, represented by the major triad C with an added major 7th (consisting of the separate notes C, E, G, and B).

SEED 1:	C	C	G	G	B
SEED 2:	E	B	B	B	C
SEED 3:	G	G	C	C	E
SEED 4:	*B*	*E*	*E*	*E*	*G*
	H	**E**	**L**	**L**	**O**

One chord of four notes, with a different note to be played in each seed just as shown above, has a possible 24 permutations $(4 \times 3 \times 2 \times 1)$—almost enough right there to reproduce the alphabet. Add just one more variable—such as adding another base (tonic) C in a different octave—and you've increased the permutations to 120 $(5 \times 4 \times 3 \times 2)$. Give *each* separate note the choice of two octaves (high C, low C, high E, Low E, etc.) and the permutations rise to 40,320 $(8 \times 7 \times 6 \times 5)$—enough to encode quite large amounts of information. The lona system is far more complex than this simple example, and yields an astronomical number of possible permutations.

VISUAL DATA

TECHNICAL ILLUSTRATIONS BY
JOEL HAGEN

CHARACTER DESIGNS BY
STERANKO

Dedicated to preserving the past, Ezekiel Bones, Ph.D., has kept careful records of his own life in the 25th century. The images on the following pages are from his personal computer files.

In the 23rd century human travel technology made significant advances, leading to the discovery of Nemesis, Earth's companion black hole. The extreme gravity flux around black holes has been harnessed to provide a practical means of covering interstellar distances, although travelers can only pass from one black hole to another.

Black hole transfer stations have made a Galactic Council of United Worlds feasible. While many independently evolved species exist, four great political alliances exercise considerable control. Each is led by one species: shri, !xaka!, humans (all carbon-based), or lona (silicate-based).

The hermaphroditic shri are atmosphere dwellers, who have developed a highly sophisticated bureaucratic system. Their planet, Griynsh, is approximately half the mass of Earth and located near the center of the galaxy. It is the home of the Galactic Museum, which houses a great many archaeological treasures.

!Xaka! are fearless, armored creatures resembling giant bugs. Their many stomachs are capable of excreting a variety of acids as well as producing a web-like substance, providing them with formidable, natural weapons.

Tiny, microelectronic insect servomechanisms, commonly called servos, now perform a wide range of helpful tasks. They can be programmed to act as warning devices, to analyze materials, or even to store images.

Since terraforming has become a standard practice, the most prestigious human military academy is now located on Mars. Students in the six-year program receive arduous training with the latest in sophisticated weaponry. The best cadets will be offered commissions in the Navy, while many of the others will ultimately join the Legion of Ares, the infamous mercenary army.

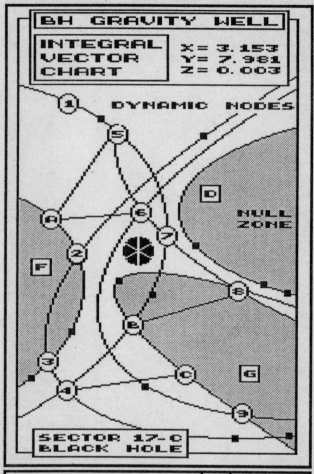

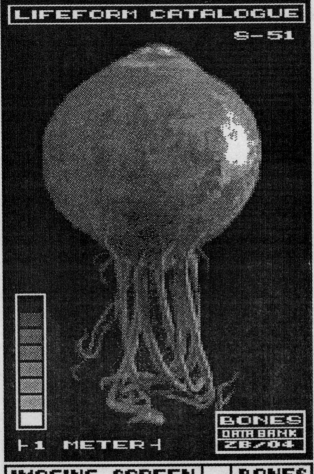

LIFEFORM CATALOGUE
S-51

|— 1 METER —|

BONES
DATA BANK
ZB/04

IMAGING SCREEN · BONES
SHRI (EXTERNAL)

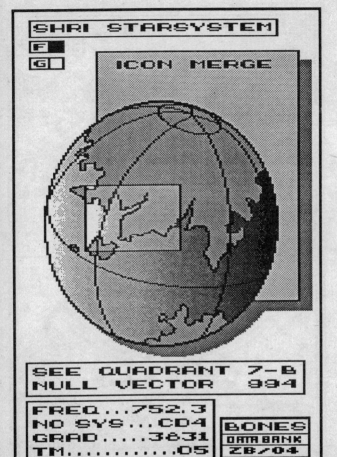

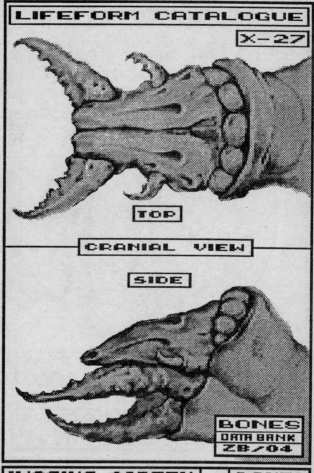

LIFEFORM CATALOGUE

X-27

TOP

CRANIAL VIEW

SIDE

BONES
DATA BANK
ZB/04

IMAGING SCREEN | BONES
!XAKA! (EXTERNAL)

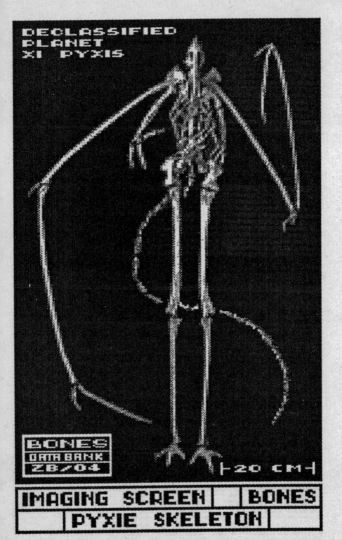

DECLASSIFIED
PLANET
XI PYXIS

BONES
DATA BANK
ZB/04

├20 CM┤

IMAGING SCREEN | BONES
PYXIE SKELETON

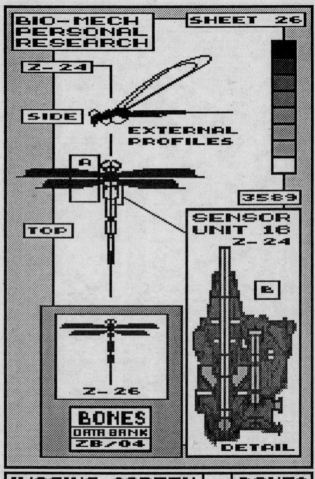

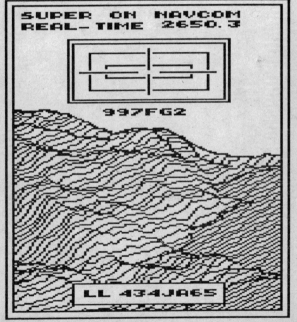

ACADEMY DATA FILE
THARSIS RADIALS

TOPO

KASEI VALLES
MID-RANGE
APPROACH

SECURITY
CLEARANCE
AREA

SUPER ON NAVCOM
REAL-TIME 2650.3

997FG2

LL 434JA65

IMAGING SCREEN   BONES
MARS BASE APPROACH

ACADEMY
TRAINING
EXERCISE

BONES
DATA BANK
ZB/04

IMAGING SCREEN | BONES
INTRUDER TRANSMISSION

ACADEMY FILE   41

FORWARD
SECTION
LINKING TUBE
ATTACHMENT

ACADEMY
TRAINING
EXERCISE

BONES
DATA BANK
ZB/04

IMAGING SCREEN   BONES
INTRUDER SHIP

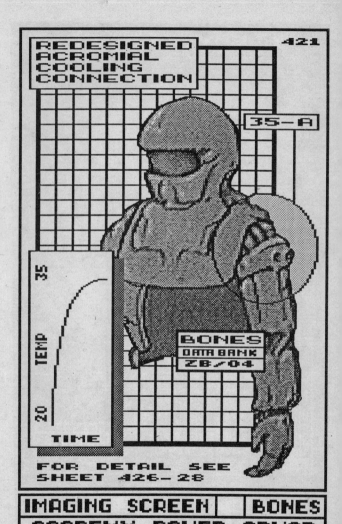

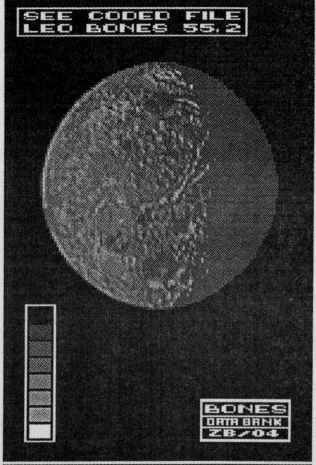